THE HAPPINESS FACTORY

THE HAPPINESS FACTORY

Jo McMillan

Bluemoose

For Isobel: wife, mother, survivor
with love

Copyright © Jo McMillan 2022

First published in 2022 by
Bluemoose Books Ltd
25 Sackville Street
Hebden Bridge
West Yorkshire
HX7 7DJ

www.bluemoosebooks.com

All rights reserved
Unauthorised duplication contravenes existing laws

British Library Cataloguing-in-Publication data
A catalogue record for this book is available from the British Library

Paperback 978-1-910422-85-4
Hardback 978-1-910422-86-1

Printed and bound in the UK by Short Run Press

Excitement

兴奋期

Chapter one

Where the skin of the earth shudders into the foothills of the Shunhua mountains, in a clearing above the mist and fringed with frangipani, Mo Moore set up a factory which, to this day, makes happiness.

Actually, it makes sex aids. Her goods sell all around the globe, and her biggest buyer is a British high-street chain. The boxes say simply: *Made in China*. In fact, they come from the place where Mo made a family and that she still calls home, a place too small for any map – the tiny, teetering village of Pingdi.

China began where Mo's father ended. It began with a letter addressed to the Night Duty Officer, Eden House Care Home, and said:

Dear Ms Moore,

You are unaware, I believe, that your father passed away in June. May I offer my belated condolences.

As Executor of his Will, I was instructed to liquidate the family firm and other assets, which task is now complete. All relevant taxes and fees have also been paid, and his affairs, I trust, are finally settled. Please find attached all relevant paperwork.

My apologies for the delay in informing you of events, but with your change of name and the long-standing severance of family ties, an address was not easy to come by.

With all good wishes for the festive season and for the New Year.

And a signature Mo didn't recognise. She read the letter again. *Long-standing severance of family ties.* She thought: you mean running away, and going into hiding, and changing our names in case he found us?

And now he was dead.

Carol delivered the letter at the end of Mo's night shift. Mo listened, as she did every morning, to Carol parking her car – in and out and in and out – the furry dice swinging from the rear-view mirror as if casting her fate for the day, until at nine on the dot, she'd lined it up exactly in the space marked MNGR. Then the slam of the door with a hip. A kerfuffle of bags in the corridor, which was Carol collecting the post, and the knock at Mo's door – always the same, Beethoven's Fifth. 'Now there's a turn up. Hey ho, Mo, four in a row.'

Carol said things like that.

And she would know about things turning up, about statistical anomalies like Mo getting four letters in one day. Carol, Manager, Eden House – Men's Wing, kept a keen eye on the comings and goings of the care home. She had an infallible memory and the kind of brain that could juggle numbers and come up with the likelihood of anything. She knew the risk of Mo getting diabetes due to working nights, of Eden House taking a knock in this year's winter flu, of a meteor striking earth and causing mass extinction.

Carol's wrist, slung with good-luck charms, reached into the darkness of the room. 'There you go, Mo,' and she handed Mo what turned out to be the Death Letter and three Christmas cards from Yorkshire. 'Sleep well,' she said, her voice in retreat because her phone was already ringing.

Attached to the solicitor's letter, a Statement of Assets for O'Shea & Sons, the family firm handed down through four generations. And now it had been liquidated. Listed too was the Dunn & Dunn Quality Home of Character, the house where Mo had spent her first eleven years, with the Doric columns and the weather vane that spun to Atlantic depressions, with the orangery and double garage with two cars – both of them his and one of them vintage. He shammied them every Sunday while her mother vacuumed the insides, fingering the dashboard and wondering where she'd take herself if she ever learnt to drive.

Also released were insurances, pensions and a 'portfolio of investments,' the papers said, and a column of financial acronyms Mo couldn't begin to decipher. Then, at the bottom, almost a footnote, the sale of 'assorted military memorabilia'. Selwyn had liked his weaponry. He'd put together a prized collection on long weekends and on bank holidays, when he'd browsed the antique shops of northern market towns, while his wife read the boxes of dusty yellow postcards and his daughter stared out of the window, cracking sherbet lemons and willing time on.

Which meant Sold: the sabre that had charged with the Light Brigade. Sold: the Luger from the Second World War that her father kept under the bed, the tip worn to a shine, wrapped in a Taylors of Harrogate tea-towel, placed out of reach 'and don't you dare ever go near it.' Which meant Sold: the musket balls from the English Civil War. And, suddenly, her father's patter came back to her about men and their Roundheads as his friends and their wives arrived for dinner, and her mother took their coats.

Also in the solicitor's envelope, a copy of *Adult Toys International Trading*, a magazine Mo hadn't seen since the day she and her mother had walked away from the family home into freezing sleet and left him. On the cover, 'The Gay Issue' and a smiling map of Ireland. The Republic had just decriminalised. The question exciting the industry: 'Is this our biggest breakthrough market since Hong Kong?'

Selwyn would have said: 'I'm not happy at all about the gay thing'. He was either happy as a sandboy or not happy at all. Nothing in between. He wouldn't have been happy at all because, as he used to say, everything had its place: coats went in the coat cupboard; shoes went on the shoe rack; men's privates went in women's privates. 'Privates' was the term he used in front of his daughter. It's what he would have said if he'd read 'The Gay Issue' over family breakfast, spooning down his porridge while Sue sliced the bloomer and put it in the toaster and stood ready with the lever the minute he was done.

Adult Toys International Trading was bookmarked, and when Mo opened it, there it was: the black-rimmed notice that Selwyn Roderick ('Roddy') O'Shea, former Treasurer of the British Adult Toys Association and Honorary Fellow of the International Guild of Adult Toy Makers had passed away peacefully at home after a short illness. His funeral had taken place in the Norman church in the town where she'd grown up – no flowers please, donations to the Rotary Club or the Yorkshire Stroke Society. He'd been buried in the graveyard that stippled the hill in sight of his workplace office. It was the graveyard too, where Vanessa Francine lay, having died of something pernicious before the age of thirty. That was all Mo had ever known about her father's first wife. That, and that her white-pebble grave was tidied by a man in a gardening apron who picked at weeds by annual subscription. And that one time, under a bright July sky, her mother, Susannah Moore, had got chatting with a man who'd brought flowers – gorgeous red gladioli – to the grave of a woman called Vanessa.

Once every year, Susannah went to the cemetery and spent time among the children's graves. She found them the saddest – the diminished plots, far too small for that much loss; the toy windmills that spun across the years the child hadn't lived to see; the cast of a palm, make-believe small, but proving this child too had been here and had also left its mark.

Susannah, though, didn't have a grave, so she borrowed other people's.

And that, Mo thought, was the problem with cemeteries: people chatted, they bonded over ghosts, because there's nothing so attractive as another person's loss. In this case, they chatted about her 'lost child' and his 'dear first wife'. Which meant Selwyn was counting on a second.

Mo pulled down the blackout blind, got into bed and told herself to sleep. But her father wouldn't let her. She tossed and turned, trying to find the comfy dent in the mattress. The room seemed smaller than ever, the walls closing in.

At the last Eden jumble, she'd tried to make more space by giving away the clutter – the books from college she'd lugged around for years; the dumb-bells, the bread-maker from David Dave, never used and still in its wrapper. And one time last autumn, when the light had slanted in and shown up all the dust, she'd packed everything away, done a clean, and never really unpacked again. Just-Ex Dave had said, 'There's less of you every time I come here.'

Which was true.

Mo was – though she didn't know it at the time – absenting herself from Dave. She said, 'Sometimes you have to put your life into boxes to see how much life you have left.'

She had one box. A big box. But just the one.

Now Mo got out of bed, opened the blind and re-read the solicitor's letter. The word 'liquidate' struck her. Not 'wind up' or 'close down'. 'Liquidate' sounded like exterminate, annihilate, eliminate. When her father put an end to things, it was always total destruction.

So, she thought, Selwyn had decided that he would be the last O'Shea and Son, the end of the line. He'd decided that his estranged daughter would have no interest in taking on the family firm.

Definitely no interest in that.

When Mo was seventeen, the careers advisor at her school had asked what she wanted to do when she left. She thought: well, at least you didn't say 'when you grow up'. Because by that time, Mo already felt old. She felt ancient – exhausted by her mother's state, by her father's campaigns against them.

It was break-time. Through the window, Mo listened to the hard jar of footballs hitting walls. 'I want to work with kind people.'

'Nursing, perhaps? Nurses are kind.'

Mo thought about that, picking at a picked-at scab.

'Or a midwife?'

She couldn't cope with babies. She couldn't, at that point, cope with much at all. But *babies*? They were so complicated and underestimated. People had no idea of the enormity of what they were doing when they made them. But Mo didn't say that. Instead she said, 'I'm not keen on the word "wife".'

'Or a vet, then?'

'They put things down.'

'But only out of kindness.' The careers advisor looked at Mo. His eyes closed. 'If you close your eyes, where do you see yourself ten years from now?'

Mo watched his eyelids flutter. Long lashes. Smooth skin. A young man, new to the job. 'Hopefully, I'm still alive, I'm still breathing.'

He opened his eyes and laughed. He loved this job, she could tell. Teenagers and their skewed ambitions: they had too much of it or none at all. It was be the Prime Minister or just have working lungs.

Mo said, 'I just want to survive.'

A different careers advisor might have said, 'Is everything all right at home, Mo?' This one listed jobs that involved survival skills: ambulance service, mountain rescue, RNLI.

'I want to work with people who've done it,' Mo said. 'People who've got through life, despite everything.'

'That'd be *old* people. You don't mean old people?'

But maybe Mo *did* mean that.

And that was how she went into Elderly Care. Now she looked after people with loose outlines who sat in hard chairs and napped to daytime telly. They drank warm squash from plastic beakers and urinated into nappies. Most days somebody died. Then relatives would arrive looking sad, or relieved, or both.

Would Selwyn O'Shea ever have imagined that his daughter was now Night Duty Officer in a place called Eden? If she opened her window, smells crept in of custard, gravy, soup – anything that didn't need teeth – and on stormy days, the shipping forecast because the Head Chef's husband worked on the trawlers. If she stood on her bed and the mist cleared, she could just see the Isle of Wight.

What would Selwyn think if he knew where she was now? He'd say, 'It's all very well looking after other people's fathers, but isn't blood thicker?'

Mo opened her Christmas cards. They were from people she knew up north – people, at least, she *used* to know. Mo hadn't caught up with anyone since she'd moved away for this job, and wouldn't now till who knew when? Tina, her neighbour at Number Two, had sent her 'Help the Aged'. Mr Sadler at Number Six, who hadn't left the house since his cerebellar stroke, had gone for 'Save the Children'. And her best mate, Spud, had dipped her baby's hand in paint and pressed it onto a cereal packet.

But then, they'd all done that: all her friends had moved away – to big houses in small towns with buttery kinds of names – and were now mostly mothers. Their husbands took reliable trains on scenic lines to the office and were home in time for *Blue Peter*. They had back gardens with trees that grew golden pears and giant peaches, and from time to time they'd ring Mo up and fight wistfulness on the phone.

Now Mo heard voices outside her door. Two residents were taking a long time to say hello in passing. Then, coming down the corridor, the whistle of Larry the Handyman. He worked his way through the Wing every morning, tightening loose things, loosening tight things and knocking out 'Chopsticks' on the piano. And against it all, the crash of pans from the kitchen, the squeal of gulls caught on gusts of wind and, from the morning mobility class, the awful cries of men battling their own bones.

When the job advert said 'live-in' Night Duty Officer, Mo had imagined a flat in the Eden House grounds with a walk along a strip of crazy paving to get to work. In fact, she had a single room with a shower and a fridge and a view of the garden wall. Mo's room was on the Red Corridor. It was like living on the Central Line.

It was the first time Mo had lived with anyone since she'd left home. She hadn't moved in with any of her three Daves: not Radio Dave, not David Dave and not Just-Ex Dave, even though he'd bought a two-bed – one room each. He'd be a flat-share lover, if that's how she wanted it.

But *why* won't you live with me?

Because she needed her own front door.

Because she sometimes wanted to be unavailable.

Because separate addresses made it easier when it came to splitting up.

Because life was complicated enough, wasn't it? Living itself was a feat, just keeping the show on the road. But living *with*? It multiplied all the complications.

But Mo hadn't said any of that. Instead, she'd moved a *bag* in – a truckle case with pyjamas, earplugs, bed-socks, nibbles. And twice a week, she'd taken the bus to his place until she'd got this job. It was promotion. It was Management. It was more money. So, until a couple of months ago, they'd commuted to each other, travelling end to end of the Great Escape Rail Link: his turn, her turn, his turn, her turn to travel.

At the end of the day shift, Carol called round to Mo with tea and dockets, and a rundown on the day's events and *Neighbours*. She fanfared the headlines: into three figures on the Christmas raffle, and light-fingered Lou lifted three thousand dollars from the Ramsey Street coffee shop, and… Carol stopped. 'Are you all right, Mo, or is it the lighting, only you look pale…'

'My father's died.'

'Oh, pet… sweetie-honey, I'm sorry.' Carol put down her *Love Is…* mug and reached an arm around Mo's waist. 'And I was the messenger too, wasn't I? That big envelope. I thought it was heavy. Have you kept it to yourself all day? You should have come out and said something, it's not good keeping it all bottled up.' She squeezed Mo as if she might contain ketchup. Mo felt the pinch of Carol's rings. She had more rings than fingers: signet, engagement, wedding, anniversaries and meaningful gemstones to ward off the worst. 'You know what'll happen now, don't you?'

He'd already had his funeral.

Carol picked up her mug and stared into it. 'You'll get pregnant,' as if she'd seen it in the leaves. 'It's what happens.' It's what had happened in her family. She named all the people who'd been conceived straight after a death, and Mo couldn't help wondering what plague had struck the Chaffeys that so many people had died.

'I think pregnancy's unlikely.'

'Unlikely doesn't mean it won't happen. Do you know how unlikely *you* are, Mo, what the chances are of you being here on this planet?' She said of all the gazillions of sperm Mo's father had made, and all the eggs her mother had carried, the two that happened to meet were *her*. What were the odds? Nigh-on impossible. And yet it had happened. 'Imagine if it hadn't been your sperm, if it'd been one of the others. What then? That's what I think if it's been a bad day at the office: at least it wasn't One of the Others.' Carol felt her wrist and tinkered with her lucky charms. She said, 'The reason why it happens, and the reason why I say pregnant, is the reason why Todd and Phoebe came up with that name for their daughter.'

Mo had made a point of never watching *Neighbours*.

'Hope.'

Then Carol said she'd have a quiet word in key ears, and soon after, Larry called round. 'I don't think I knew you even had a father.'

'I *didn't* have a father.'

A shrug of his huge shoulders. 'I suppose death is something that touches us all at some point in our lives.' In Larry's hands, a bouquet of hammers and chisels, a bunch of metal flowers.

Then the Head Chef came by in her bloodied apron bringing condolences from the kitchen. 'When my dear Dad, God bless him, passed...' and she described a state of magnificent grief Mo simply couldn't imagine. 'We're all very sorry for your loss.'

'No need. We weren't that close.'

'But *still*...'

'I know. I know.' Though the Head Chef didn't. Very few people had any idea about Selwyn.

That night, Mo did what she'd done every night since getting this job – went to the lounge and drifted through the magazines. She picked up *My Life*, which Carol brought into work 'in case family want something to browse, to pass the time while Dad's sleeping.' The crossword was half done, the horoscope annotated, the telly ringed. Mo did the personality test. She found out she had a tendency to be impulsive, was more superstitious than she realised, and dependent and independent, depending. She turned to the feature 'I changed my life...and it changed me!' The women were always pearly and smiling, and caught at the end of a laugh. They looked astonished at what they'd done, their eyes so bright they could have been polished.

This woman had thrown it all in – her husband and a job in marketing – and got on a plane to Peru. Why Peru? In truth, she said, it could have been anywhere. But the one thing she packed whenever she travelled was her good luck Paddington Bear. In Lima, she'd learnt to knit. She took to bowler hats. And now she sold knitted Paddingtons all over the world, including to Hamleys.

Mo gazed out of the window. Beyond the glass was the rest of the world. Her horizon stopped at The Needles. But follow a line from the Isle of Wight and you got to France and Mali and Ghana. She knew because she liked to spend time with the atlas – the out-of-date Collins that called Zimbabwe Southern Rhodesia. She'd even been there once, to visit Selwyn's uncle before it was taken over. And Canada to visit a cousin who lived at number one-thousand-and-something because Canada was huge and needed long streets. Also Australia to see his brother Dennis, who was doing all right with sheep.

Mo picked up the atlas now. She held it to her face and inhaled. Then she fingered the pages till at the back she reached the maps of the night sky. Mo had always wanted to learn the constellations: it would help if she ever got lost at sea. Sometimes, when she heard the shipping forecast, she wondered what it would be like to be on a ship actually going somewhere and really needing to know.

Learning the constellations was like learning the positions of cricket. She'd done that once for Radio Dave – except the stars began with the Big Bang and lasted millennia, and her relationship with him had started softly and petered out after a season. But he'd seen her through her mother's death, just when everyone – except Mo – was taking their final exams. He'd been the kindest, loveliest man and had made her fall in love with Daves in general. After Radio Dave came David Dave, who wasn't a true Dave because he wanted all his syllables. After graduating, he'd gone into Social Care Management and had helped Mo get her first job. He knew why she didn't have her degree, even though – apart from the piece of paper – she was qualified. David Dave was practical, and going out with him was like walking on one of those conveyor belts at the airport, where you get to where you're going really fast without even trying. He was a facilitator, although sometimes he could be of too much assistance. One day he announced he wanted to facilitate Mo's well-being. 'I want to look after you. I want to take care.' Which was kind, but also depressing because it meant she needed looking after. And it turned David Dave from a boyfriend into something else. It was the word 'care' that did it – odd, really, given that Care was what they both worked in and cared a lot about. Which shows how careful you have to be with words.

Also with people.

Mo had left him after that.

He said, 'You *always* do a runner.'

'I *don't* do a runner. I remove myself from situations.'

'That's just a question of speed. *If in doubt, run*. It's been the motto of your life,' and he recited all the things she'd run from – her father, of course; jobs that weren't going well; university, which wasn't fair; the Brownies. Did she really tell him that?

Then there was a pause. A fallow patch. A long one. And then, finally, came Diploma Dave, who was now Just-Ex Dave. He was the one who'd suggested Mo did the BTEC in Grief and Bereavement. A diploma like that would mean she zipped up the career ladder, death not being something many took as a specialism. And it was the BTEC that had got Mo this job at Eden House. When the contract went out to tender, they had to have someone on the staff who could deliver the Service Level Agreement, who was trained 'to interact meaningfully with a close family member before, during and after their Loss'. Also to show that 'we *will* care, we *do* care, and that we *have* cared,' to care in all the tenses.

'It'd be a useful experience – in so many ways,' Diploma Dave said. 'Everything you do...' He reached out his arms. 'Come here,' and Mo flattened her face in the smell of the spaghetti he'd cooked the night before. '*Everything* you do is defined by loss. Of your mother. Of your father.'

'I'm *not* defined by my father. Everything I do is the *opposite* of my father.'

'Exactly.'

And that was the thing: Daves understood. They were untroubled, understated, unironed, uneventful men. And not one of them liked Perry Como, or Pontefract cakes, or had a vintage car.

Now Mo picked up the local paper. Selwyn, apparently, was out tonight. Aries was bright and clear at nine o'clock in December. He was a Ram, born on the first of April, which made him the butt of easy jokes. He wasn't happy at all about his birthday, so he always said he was born on the second and it was 'close enough to midnight to be true.' Selwyn's mug bore his zodiac sign – a ram's head and horns. It was drawn in outline, and sat on the breakfast table facing Mo and her mother like a womb and fallopian tubes. It was a big mug with a fat handle for a slow cuppa while he read the *Telegraph*. On his side of it, the inscription: *Aries demands love for, like the infant, without love Aries dies.*

Not that Selwyn thought much of the stars. They'd always been there, he said, and always would be.

'Not *always*. Not before the Big Bang.'

He said they were just like the pattern in the wallpaper – and who got excited about that?

'But the stars *change*.'

'No, they don't.'

'Yes, they *do*.'

'No, they *don't*.' Just like Punch and Judy.

And so it was. Selwyn took command of the night sky. He ordained that the stars were still and eternal. And so, for the eleven years that Mo lived with him, that is what they were.

Still and eternal.

It sounded like the kind of thing you'd find on a gravestone.

Mo hadn't seen it in years, but she could still picture the cemetery that overlooked their Yorkshire town. She wondered who her father's neighbours were, how much elbow room he'd got for himself, what view he commanded, how close to the top of the hill he'd managed to secure his plot. Was it an eternal Quality Home of Character with the Burmese marble that his father, Stanley, had? She wondered about the wording: *Loving husband*? *Loving father*? The things that gravestones said...

And that was when Mo heard her name. Mr Nash, bent out of shape by compression of the spine and reflections in the glass had tottered round to find her all the way from Room 42. It was the meaning of life, though he didn't know it – he was way too old for things like that.

She opened the lounge door.

'Can't you sleep, Mo?' he said. 'Do you know what I do when I can't sleep?'

He was doing it right now. He called round and delivered messages that, at three in the morning, often felt like the meaning of life. Mo wasn't sure where he got them from – if he made them up, or if the preacher from the Gospel Group put them into his head. But Mr Nash stood in his pyjamas and bare feet and said things like: *You will be free of your past when you realise you cannot be free of your past.* But the one that seemed to haunt him was: *You live once, but you die twice – the second time when everyone who's ever known you has gone and there is no-one left to speak of you.*

Mr Nash didn't have any children.

'Will *you* speak of me, Mo?'

Tonight, Mr Nash had had a nightmare that this was his last winter and, given he was almost one hundred, it might well have been true. Mo came out and took his offered hand, and they sat in the lounge and watched the first snow of winter fall through a slice of yellow moon. It landed on the rockery and settled, turning the houseleeks into outsized flakes.

Mr Nash said, 'Snow makes me think of Gladys.'

They'd met in the hard winter of 1916, courted in its first flurries, declared themselves in the thick of a blizzard, and drawn hearts in the drifts in Regent's Park before Mr Nash was sent off to France. Gladys told him afterwards that they hadn't melted for months. She had cold ears for the rest of her life, he said – never recovered – the lobes like drops of ice, like frosted pearls.

Gladys was ten years dead.

Mr Nash visited her grave on the first of every month. It was his only outing from Eden, and he was devoted to it. He went in all weathers in his black worsted coat and fedora, and always took Gladys a bunch of white roses: they looked like her pearl-drop ears. And when he got back he was frozen, his nose dripping. He was smaller and older and 'each time closer to her,' he said.

Mo thought: I don't need a corpse.

Seventeen years of nothing, and from nowhere a Dead Dad.

She gazed out of the window to where a chaos of snowflakes eddied and then settled and made a cushion on the garden bench. It was where, every morning, Larry had his cigarette and polished with his overalls the plaque that said: *In Memory of All Who Sit Here.*

Mo had done her best to forget she'd ever had a father. As Selwyn himself would have said: 'Could you just do us a favour and kindly bugger off?'

Chapter two

In the morning, Carol knocked – quieter than usual – and put her head round the door. She gave Mo an envelope. It had no stamp. It was from Carol-and-everyone-at-Eden-House and the only condolence card Mo ever got for her father: a black-inked sailing ship touching the fine horizon of a wide, blank sea. Carol had already conveyed to Mo her take on loss and its reparation, and she hadn't had time to go round collecting signatures. So she'd filled the space with fat felt-tip: *YOU ARE NOT ALONE!!!*

'And a bit of good news,' and she read Mo her *My Life* horoscope: *Be ready for major change. Things you want will become available if you keep an open mind. Look in unexpected places.* It was the June issue and Mo had already read it. 'A horoscope isn't news, Carol.'

'Oh, *pet...*,' as if of course it was, and Mo must be really out of sorts. Carol believed in reading the signs. Not signs in general, but *the* signs, put out there by the designers of the universe, the makers of fate. She asked Mo how she was doing.

There were five stages of grief and, as far as Mo could tell, she wasn't feeling any of them. She was feeling dumped on. Put out. Pissed off. 'Oh, you know how it is. These things are hard to put into words.'

'Ah, bless. But of all of us at Eden House, you're the one qualified to manage things like this.' Mo's official title was Night (and Mortality) Duty Officer, but 'let's drop the bit in brackets,' Carol had said, 'for the brevity of all concerned.'

For the final assignment on her degree, they'd all had to keep a reflective journal. Her tutor had said: 'I want to know how, deep down, loss *feels* for you.' Mo hadn't had a chance to do it. She'd been too busy. Her mother had been dying at the time.

Carol said, 'This is stage one, isn't it?'

'Denial.'

'Only four more to go.'

If Mo had a reflective journal now, she'd have written *I could be furious with you, Selwyn, but I don't want to be because that's what* you *were. So instead I'll do forgetting. I'll be completely calm and make a cup of tea.* 'Would you like a cup of tea?' she said to Carol.

'Oh, hon. You're so... I don't know how you do it. *I'd* be in pieces.'

Mo wanted to say: actually, I *am* in pieces. I'm just stuck back together with glue that's proved, over the years, to be fairly durable. The lines aren't entirely straight. A professional restorer wouldn't be impressed. But then, I did it myself, with a little help from my Daves.

But Mo didn't say any of that. She said, 'Earl Grey or Assam?'

After the tea and Bourbons, and 'Sleep well,' and 'Anything I can do, you know where I am,' and a rattle of Carol's charms, Mo went to the window. She put the Eden House condolences between Just-Ex Dave's Christmas card and a pot of basil groping for the light.

Mo had written to him in October to say: *Sorry, I'm really sorry, but I just can't do this anymore.* She'd written one night when no-one was stirring on the Men's Wing, and there was no wind, and even the gulls had given up crying. She said she didn't know why she had to end it, but she just *had* to. She asked him if he knew why.

Dave had written a whole essay around Season's Greetings in nine languages from Amnesty International to say: honestly, he'd seen it coming. It'd been brewing for months. It wasn't easy, he said, commuting to a relationship in a tiny room in an institution. He had to sign in and sign out, and it made loving

Mo feel like a prisoner-befriender scheme. And when she came up to him, it was day release. 'Life's just become too small for you,' he wrote. 'You need air. Go somewhere. Do something.' He'd signed off: *Go well, Mo! D xxx*

Not love. But still, she'd got his usual three kisses, the kisses he'd press to her cheeks if they ever met again. And then a P.S.: *But the main thing is: Just go!*

Mo went to the sink and stared at herself in the mirror. There she was, Mo Moore – according to Carol, a singular human event and, despite her declaration otherwise, completely and utterly alone: she had no father, no mother, no partner, no siblings, no children, no family at all. Even when she searched for it, she found no family likeness. There was no trace of either of them – not the O'Shea jaw, not the flash of Moore auburn hair. Mo had a long, pale, cricket-bat face, which was why Radio Dave had loved her.

Mo opened the wardrobe and knelt down to the safe. The safe had been installed, Carol said, to scupper the chances of potential intruders. In reality, it was against forgetful residents who wandered in from time to time, thinking they lived there, or that Mo was their daughter or their wife.

She tapped in the code: 150176 – the date she and her mother had left Selwyn, the date that had changed everything. Inside, her birth certificate, a tin of Sue's ashes, the solicitor's envelope. Also, one or two photos of residents who'd died and thank-you letters from their family. Sometimes, Mo would take them out and hold them up to the light and say their names and remember.

Just-Ex Dave had found the photos disturbing. 'You keep *dead* men in your cupboard?' He said, 'You're not happy, Mo.'

'I'm not *un*happy.'

'Yes, you are.'

'Am I?' How did Dave know so many things she didn't?

And now Beethoven's Fifth, tapped so lightly Mo almost missed it. Carol put a hand into the room. 'Recorded delivery.'

She was whispering. 'Thought you should have it even though you're asleep.' Mo took the envelope and Carol pulled the door to.

Mo knew who it was from – she recognised the postmark. She was careful with the envelope, didn't want to rip it. It wasn't a letter this time, though. A compliments slip said:

I am pleased to inform you that you are the sole beneficiary of your father's estate. I enclose a cheque for the amount due. Your father appended one condition, namely that his grave is suitably maintained in perpetuity. I have taken the liberty of arranging the matter and subscribed to a GOLD service. I attach a standing order to Yorkshire Parks and Leisure and would be glad if you could submit it to your bank.

Mo removed the paperclip and a cheque fell into her lap. It was inscribed in effortless copperplate and issued by a London bank she thought was a wetland bird. Her eyes fell to the noughts – not so many that they blurred, but enough to have to count them twice, to say the number out loud and check against the longhand that filled both lines.

Mo paced her room. She did circuits of the rug. She knew she was really happy and really *not* happy – she didn't know why. Dave would know, if she could have asked him. Actually, *she* knew why.

She was bothered by the fact that a man who'd threatened to kill her had decided to leave her everything he had.

Why would her father – a man she hadn't seen for seventeen years – decide to be nice now?

Why not leave his estate to his brothers? Selwyn had thought a lot of Ted and Dennis. Or his niece? He'd always had a soft spot for Debbie.

Or else Battersea Dog's Home? Selwyn loved dogs – though they'd never had one because the fur would show on his Quality wool carpets, and because they needed walking, and he was too busy, and he didn't want his wife or daughter out in the park after dark, and then it's not fair on the dog. So he took passing possession of other people's, knew all the breeds, ruffled the scruff of the neck, said, 'There's my boy!'

Why had her father thought of his daughter after all this time?

Mo lay on the bed doing mental arithmetic, thinking how many years she could get by without having to work – and double that if she went part-time; or maybe she could retire if she cut back on everything and ate baked beans for the rest of her life. And she drifted off to sleep in a cloud of fractions and unlikely life-choices.

A couple of hours later, Mo woke with a start. Through the wall, Mr Turner had pulled the alarm thinking it flushed the toilet. It would take a while for the corridor to quieten, so she reached for something to read. Under the bed, the Gay Issue of *ATIT*. Mo flicked through the pages, releasing the smell of expensive ink and turning down corners of the things she'd go back to. She skimmed her father's notice. So, she thought, over all those years, Selwyn could have been anywhere – half a world away, on the other side of the globe – and now here he was, former Treasurer and Honorary Fellow, in a Gold grave in Yorkshire.

Mo's gaze slipped over the staples to the classifieds, slid across discounts on lubricants and love-beads, and then stopped on an ad that said:

> Why not fresh start in beautiful China? Come and see the future! Make an adventure! Huge space house and grounds of wild nature!
>
> Plus local handicraft factory for easy take-over.
>
> Call Mrs Su
> Pingdi, P.R.C.

Mo's hand reached for the phone. An index finger dialled. She listened to a distant ring. Then a voice yelled '*Wei!*'

'Is that really China?'

'China.'

'Oh my God,' and Mo put the receiver down. What on earth was she doing? She lay on the bed listening to her heart, wondering if that pounding was excitement or panic. She grabbed the solicitor's envelope and breathed into it, calming herself. After a while, she peered inside, found a manila cul-de-sac, a dry, dead-end that smelt of antique drawers. Mo's hand drifted back to the phone. She lifted the receiver and consulted the mouthpiece as if it were an oracle. She put it to an ear and listened to the hum of English indecision.

Years later, when Mo told the story, she said it was the fresh start and the adventure that did it. Also 'huge space' and 'wild'. The word 'factory' didn't register except as something that happened to come with the house.

This time, the voice took longer to answer.

'Excuse me, is that Mrs Su?'

'Is.'

'It's just that...well...' Mo took a deep breath. 'I've seen your advert in *Adult Toys International Trading* and I'm wondering is it still available?'

'Available.'

Oh, she thought. That complicates things. 'So...how much are you asking?'

Mrs Su quoted a figure in Renminbi. 'Which country you call from?'

'I'm in England.'

'Sterling money! Excellent.' She did the conversion in her head and told Mo how much in pounds.

Mo thought: *that's peanuts*, and then wished she hadn't. It was the kind of thing Selwyn would have said. The Quality Home had been full of things that had cost him peanuts or been going for a song. She said, 'That's a very reasonable price.'

'You are a very reasonable person to say so.'

'Have you had other interest?'

'Interest, but he is not paying English pounds with foreign connections to the outside world. I have not sold to him.'

Mo said, 'I've never been to China, but it all sounds very exciting and...'

'No buts. *You* are The One.' Her words tolled across the globe, loud enough to escape the receiver, where they hung and eddied, then drifted to the floor. She told Mo she'd meet her in Hong Kong and take her to Pingdi. 'I show you the property, the wild, the woods, the Menglang, I show you the everything. I show you future chances you cannot believe.' She said, 'You buy your flight ticket, I buy your visa. I get you F-type.'

'F for what?'

'For feasible. In Hong Kong, no embassy, no apply, no waiting, no why you want to go to China, do you have friends there, what *kind* of friends, do you have AIDS? Just, cash please.' A brief pause, but only to catch her breath. 'Come quick! As quick as you can. I am already waiting.'

And then the line went dead.

Mo listened to the sounds of the Eden House canteen – the splutter of blenders and slug of mashers, the makings of formless food. She caught the smell of semolina, which meant today was Tuesday.

Mo picked up her inheritance cheque and held it in both hands. It was like a giant business card, like a Golden Ticket to the Chocolate Factory. What should she do? Something sensible, such as invest it, or whatever it was you did when you understood money? Or should she just take the money and run?

If in doubt, run.

So Mo went to the bank. She handed over the standing order for Selwyn's grave.

The clerk said, 'What reference shall I put?'

'SOS.'

'Is that a charity?'

Did you have to feel charitable for it to count as charity? 'It's my father.'

'That's very nice,' she said, 'helping him along.'

'He's dead.'

She blushed. She fiddled with her necktie – red-and-white striped and tied in a huge bow. Why did bank clerks have to dress as clowns? She said, 'Well, you're helping him along anyway, wherever he is, wherever you go after this life...' She glanced at the standing order. '...such as Yorkshire.'

'And I'd like to pay in this cheque.'

The clerk stared at it. She stared at Mo, and then she dropped from her seat. 'I won't be a moment.' She tapped a code into a door and disappeared.

It took a while. Mo sat in the scoop of a leatherette chair and listened to a couple suggesting each other's possessions as security on a loan. When the clerk returned, she apologised. 'It was rather a large amount and it triggered our Fraud Alert. But it should have been our Privileged Customer Procedure. Can I book you an appointment to discuss your options?'

But all Mo wanted was traveller's cheques. 'And £500 in Chinese money.'

She looked unsure at that. Did they use actual money over there? So she looked it up, and it turned out they did, and it would take three days to arrive from London.

Then Mo said to expect a large withdrawal from Hong Kong.

'Visiting family?' She said she'd always wanted to visit family. In Australia. For her eczema. But she was stuck in a booth behind bullet-proof glass in a bank overshadowed by Woolworth's. A painted nail worked at a patch of skin.

'I'm emigrating,' Mo said.

'For real? For ever?'

Yes, for ever. For ever and ever amen. 'For now,' Mo said. It made her sound less reckless, including to herself.

Then Mo went to Thomas Cooks and bought a one-way ticket to Hong Kong. She borrowed a phrasebook from the library and learned to say 'hello,' 'thank you' and 'goodbye' in Chinese. She got jabs for hepatitis and jaundice, and tablets in case of the water.

When she told Carol she was quitting her job and going to China: '*China*?' A pout as if to place it. 'That *is* unexpected. But didn't I tell you? Or rather, didn't the stars?'

Then Christmas came. The choir from the boys' school gave a carol concert – real-life children with voices and hearts that hadn't yet broken. Mistletoe hung in the lounge for anyone who could purse their lips and stay steady enough to kiss. There was an advent calendar, and residents took turns to open it, taking pleasure in counting down their days.

The day Mo left, Carol gave her the latest issue of *My Life*. Under the Editor's Letter she'd written in that loping hand of hers: *Send us a Paddington Bear (or whatever it is they have over there)! Love you! Miss you already!!!* Mo also got a present, a pannier for the bike she was sure to ride in China, made by the Wednesday rattan class. She spent that day as she had every day of the last eleven months: listening to stories with unreliable names, and managing the basic functions of whatever life was left to the people who called this home. She made Mr Wright his last cup of tea – two bags, not stirred, not shaken.

Mr Turner said, 'Does it have to be China? It's an awfully long way to go to get away.'

Mr Nash said, 'What'll I do now when I can't sleep?' His fingers fluttered upwards and landed weightless on Mo's palm.

'Have you ever done anything impulsive, Mr Nash?'

'I'd do everything impulsively if I could see where I was going.' His hand slid back to his lap. 'I'm sorry you won't be here for my centenary.'

There'd be a scattering of nieces and nephews holding paper plates of white-triangle sandwiches, spreading out in the lounge and trying to fill it. 'You know what you are to me, Mo.' He put his hands to his face. It could have been Hide-and-Seek: he'd count to one hundred and come to China and find her. Mo knew she'd remember that moment. Of all the pictures of all the residents, that was the one she'd take with her. She pressed her lips to what was left of his hair and kissed him, his skin cool and dry and smelling of the baby lotion he'd won in the summer raffle. You weren't supposed to do things like that. It crossed professional boundaries. But then, Mo didn't work here anymore.

She looked away. In the garden, Larry the Handyman was putting the finishing touches to his farewell monument. He'd swept up the snowdrifts and turned them into a sailing ship. Mo was taking the slow boat to China.

She had her last meal in England in the Lucky Star Noodle Bar with its All-You-Can-Eat Seasonal Buffet. Mo sat next to the counter, at a table too small for two. Beside the till, a golden Buddha laughed at everything, its lap heaped with fortune cookies. From the speakers, Boyz II Men sang 'End of the Road'. Early the next morning, Mo would be on her way to Hong Kong. The plane would tip away from the earth, and something heavier than air would take to the air – that was the magic of it. She'd press her face to the window and wave to the shrinking tentacles of suburbia, and say 'Goodbye England. I'm never coming back.'

Around her, families ransacked kettle-drums of cooling noodles. Brassy laughter filled the café on this sunny winter afternoon. Tomorrow, Mo thought, she was heading to an entire land of noodles – of firecrackers and lanterns, wild tigers and paper dragons, triple-jointed acrobats and one-hundred-year-old eggs. A Forbidden City of concubines and eunuchs. Men in silk pyjamas with plaits to their waists and women with bound feet.

Or did she just make all that up? Actually, she had no idea what China was like. She had no idea what *life* was like when you didn't work in Elderly Care, when you weren't on call against final indignities, against life's last loss.

Mo watched the diners. She matched fathers with daughters, and mothers with sons, picking out shared features and tied fortunes. And her thoughts edged, despite themselves, towards a grave in Yorkshire. She couldn't imagine that towering man, her father, shrunk and weak and wistful like the men in Eden House. She couldn't imagine his rage and thunder, cold and stilled. She had no idea what was left of him now, how long a body lasted in rained-on northern mud – the flesh, bones and gold teeth, the hardwood and brass handles. She was sure he'd have had brass handles.

Mo could have taken the train, gone to the cemetery, seen how close he was to the first wife whose early death had set all this in motion. She could have lain flowers, memorised the headstone, had a word. But what would she have said? There was so much to say, and none of it sayable. Mo had more words of Chinese than she could offer to Selwyn Roderick O'Shea:

Hello. Thank you. Goodbye.

Mo flew through twelve hours of darkness. She watched *Far and Away* over and over, drifting in and out of sleep. She didn't know which curves of the earth they were following, which countries were down there, which languages they were flying through. She half-heard conversations she couldn't understand. The cabin was hot and sounds were muffled. It was like being back in the womb.

The plane was blown on favourable winds, and Mo was delivered an hour early into bright Chinese sunlight. On the approach to the airport, she leaned across laps scattered with salted peanuts, and stared at the miniaturised spread of Hong Kong. In the harbour, tiny ships trailed silver wakes. Money sparkled on the mountainside and rose sleek and even, like perfect columns of casino chips. And somewhere down there in that touchable distance, at that point where there was no difference between earth and sky, lay Pingdi. Mo couldn't see it – she wasn't even sure where it was – but she knew that when she got there, she'd never have seen anything like it.

Mo thought she'd have to wait for Mrs Su, but when the doors slid open into Arrivals, there was a woman – solid, square, her elbows wide on the barrier, angling out taxi touts – with a sign that said *Su-Mo*. Her gaze grabbed hold of every new face. And then she saw Mo's wave. 'Here, here! Here, here!' – the low drone of Parliament – broadcast over and over until Mrs Su had secured Mo's hand in hers. It was a hot grip, a relentless, sticky welcome to Hong Kong. 'How you feeling?'

Mo felt abroad. Fabulously abroad. She'd never seen so many Chinese people in one place. Mo was too excited to speak.

Mrs Su said, 'You need calm. You lean on me,' and she offered Mo her bulk. Mrs Su scanned each new face as if expecting someone. 'So we just wait here.'

And so they waited. Mo was sweating in her padded winter jacket. She'd flown six thousand miles, across continents, across seasons, into T-shirt weather, into air full of warm water and the smell of purple treacle she knew from the lanes of Soho.

Mrs Su checked her watch. 'Did he get separated as you got off?'

'Who?'

'Your husband.'

'*Hus*band?' It came out sounding like '*Hand*bag?'

'You do not have one? And no friend either? No nothing? You are here *all alone*.'

Which sounded like a fairy story. Not that Mo minded. Wasn't that how adventures began?

'Bah! Husbands!' A flick of the wrist deferring them till later. 'You still have time. You are young.' Mrs Su took a step back and scanned Mo's face. Then she caught another angle, saw her in a slightly different light. 'But also a little bit old. Or perhaps it is just the jet-lag journey. You are not too tired I hope. We have a border to cross, a train to catch and a long road ahead.'

They took the Extremely Fast Coastal Train and headed west. Every seat was taken and every aisle full. Mo sat by the window and soaked up her first sight of China. They rocked through squared-off towns that were lit with neons and tiled like bathrooms, the air pitted with the beat of Hong Kong pop. Men rolled their vests up to their nipples. They smoked and coughed into their luggage and held chickens by the feet, their throats fresh from cutting. Women fanned themselves with a hand. They peeled tangerines and fed segments to their children. They cleaned their nails with dirty knives.

Every so often, someone pointed at them and said something till in the end Mrs Su turned around and told them off. Then she leaned against Mo, bonding at the shoulder. 'I said they should make you feel welcome, not point and stare and say "foreigner". I told them *everyone* is a foreigner depending where they are. I said in England, *they* would be foreigners and how would *they* like it?'

'And what did they say?'

'That I am full of bull's shit. They will never go to England. They can hardly afford the local train. So then I told them that you just lost your father. They will not bother you now.' She patted Mo's hand. 'Everyone understands dead fathers. They are everywhere.' And Mrs Su told her about her own father, who'd died when she was twelve years old, fighting in the civil war. His body was somewhere in Manchuria.

Mo didn't know the Chinese had had a civil war.

He'd died heroically, she said, in hand-to-hand combat, killing a soldier from the Guomindang. Which meant, probably, another dead father, and that Mrs Su was twinned, in a way, with the child of the man her father had killed, who'd tell a similar story.

Little by little, the train fell quiet. Hours passed. The track narrowed. The fast train emptied. It slowed. Cars overtook them. When they reached the end of the line, they changed onto a bus and hair-pinned into the mountains. They climbed through forest so dense that the driver used fog-lights and left an elbow to sound the horn. Mo had no idea where she was. Was this still China? Some countries went on and on.

Finally, they pulled into Dadu station. It was the last stop, and they were the only ones left on the bus. *The Happiness Factory* van was waiting for them, a tall figure propped against the bonnet. Mrs Su waved. 'That is Milton Jin. You notice he is noticeable. In China, generally, this is not a good thing. But if unavoidable due to genetics, then best to be a crane. And this, you can depend on: Milton *is*. He is multi-purpose. He can everything. He is driver, handyman, bookkeeper.' Mrs Su dropped out of the bus and walked as if she had no knees over to the van. She introduced Mo. Milton's hand was warm from the bonnet, his fingers all articulation – bone, knuckle, bone, knuckle, bone. 'Milton speaks excellent fluent English. He is also the village translator and conversation tutor.'

Only, Milton didn't speak. He held his face close to the windscreen and searched the twilight for danger and snags in the road. As he drove, Mrs Su did the talking for him. She said Milton was the only person in the village ever to go to college, ever to have even *seen* a college. He won a competition of the Provincial Agriculture Committee and his prize was a course in Irrigation. 'But it was 1979 and Reform and Opening to the Outside World.' It was the launch of China into the future, so what was the point of studying feudal waterworks? Instead, Milton spent his college year in the library, learning all he could about finance and accounting. He was 'Milton' after Friedman. He made his way up to be Treasurer of the Entrepreneurs Club and gave the end-of-year talk on Trickle Down. He swapped two bags of mountain mushrooms for a room-mate's notes on double-entry bookkeeping. And he joined the English Society, learned to play Monopoly and traded useful phrases on revenue and taxation with a man from the Gobi Desert.

Now the van swerved and started to climb. Mrs Su pressed a finger to a fogged-up window. 'Please pay attention, for we enter

The Mist!' Mo peered into the darkness, watched it deepen and cool. 'The Mist is famous. Like your London fog. Some people say The Mist explains everything.' Then, against the night, red dots appeared: pin-prick constellations that grew larger and brighter and rounded into lanterns that hovered over the village. Milton eased through the South Gate. A red neon saying *HAPPINESS* floated against the black. They drove at walking pace down Pingdi's only street. Bunting criss-crossed the village, strings of good luck lacing up the houses. 'Everyone is here! See the crowds!' Faces craned at the van. Strangers waved at Mo as if they knew her. Mrs Su wound down the window. 'Hear the clapping!'

It was an unexpected reception. But then, Mo thought, villagers in England lined the streets for odd enthusiasms too – to roll giant pork pies along the Calder valley; to beat children dressed as wolves down the high street and out of town.

'Hear the chanting!'

Mo paused. 'Is that English?'

'English. The slogan is: "We know you can, Superman." It is the mixed-up words of a pop-hit song. Which one, Milton?'

'"Land of Make Believe."' It was the first time Milton had spoken. The sounds came from vocal cords that were long and precise, his words clipped, his accent straight from the BBC.

'He uses songs for his teaching English. No textbooks available, so use what you have. He has a Bucks Fizz tape and does grammar with the vocabulary.'

Milton pulled up at the Grand Pavilion and opened his door to the bleat of goats and the gasp of homemade fireworks that flew higher and burst brighter than Mo had ever seen.

Mrs Su dropped to the ground and patted the creases from her trousers. 'That song has how much vocabulary?'

'Approximately one hundred different words, many of them useful.'

Mo watched faces edge towards them. 'We know you can, Superman – do what?'

'*Anything.*' Milton got out of the van. He ducked under pavilion beams carved with lotus flowers and lit by showers of sparks. 'If you can get here alone, knowing no-one, across oceans and rivers and through The Mist, there is nothing you cannot do.'

Chapter three

Mrs Su led the way, brisk and business-like, to sign the papers for the transfer of ownership. The mayor was waiting for them in *Lao Difang* – The Usual Place. It was the village's only restaurant and it had no menu. It was run by an elderly couple, Mrs Su said, betrothed to each other as children, since when they'd spent every day together. They'd grown so close over eighty years, there was now no telling between them.

Mo turned a corner to find two bow-legged figures in black pyjamas leaning out of a doorway. Hand-in-hand they scuttled to the back of the house, brushing past cobwebs that hung like thick tan tights, weaving under vests and Y-fronts that steamed by an open fire, and tripping over dogs slaughtered by the heat. Their Banqueting Room had one table. Four places were laid with bowls of noodle soup, three of them cold and one of them empty. The mayor jumped to his feet and looked up at Mo with eyes blown into surprise by the thickness of his glasses. He reached for her hand. It was like putting on an oven glove, warm and inaccurate. He said how delighted, enchanted and fascinated he was to meet a woman from England, his first ever citizen in real life of the United Kingdom, though he had heard the voices of many, thanks to the World Service. 'My favourite of all is *Just a Minute*.'

Mrs Su glanced at the clock. She held out a chair for Mo. It was within range of the restaurant's only fan. On the table, the Terms of Transfer caught the edge of the breeze. They were brief, a single sheet. Mo's eyes ran down the page. 'It's all in Chinese.'

'That is because we are all in China.'

Mo stared at the Terms. For the first time since *Janet and John*, she realised she was illiterate. She squinted at the characters, tried to make out pictures, because that's what the phrasebook had said: Chinese characters were pictograms. Or picturesque, anyway.

'All very simple.' Mrs Su unscrewed the lid of an ink-pen.

'Simplified characters in the PRC. But your alphabet is even simpler.' The mayor said he'd learned his ABC from missionaries back in the '30s. 'The Lord's Prayer gave me my first ever words of English. You know it, of course. You can recite it off by heart backwards in your sleep. "Our father..."'

'"Which art in Heaven..."'

'Et cetera, et cetera. Amen.' Mrs Su held out the pen to Mo.

'But could someone translate them?'

'Could.' Mrs Su glanced again at the clock. 'But not now.'

'In a couple of minutes it is Pingdi Lights Out,' the mayor said. 'The generator shuts down. There is no more electricity. Then the village sleeps.'

Or give her a summary? At least give her a clue.

'Clue is: you take it over. Instead of Su family is the owner, *you* are.' Mrs Su pushed the Terms closer to Mo. 'A.S.A.P. they bring you the translation. Meanwhile...' There were three dotted lines, one for Mo's signature, one for Mrs Su's and one for the mayor's as witness.

The minute hand moved on a place.

The mayor said, 'After the revolution, the missionaries left and took their Biblical language with them.' But he'd served in the People's Liberation Army, intercepting foreign radio, and as soon as he could, he'd erected a mast on the far side of Soaring Magpie Mountain and tuned in to Bush House. He had the schedule of the World Service pinned beside his bed. 'I can recite the entire shipping forecast.'

'But not now.' Mrs Su leaned forward. Mo felt her breath on her neck.

Looking back, Mo could remember how quiet the room fell – just the scratch of the nib, the rub of ball-bearings, and an off-kilter breeze that rattled the lucky paper-chains. And in her head, *Viking, North Utsire, South Utsire, Forties, Cromarty, Forth, Tyne...*

When they were done, the mayor poured a round of his Moonshine. When finally he spoke, his voice was slow and hypnotic. 'This is Apple 1972, the fruit from my own trees and distilled in my own gardening shed. 1972 was an exceptional year.' He waved the glass under his nose. 'Notes of sugar and spice and diplomatic niceties established between China and the United Kingdom.' Then he tapped with a spoon and called for order. 'With great pleasure, I welcome you, Momo – if I may be so familial – to Pingdi.' The village, he said, was the ancestral home of the Su clan and Mr Su had built his factory here to show gratitude, to offer something back: receiving and giving, reaping and sowing, in the eternal circularity of things. 'He built the factory in the shape of an "H" as in H-for-Happiness. He built the house in the shape of a "U" so that together, from the bird's-eye view, they say "HU".'

Milton drew it with a chopstick in the skin of his noodle soup.

'In Chinese, "*hu*" means "household". It also means "keep safe". It also means "mutual". It is a sign that one for all and all for one, we take care of family.' He said that in China, everything has many meanings. Every word we say, every word we write can be understood another way. 'My advice is: speak slowly. Read slowly. In China, everything is between the lines.' Then he raised his glass and they drank a toast to multiple meanings. Mrs Su seemed thirsty. She knocked it back. The mayor also downed it in one. Milton was self-contained. No Moonshine seemed to pass his lips, and yet his glass emptied.

'Milton is a one-off man,' the mayor said. 'Extraordinary and very kindly. He will help you with Mandarin, show you the ups and downs and ins and outs. The language is easier than they say. The tones, they are singing, the grammar it is Lego. Only the writing is boot-camp.' Mo had to learn Mandarin, he said, because Pingdi was on track to be the first bilingual village in the country. When Mrs Su had put the advert in *ATIT*, they knew they had to be ready for foreign responses. So, on 1 October, which was China's National Day, they had marked *Inter*national Day. Within a year, everyone would speak one hundred words of English. 'They say a picture is worth a thousand words. We will prove that a hundred words are worth a thousand words. You speak how many languages already?'

Mo did A-level French. Her teacher had found love in a Parisian garret and taught vocab from chansons d'amour. Every lesson, he sang *Ne me quitte pas* as the class filed out the door. And she'd learnt German from Herr Janascheck who wore checks. He was a former bookkeeper and he filled the blackboard with his passion for tables and double-entry grammar.

Now the restaurant clock struck nine, the fan sighed and the bulb fluttered and died. The Banqueting Room door opened, and the landlady, or maybe landlord, swung in with a lantern, and Mo, the Mayor, Milton and Mrs Su shuffled from The Usual Place to the lick of a tallow candle. Mo looked up to a bright scythe of moon and enough stars to drown the constellations. The mayor pointed in the direction of *HAPPINESS*. The factory name was the only light in the village that never went out. The house and factory were that way: a ten-minute walk through the North Gate and along the track towards the Pink Pagoda. Tonight she'd sleep at the mayor's place, and he'd show her round in the morning.

The mayor threw Mo's rucksack over a shoulder as if it weighed nothing. 'You come with so little baggage.'

If only he knew.

'The rest comes by ship?'

No, the rest was in a box in Carol's attic: most of her clothes, her new rattan pannier, the photos of her dead men, her mother's ashes. She'd thought about bringing those, but what if the men at customs sniffed the tin and took the powder away for tests? So the ashes were in Carol's safekeeping. 'Of *course* I'll look after Mum,' she'd said.

From the darkness, Milton's deep voice: '*Zaijian*, Mo.'

'*Zaijian*.' It was one of her three words. That was almost conversation.

The mayor said, 'You know it means "goodbye," but actually, "see you again".'

'*Zaijian* in the morning, Mrs Su.'

Silence.

'Mrs Su?'

Mo tried to make her figure out – a thickening of the darkness, the solidity that had to be her. She thought she caught the distant click of footsteps. 'She hasn't *gone*?'

A gasp from the mayor at the delight of Chinese. 'The word "su," it means "fast". It also means "stay overnight". But not tonight. Mrs Su has urgent things to do.'

Mo slept long and fitfully in the mayor's spare bed. She was roused several times by the roar of the river and the stir of whatever animal lived under the roof. She dreamt she'd bought a house and a factory without even seeing them, and when she woke up she realised that she really had.

Mo went to the window. Down in the yard, snails had trailed disco glitter as they'd crept home at the end of the night. Geckos basked in the morning sun. In one of the trees, a flock of something tiny swung from the tips of the branches, turning it to a candelabra lit in electric blue. Mo threw open the window to the smell of fresh coffee coming up from the kitchen. She got dressed and went to find the mayor. He'd fried eggs, to make her feel homely, he said. He apologised that he couldn't make toast, only China didn't eat bread. He said sorry there was no butter, or ketchup, Daddy's, baked beans, waffles or bubble. He listed all possible parts of a full-English breakfast, stringing it out like a round of *Just a Minute*.

Mo ate her eggs with a knife and spoon. The nearest fork was in Dadu.

While she ate, the mayor spoke. He said, 'I am sorry you had to leave behind your father.'

Mo didn't tell him that was the point.

'He will be cared for? Someone will look after his resting place?'

Someone will, she thought; she had no idea who.

He said, 'The dead have to be cared for as much as the alive. They *are* alive, in our thoughts. Just like the missing. They are found again when we think of them.' And the mayor told Mo that he had a hole in his heart. Actually he had two. One for his wife and one for his daughter – both missing, presumed alive.

He showed Mo a photograph of his daughter, Dan, aged twelve, with pigtails that stood out like horns and a face that said life was even better than expected, and could the photographer please hurry up so she could get on with it. He hadn't seen her since he'd been denounced by a Red Guard neighbour as a 'bad element'. That was one of the Five Black Categories and his family had 'drawn a clear line' between themselves and the man who'd cherished a radio for its long-wave BBC English. He spoke quietly and reluctantly. Or maybe willingly, but with sadness.

The mayor had written many times to the old family home, hoping his letters would be passed on. But his wife and daughter had changed their name, he'd heard, from Lin to Something Else. But he'd never given up hope of seeing Dan again. 'I have stayed Lin Hongmeng. *She* could find *me*. But then, why would she? It has been nearly thirty years already.' He tipped his mug and said to the dregs of his coffee. 'But then, it has been nearly thirty years, so why would she *not*?'

He put the mug down, wiped a hand across his lips. 'Was your father a keen radio-listener?'

Selwyn thought radios were for stick-in-the-muds and blind people. His favourite gadget was their 22-inch colour TV with remote control and Teletext. He loved *The Six Million Dollar Man* and *Tomorrow's World*, and that turned into *Top of the Pops*, which he watched on mute till Pan's People came on. At that point, Sue, who was in the kitchen, called Mo in to help with the tea, and covered up the dancing with cupboard doors allowed to slam and the drawn-out hammering of steaks.

When they'd finished breakfast, the mayor presented Mo with Dan's old bicycle, her favourite possession, but left behind the day she and her mother vanished. Dan used to take off on her Flying Pigeon for whole days, he said. She came from *Zhongguo*, the Middle Kingdom, and she wanted to know how long it took to get to the edge. She wanted to know what life was like if you didn't live in the centre of the world. It was why the mayor was sure Dan now lived abroad and spoke English and knew the BBC. 'The radio pulled us apart and the radio will bring us together.' He believed in patterns, and cycles, and things working out in the end.

They walked along an unmade road rutted with bike tracks towards the factory. Over their heads, swallows wheeled and screeched, snatching at insects. Red kites circled on thermals, their wings describing the structure of air.

'Do you hear that?'

Mo turned an ear, caught the distant sound in the woods of birds chipping away at their day. 'Like woodpeckers, but actually villagers. They are all over these mountains. They tap the sap of the *Ficus Elastica*. They also fell hardwoods for the factory engine room – walnut, hawthorn, blackthorn, ash.' Everyone in Pingdi played their part in The Happiness Factory: as vegetable dyers and mould casters, as washer-driers and quality controllers, as packers and in dispatch.

'And here, look, The Twins, as choppers of wood for the boiler.' They waved at Mo in unison. The Happiness Factory was steam-powered, the mayor said, 'the engine salvaged from a train abandoned on its tracks when the British Empire crumbled and you pulled out of the region. It is the Pingdi way – to recycle, reuse. You see, Momo, what you have bought is not a factory in the *modern* sense. It is not an East Coast, Special Economic Zone kind of wonder. But it *is* special. And it *is* a wonder.'

They entered the factory at Coloration. Golden cauldrons brimmed with indigo dye. The air was hot, steamy and sweet, like Eden House on Thursdays, which was treacle sponge day. 'Our handicrafts are unlike any other,' the mayor said. The indigo plants were harvested by the Nasu clan, who snaked down the mountain and swapped cakes of dye for things you could only buy in Dadu: cigarettes, magazines, lottery tickets. The mayor showed Mo a photo of them, their skin pleated, their hands blue, like living works of tie-dye.

Then he eased open the door to the Production Hall, to a swirl of sawdust and the smell of linseed oil that for a moment brought back Radio Dave. A conveyor belt ran through the hall and the mayor led Mo along it. This was the mixing vat, where the hint of rubber inner tubes was overlaid with something close to vanilla. These were the rinsing tanks, and this was blow-dry, and here we have Quality Control. 'Please note the callipers and balance, the slide-rule, log book and loupe. And to test resistance to possible stresses: the vice and electrodes, bike pump, hammer and tongs.' Through a glass panel, villagers held purple dildos up to shafts of sunlight and dabbed at dust with lengths of sticky tape.

Mo leaned in for a closer look. Yes, they *really* were. Purple. Rubber. Dildos.

The mayor said, 'Each item is not quite the same, each one carries the mark of the maker.'

Mo had never seen anything like it. She loved it.

And she also loved it because Selwyn would have hated it. He'd have said: a bunch of peasants making stuff so appalling you couldn't it give away.

The mayor said, 'You are surprised they are so homemade? You expected technology? In Chinese, we call our handicraft "*jia yinjing*". Word for word it means "fake penis". In English,

Milton tells us, it is...' and he reached into a pocket and pulled out a notebook where he'd written: dildo (*sl*) IPA: /ˈdɪldəʊ/ *(check!)*. But was that really how you said it? He tried it several times, wrapping his tongue round the unexpected shape of the vowels. 'I am sure you know the exact etymology. You come from an ancient dildo family.'

The O'Sheas had been making sex aids since 1888, a line of men she knew from the portraits in her father's office: Selwyn, her father; Stanley, who was white-haired from the First World War; Samuel fat; Seamus thin. And they all had that O'Shea face – the wide-cast eyes, the set-to jaw, obstinate and reckless every one of them.

Seamus had farmed two score black sheep on the banks of the Shannon, but was turned off the land for being overly shy of God. He and his family had had nothing when they took the boat over and landed in Morecambe Bay. But they were grafters, the O'Sheas – that was how Selwyn liked to put it. They took risks and opportunities and made useful marriages. His grandfather, Samuel, had married into a Manchester family making money from treatments for the diseases of the age: tuberculosis, scarlet fever, cholera. And in their catalogue of Victorian contraptions was a device for treating neurasthenia. It induced pelvic spasms. The Rippleator was hugely popular among literary types in London and their high-strung artist-friends. They did a roaring trade in Harley Street and around Bloomsbury Square.

Stanley took over the firm from Samuel and saw it through the Second World War. He said the Germans did the business a favour because it took O'Shea & Sons into prosthetics, gave them a head-start in replicating body parts. Then in 1961, the year the contraceptive pill came out, Stanley handed the firm over to his eldest son. Selwyn decided it was time for O'Shea & Sons to have its own sexual revolution. He was going to be up-front about what they made, no more 'home massage devices'.

Briefly, he tried to rename the factory, to take down all the letters of the family name apart from the 'H' and the 'E'. It was modern, and the brand of his underpants. But Stanley, who still went to church every Sunday and referred to God as if capitalised, said, '*HE*? Does the Lord God Almighty own the factory now?'

So the company had stayed O'Shea & Sons.

No matter.

Selwyn was going to do things differently. He was going to get out there and 'thrust,' as he put it. He subscribed to *Adult Toys International Trading*, went to every trade fair, handed out business cards, invited people up to Yorkshire. Some even came. He was elected President of the British Adult Toys Association and Honorary Fellow of the International Guild of Adult Toy Makers. He ran a thriving business, and the proof was gilt-framed on all his office walls. His name was stencilled in block capitals on the glass of his door, and people knocked and waited without complaint for the frosted face of SELWYN O'SHEA, BATA (Pres.), HFIGATM to turn their way and say: 'Your seat's getting cold. Come on in.'

The mayor led Mo by the back route to the house, along the banks of the river. The Menglang started in glaciers high in the mountains and ended with shipping in the South China Sea. But here, its waters were clear and flecked bronze with shoals of fish. Over the surface, dragonflies flew out of the Age of the Dinosaurs, bright blue and luminous, like neon flashes of modernity. Mo strolled in the summer smells of December, while the mayor named the flora: azaleas, rhododendrons, primulas, clematis – names she knew from Larry, and from the residents of Eden House who could all raise an approximate finger to the window and come up with names for flowers. The mayor pointed out the telegraph poles that loped across the fields. The low-slung cable was used by migrating birds to roost and by villagers for shuttlecock. Mo's line had been cut for now, he said, and his was the only working phone in the village. 'Where you live, it is simple-style. But even so we call it the "Palace".' It was named after the People's Palace, which was where Mr Su had started his career in theatre.

'Mr Su's an *actor*?'

'Was. Acting also *ended* his career...' A deep heave of his barrel chest. The theatre, the mayor said, had been everything to him. He'd even met his wife-to-be there. Mrs Su had gone backstage and demanded more fireworks. But then, she'd trained as a rocket scientist. Mrs Su needed spectacle.

Her parents were worried about them seeing each other. Was an actor safe? On the other hand, he had urban household registration, so if she married him, she could swap her rural one and have all the advantages of town life. Acting was a step down. But the *hukou* was a step up. They dithered.

'Mrs Su told her parents: "He is a dreamer. I am a scientist. Equal and opposites. We are a couple made by Newton's Third Law. Also by the Marriage Law 1950." All future matches are by free choice. No arrangements. No meddling.'

The mayor turned away and stared as if into the future.

Mo followed his gaze. And there, bowed and bright and the windows throwing back sunlight, was the Palace.

The mayor handed Mo her keys – a huge bunch, theatrically large – although the door was never locked, he said. She stepped into the hall, which Mr Su used to call 'the foyer,' and into columns of sunlit dust. The mayor led Mo through the Palace, down long, echoing corridors. On the stairwell, posters from Mr Su's productions. 'Ever since Reform and Opening, China has had Shakespeare fever.' He'd dreamt of putting on the plays at the Palace. 'Here, he is cast as Romeo. Here he is Bassanio. But in China, you cannot do any old Shakespeare. Cautious how you do Hamlet. Best not Julius Caesar. Never Titus.' He turned to Mo looking wistful. 'But to come from the very *Land* of Shakespeare...'

Mo had gone to a school that never did Shakespeare – though they did do Typing. The teacher said that if you typed at random, one day you'd type Shakespeare, so just imagine what you'd produce if you actually had control of the keys.

They went through to the kitchen. It was huge and mostly empty: a camping stove, a cold-water tap, a thermos flask for hot water, an enamel bowl for everything. There were plastic stools and a kitchen clock that was stuck at a permanent four. 'Many foreign visitors like this simple way of life. Milton has seen them getting off trains – tall, pale people who come all the way to China to live from a single bag. We hope it is also your style.'

They went to the window and looked out at the garden, where a line of pines had scattered their cones like a thousand Walnut Whips. Paths wavered through wild meadows, and criss-crossing streams fed into the Menglang. And there, between two fruit trees, and in the scent of warming lavender, the hammock she'd always wanted. Mo said, 'How far do the grounds go?'

The mayor flapped a hand vaguely in the direction of Burma.

So, Mo's garden went up into the mountains, and the wild of the mountains came down to her front door.

'You could live from the garden alone,' the mayor said. Milton had arranged the vegetable patch in columns and rows, labelled and dated, as if gardening were bookkeeping. 'But if you need protein, such as eggs, I have chickens. If you need milk, I have goats. If you need fish, I can fish. If you need company, I have time.'

That was nice of him, Mo thought. What a nice man. How *nice*. But also, how earnest. How eager. She watched him bounce on the balls of his feet. He was restless. Fretful, even.

The mayor said, 'Do you come with busy plans?'

'For what?'

'For the factory.'

The factory was perfect, it didn't need plans. Mo loved it just as it was. Her only plan was to have no plans, to make things up as she went along. She wandered to the end of a corridor and watched the parallel lines of the Palace converge. She inhaled, letting her lungs expand. Was she really owner of all *this*? All this room to breathe. This quiet. This perspective. The Palace was even bigger than the Quality Home, and that was the biggest in the Dunn & Dunn catalogue. It was 'deluxe' as Selwyn used to say, and visitors were always given his Grand Tour. It started with the English Civil War and ended in the orangery fifteen minutes later with Harrogate tea and a cake-stand of canapés that had appeared from nowhere, though in fact from his wife.

What would he have made of all this?

He'd say: all very nice and you've one-upped me there. But it's different when it's been bought with your own money.

But it *was* her own money. He'd given it to her.

He'd say: but did you *earn* it?

Did she?

Her mother always said that he'd got away with everything, that Selwyn had never paid for what he did.

Now there was a knock at the front door and Milton came in with the translation of the Terms of Transfer. The mayor sat beside Mo and read them out, explaining as he went. Milton had done them 'A.S.A.P. as in as *soon* as possible, but also as *scrupulous* as possible, because we need to be sure you agree.' He pressed a hand to the page, ironing out the creases.

Milton said in an undertone, 'Please note the footnote.'

Mo read:

> *p.s. The Purchaser agrees to accept uncondi-*
> *tionally the aforementioned Factory and heretofore*
> *Residence exactly as found with no recourse*
> *to Complaint or Claim of any kind e.g. legal,*
> *financial, moral etc. against the Seller (i.e. Mrs*

Su, in Chinese: Su Wufen) or the Seller's extensive family.

Well, that was fine. Mo *did* accept it unconditionally. This wasn't Eden House; this was as close as she'd ever been to actual Eden.

The mayor looked anxious. He ran a hand over what was left of his hair. 'Have we sold it you, Momo?'

'You don't have to sell it to me.'

'I know, I know, Mrs Su sold it to you already. But we want you to like it, or at least the *idea* of it. We are afraid that you might leave.' He glanced at Mo. He glanced at the clock. It wasn't yet lunchtime, but the clock said four. 'Is it time for afternoon tea?'

Milton opened his bag and produced a thermos flask.

'Then we can explain about the Sales Order Book.'

Milton said, 'I am not, in fact, Milton for Friedmann. I am Milton for *Paradise Lost*.'

'What's a Sales Order Book?' Mo took the mug that Milton held out to her.

'I am sorry to say it is empty.'

Plateau
平台期

Chapter four

Mo had never seen a Sales Order Book. She had no idea how big they were or how many orders you needed to fill one. She went to the kitchen window. It was a big garden, full of things growing without even trying. In the distance, the mountains looked tiny, as if you could take them in a single stride. Mo thought, if someone said to me: *Would you buy a dildo handmade in those lovely mountains?* I'd say: *Of course I would.*

And so would Carol.

And Spud.

And other mates from college

And Tina, her old neighbour, probably.

Maybe *not* Just-Ex Dave. He'd wonder what Mo was getting at.

But Radio Dave. Definitely him, if he was still at the same address.

Plus there was everyone *they* knew, and everyone *they* knew, and that's how things took off, wasn't it? Look at kaftans and fisherman's pants and Goan tattoos. No-one had heard of them, and all of a sudden they were everywhere.

Outside, sparrows heckled each other as if they were at the Stock Exchange. In the flower beds, bees had their heads down and were humming like the Bingo just before the call. Mo said, 'I know people who'd buy our dildos.'

The mayor clapped. He rocked on the legs of his pink plastic chair. 'You see, Mo, we have hundreds of Awaiting-sales. But you have hundreds of foreign contacts.'

'Well, not *hundreds*, exactly...'

'We were *sure* there is a market for our goods. We just needed the right person from abroad.' And he looked at her with a misted gaze as if she were something religious.

A few weeks later, Mo heard back from Carol: *What are you like?!? OK, I'll be the Avon Lady of sex aids for you!!!*

Spud said: *Jealous. You make everywhere you go sound exotic. Got one already, but not one of yours. ps: Expecting again.*

Tina wrote: *Thank you for your sample. I appreciate the thought, though please another time, discreet packaging. What money do I pay you in?*

And Radio Dave, who took longer than anyone else to reply, said: *Messages like that make me miss you. When are you coming back?* And when, months later, Mo's bank statement arrived from England, the reference for his transfer was: *WHY DID WE SPL*

Mo was proud to be keeping the village craft alive. Because Pingdi had a history with sex aids. For three hundred and fifty years, for the entire reign of the Qing, the village supplied the Forbidden City with pink jade dildos. Other places, the mayor had told her, were bonded to supply their own local material. Yizheng cast them in bronze. Tengchong sculpted them from pumice. But the silky mottled pink jade locked in the Shunhua mountains was every emperor's favourite. From 1644 up to 1912 when Puyi, the last emperor, abdicated, Pingdi had equipped the royal bedchamber. 'All sizes, double-ended, triple-spoked, anything you can think of,' he said.

The mayor told her that when Mr Su had inherited, he'd come back to Pingdi to sort out his parents' affairs. And one night, standing at his childhood bedroom window, he'd looked out at the Pink Pagoda and had a vision of using the money to revive the lost skills of the village. But this time, they wouldn't make jade aids to satisfy just an elite. His factory would serve workers and peasants. 'As Chairman Mao said: *"Wei renmin fuwu!"* They would serve the people.

Mr Su had grown up with the planned economy. He wanted to employ the whole village – guaranteed, and for life. Pingdi deserved its own Iron Rice Bowl, he said. Milton warned Mr Su about his business model. They were no longer a monopoly supplier to the Imperial Court. China had a free market now. It was socialism with Chinese characteristics. There was competition, and he should think about overheads and turnover and efficiencies of scale and other things that were in Milton's college textbooks. 'Please remember it is just a dildo,' he said, 'not a political manifesto.'

But Mr Su was Old School, and he wouldn't be warned.

At first, it seemed, he'd been right. Mr Su contacted his theatre circles. 'He knew they would all be keen to buy one, and he knew *their* friends would buy one – at least one. Everyone is everyone's friend in the theatre.' And in the first couple of months, there were healthy sales in the arts.

But soon, that market was saturated, and Mr Su had to look for other openings. He gave samples to migrants who worked on the east coast and asked them to tout them round. But when they came home for the Spring Festival, it was with word that city people weren't interested in country crafts. They wanted modern electronics, with flashy names, from abroad.

In the end, the mayor confronted Mr Su. 'The villagers, they need wages. They need to be paid in yuan, not hopes and promises. We all have bills, fees, debts. We have to eat.' A few days later, Mr Su announced he had an important business meeting in Guangzhou. He packed a small bag and left. Mrs Su waved him off at Dadu bus station, and that was the last they'd seen of him.

'What happened?' Mo asked the mayor.

'No-one knows exactly. All we know is Mrs Su uses your money to commute her husband's sentence and get him out from solitary.'

* * *

Then Chinese New Year came, and the Lantern Festival, and Insects Awaken, and there were still no new orders from England. Milton said, 'I think we have exhausted your friends. We must cast our net more widely.'

Mo didn't have any enemies.

'But you have *Adult Toys International Trading*.'

Mo sighed. She really didn't want to talk to England. 'Can't you do it?'

'You have native English. And an understanding of the culture.' He knew not to mention her family history, her father's name in the trade. 'And a kind and persuasive heart.'

'That's just buttering me up.'

'It is being kind and persuasive.'

So Mo and Milton went to the mayor's house to use the village phone. She prepared herself for the odd sound of English spoken with an English accent. At first, she didn't mention Selwyn or O'Shea & Sons. She just said she was 'a British woman calling from China and would they be interested in handcrafted dildos?'

'Sorry?'

She said each one was unique. A work of art. Every dildo was an expression of the human soul that had made it. Each was beautifully flawed. She said all of those things to fill the silence at the other end of the line.

And then click, and the line went dead.

So then Mo tried mentioning the family name and voices perked up. Some were long-standing O'Shea customers and were glad to have news of the company.

The supplier of the Big Bertha Inflatable Love Cow told her he'd known Selwyn personally, had shared a table at the last Toys Dinner. 'He'd seemed on such good form then. Full of stories, the life and soul, as ever. And then, just a few weeks later...' A sigh, a gust of collegiate sadness. 'A light has gone out. He was a true trailblazer...'

Selwyn had a cabinet of prizes. He'd won the International Forward-Thinking Cup for a vibrator 'indistinguishable from the real thing,' the Chairman of Awards said, 'with a level of verisimilitude that left the Committee impressed and, in all honesty, agog. Mr O'Shea has done away with euphemism and acknowledged what women really want.'

But who had Selwyn modelled it on? Mo had always wondered that. His brother, maybe? Ted would have liked the idea of sleeping around without having to go to all the bother. Not on himself, she was sure of that. Because *his* privates were private, for his use only, and he'd do what he wanted with them.

Once, Mo had made a papier mâché model of men's privates from leftover *Daily Telegraphs*. She'd hung it from her bedroom ceiling like you do with Airfix planes.

Her mother had said, 'I wouldn't let your father see that.'

When he saw it, he paused and circled with that jutted-out jaw she knew from when he did Spot the Ball. 'Is that what I think it is?'

Mo shrugged. She never knew what her father thought.

He went to her desk and found the safety scissors. He stood on Mo's bed and tightened the cord on his dressing gown. Then he reached up and cut the string and let the model thud to the carpet. It was the easy way he rocked his weight that stayed with her, the maroon leather slippers that clung to the shape of his feet. Dust rose and sparkled the way icing sugar does, and for days after, the sweet smell of flour glue.

Down the phone line: 'Selwyn was a fine man...'

It was what they all said. It was what they all believed. And life *was* fine in the Quality Home as long as his shirts were ironed, and his sleep wasn't interrupted, and you stopped your bloody swearing when he told you to.

Should she put them straight? Mo said, '*Well...*'

'Exactly. Well-mannered, well-dressed, well-thought-of, well-heeled – lucky you.'

It was the same story with every number she rang: they'd all known her father, and all said how sorry they were that the industry had lost a leading light, and of course – for Selwyn – *anything*. Send us a few over.

The next day, Milton drove Mo into Dadu to send the parcels off. Mo was quiet. The conversations with England had left her subdued. She hadn't come all the way to China just to get on the phone and ring up her past. Would Selwyn never go away?

Milton noticed the mood. He chatted to cheer her up. He talked about the freedom of the road, and the most stunning parts of China he'd seen, and that one day he'd take her on a road trip all the way round China's border. Milton didn't own a passport. Or else she could join him on one of his deliveries. He often had a drop-off in Guangzhou. 'Also, I have to make appearances from time to time.'

'Family?'

A nod to the windscreen. 'Appearances are everything.'

'Parents?'

'My mother is dead and my father is dead to me.'

'That sounds bad.'

'It is bad.'

'For years?'

'Thirteen.'

Which meant he was counting.

'A specific thing, then? An event.'

Milton slowed to let sheep cross the road. He pulled on his fingers making the bones click, all but the ring finger, however much he tried. 'This is such a huge country, Mo. And all of human possibility lies in it. And so little of it is allowed.' He reached for the glove compartment and rummaged through tapes. 'This one. Like us, with rural household registration.' And they listened to Village People the rest of the way into town.

Milton parked by the bus station. 'You know this side of The Mist is what we call Real China. You have seen already people are a little different. They ask personal things about you: which country you are from, how old you are, which star sign. It is best to answer, otherwise it is rude. But no need to answer truthfully. The truth is not expected. Only the expected answer is expected.'

'But wouldn't that be lying?'

'It would be meeting expectations.'

The Post Office was on the market square between the Everbright Bank and a shop selling plastic shoes. Speakers were strapped to the maple trees and love songs drifted out and hovered over the heads of Dadu's elderly men. They talked to their caged birds; they ran through dance steps on their own; they kissed the air in their sleep.

Mo and Milton joined the end of the queue and stood in the smell of sandalwood that curled behind the counter. Mo heard the word 'foreigner' ripple down the line. She listened to Chinese she couldn't understand, and to the tick of a clock counting down the days to the handover of Hong Kong. When they reached the front, Milton interpreted and filled in forms in triplicate. The cashier stamped them. Mo showed him her passport. He told her which country she was from, where she was born, how old she was, wished he was a dragon instead of a snake. He tugged at the China Post shirt that he now over-filled. 'For China Customs, what do I write?'

Mo said, 'Chinese curios?' But then she thought that might make customs curious. So she said, 'Put *Nothing Worth Opening*.'

The clerk nodded, scribbled something, said with luck they'd get out of the country and with even more luck, they'd get into hers. He hoped for the sake of *Happiness* that they did. 'But expect a wait...' He rolled his eyes towards the Hong Kong clock. 'England...' A sigh so deep it reshaped the incense. 'You make so many problems, for such a small country.'

And so Mo waited.

Every so often, she dipped into her inheritance to keep people paid and things ticking over. A slow trickle of letters arrived at the Palace with smudged postmarks and dirtied portraits of the Queen – letters that had been opened and taped shut again, and all of which said the same. With each one, Mo noticed how strange English sounded now. Or maybe it was the remote and estranged way people put their refusal: 'We considered your samples with utmost care, but regret to have to inform you...'

Summer came, and Grain Full, and Grain in Ear. Mo let the garden grow even wilder and she lay in the long grass sipping homemade lemonade and learned Mandarin with Milton. They swapped sex vocabulary. The words Mo needed weren't in her pocket dictionary – weren't even in the mayor's *Complete and Unabridged Modern Chinese Dictionary*. She had a notebook and wrote down the Chinese characters and the pinyin and the tones. Especially the tones. Milton was keen on those. Because otherwise you could mix up such things as 'pen' and 'cunt'. And you must never suggest eating chicken, or you're suggesting eating cock. He told her about the second oldest, and the little younger brother, and hitting the aeroplane.

Milton knew a lot about male anatomy. And they knew each other well enough to talk about such things.

All summer, Mo practised her new vocabulary on people in the village, who really didn't seem to mind, and all summer, Mo waited for an *ATIT* call to come good.

Then autumn arrived and Limit of Heat and White Dew. In the garden, the apples fell and fermented, and the wasps got drunk and brawled. The walnuts burst and the last rose buds decided not to open. The wind changed direction. It brought hungry buzzards that circled over Mo. Sometimes she caught the sound of The Twins splicing wood for the boiler and singing 'The Year's Lament'. They sang like eternal angels, were known throughout the province for their uncanny voices. They sang at funerals, Milton told her, especially those of the higher-ups, when it was important that everyone wept. Then the equinox came and the smells in the garden tipped from ripe to rotten.

And that was when Mo knew she had no choice but to pick up the phone and ring the one person she really didn't want to speak to. Bernard had a full-page spread in the *ATIT* classifieds. He had money, connections, clout. But he'd also been her father's closest friend. He'd come to the Quality Home most weeks and sat on the sofa and been entertained. She could still picture him – the Fred Perry polo shirts, the canine way he had of sniffing the air and following Selwyn about with his eyes.

Bernard paused when she gave her name. He said, '*I* remember *you*. You won't remember me. In fact, I remember the day you were born. You came out the wrong way round. Well, well... Long time no anything. Anyways, to what do I owe the pleasure?'

Mo explained about the factory, about China.

'*China?* As in Japan?' He said, 'It's cheap labour over there, isn't it, and so many *of* them. Trillions now. Is it true they're all identikit and live off boiled rice?' A cough reached her from Yorkshire. 'I'd never have guessed you'd stay in the family line, though. Just shows what genes can do. He had strong genes, did Selwyn. Strong everything.'

Muffled sounds. Was he getting a cigarette? Settling in for a chat?

'You always were an odd one... Do you know how I remember you? Me and the wife came round to yours one day. And you were in the garden up to your waist in mud. And do you know what you were doing? You were digging a tunnel. You says, "My name's Pat and I'm getting out of Colditz."'

It wasn't a cigarette. Bernard was chewing gum. It always seemed to happen: men got to the age when their belly crept over their waistband, and then they started to chew.

Selwyn had chewed. Wrigley's Spearmint. And he wrapped the silver foil around his little finger and made it into a trophy, which he awarded to himself.

Mo had never liked the name Bernard: as in Manning and Matthews and Bernie Inn. And there was a boy at school called Bernard who cornered girls in the cloakroom and stuck his tongue down their throats. He was doing it alphabetically, working his way through the register.

Bernard must have expected more acknowledgement of his chit-chat: 'Hello? Hello, China? You still there?' Then a pause while he re-settled his chewing gum. 'You and your mother just vanished. Thin air.' He said, 'Bereft he was, your father, when your mother left. He came to stay with me and the wife for a bit. The dogs helped him get through it, Kiki Dee especially. He loved that dog. That dog loved him.'

Her father had a soft spot for Boxers. The temperament. The name. Selwyn had been a boxer in his school days. He'd been born 'early and poorly,' as Nanastan used to say, so to toughen him up Stanley had put him in the ring. His parents had kept a photo album of his boxing career – from the first win looking cave-chested and in gloves as big as his head, right up to the Famous North-of-England Knockout. Selwyn had kept a framed print of that on his bedside table.

Mo listened to more about dogs and the business and the wife, and then, finally, Bernard said: 'Tell you what, send us one over. I'll be honest with you, I have my doubts. But if it's for your father, if I'd be doing *him* a good turn...'

After the call, Mo got on her Flying Pigeon and hurtled towards Dadu, burning Bernard off. Villagers waved at her. They took it for exercise. 'Add oil! Add oil!' which was urging her on, but in literal translation. As she sped past, she caught the tail-end of compliments: 'How fit! What fine form!'

Mo wasn't in fine form. She was in a state. In a rage. That voice, which she'd heard so often rumbling agreement to whatever Selwyn said, had just been in her ear. Which meant it'd been inside her head. It had *penetrated*.

Mo hated phones.

And I hate you, Bernard, with all my heart.

She pedalled like a maniac, bumping along the track, ranting aloud, till she was too breathless to speak. Then she cycled slowly back home, letting the wind cool her off, and she dropped the bike in the yard.

Though, actually, not with all *of it.*

Mo picked the bike up and checked for damage.

And, actually, I don't hate you, Bernard. I just hate what happened – of which you know nothing.

She closed the Palace gate, and opened the shed, and put the Flying Pigeon away.

The next time Mo met Milton it wasn't for a vocab swap. He came to her office with the Factory Accounts for a lesson in financial literacy. He retrieved his college textbook from under the table. Mo had used *Free-Market Economics and How to Apply Them* to even up a leg. In front of her, he placed a pencil, rubber and a bottle of water, as if she were now under exam conditions.

Milton sat opposite, hunched in the brace position. 'You understand the meaning of numbers are red?' He turned the pages of the Accounts through the nine months Mo had been in Pingdi back to the start of Mr Su's debts. He showed Mo his working and put a final tally on the bad news. On the cover of his textbook, liquid in a golden pool looked unlikely to trickle down. 'We had the supply and nowhere the demand.' Milton zipped a thumb against the corner, a skid from the first page to The End, releasing the smell of a remote Agricultural College. Then a look of resignation spilled over his face, and they sat in silence and tried to resist the downward slope of the table.

After a while, Mo said, 'What happened to Mr Su?'

According to Mrs Su, when her husband got to Guangzhou, he went into Bankouro, claimed to be the famous but reclusive Ronaldo Wang, and asked to withdraw one hundred thousand yuan. Ronaldo Wang was the owner of Magellan Enterprises. He lived with a pit-bull terrier on a yacht off Macau, and every night sent a runner to place bets at the Grand Lisboa. The bank teller – junior and new in the job – didn't see past his Gucci shades, and was swayed by the accent with that no-man's-land lilt of someone who lived off-shore. So he went to the vault to fetch the money.

Mr Su was almost out of the door, his snake-skin holdall banging against a knee and the heat of the sun on his face, when the security guard noticed something. It was a sound he never heard at work, but he knew it from his dormitory. It was the squelch of the plastic shoes people wore when they went for a shower.

'Poverty has its give-away noises,' Milton said.

Mo thought about the story. Through the open window, the sound of sheep chewing sorghum. 'Is it true?'

'There are a thousand ways to get rich in China, and a thousand ways to fail, so why not that one?' And Pingdi was a kind place, he said, so when Mrs Su told the story, people listened and nodded, and now it was village lore.

What would her story be, Mo wondered. Would it have a happy ending? And if not, would the village give it one? She gazed outside, to a trail of wood-smoke and a sky dotted with cloud. Money was her blind spot, she knew that. And she'd made a point of keeping it that way. Not that her father had been a Scrooge. He hadn't sat up in his nightcap and run coins through his fingers by candlelight. He'd sat by the fire in his leather wing chair, and Sue had brought coffee and slid it onto the nest of tables. A hand reached round the edge of the *FT* – a gold cufflink engraved *SOS*. 'Thanks, love,' said to the stocks and shares and bonds and whatever else they were, these columns of figures that were more interesting than his wife.

Mo said, 'Can't we take whatever's left of my inheritance, and move it around a bit?' It was what bankers did for a living. It was how the pros raised money, even though it was more of a sideways shuffle. She took a note from her wallet and held it up to the window. Weak September light poured through it. Mo thought: how can a piece of paper, worn thin and sticky with use, be worth the same as a week's supply of food? And if money was nothing more than paper and ink, couldn't they just print some?

'That would be fraud.' Milton ran a finger down the spine of his book and picked with a nail at the College Library sticker. 'Also, printing money causes inflation.'

'Or else, gamble on the stock exchange?' Mo knew you could take a punt on the Chinese economy in a corner casino in Dadu. She'd seen the man with broken teeth waving raffle tickets and give-away bottles of Hong Kong Coca-Cola.

Milton said, 'What is left to gamble?'

'Or call in help?'

'The receivers? That would mean we are bankrupt.'

Mo turned the banknote over, to where Mao Zedong's hairline receded and his misted gaze saw things in the distance that no-one else could see. She said, 'Are you superstitious, Milton?'

'The whole of China is.'

Because in her copy of *ATIT*, Mrs Su's ad was directly opposite her father's notice. It meant that when Mo closed the magazine, the two touched. And not just touched; they lined up exactly. That had to be a sign. What were the chances of that being chance? It was the kind of thing Carol would know.

Mo hoped Milton would say: of course it was a sign. It was preordained that she spent her inheritance on a factory going under. That *had* to happen in order that something else could happen after. Instead, he said. 'You have given away life and limb.' Did he mean her father? 'You have tried, Mo, and for this we are all grateful. I do not know what we do now, but there can be no more of this.' Milton offered her his hand – his arm long, the man himself distanced. 'I am truly sorry for your loss.'

A couple of weeks later, Bernard's reply arrived at the Palace. It was Mo's last hope, the letter she'd been waiting for. But she knew from the envelope – the slap-dashed address, the twenty-odd stamps that just about made up the postage – that this was not good news.

> *Dear Simone,*
>
> *Thank you for sending me your Sample. There are types that like that kind of thing, but I can tell you straight up they're not in my circles, not on my books.*
>
> *For future reference, it didn't help that the Sample you sent me got bent in the post, unless you meant it like that. But that kind of thing doesn't go down well with your average punter. If there's one thing I've learnt over all these years in the business, if you want to make money, pander to normal.*
>
> *So, much as I would like to help your father's memory, that Sample was just too 'culturally specific,' I think is the term they use these days, and as such is not commercially viable. At least, not in this culture, where I live.*
>
> *Anyways all the best,*
>
> *Bernard*
>
> *PS: Did you know the down-there part on a lady is as acid as a tomato, I don't know what it's made of, but your Sample doesn't have any kind of coating and that stuff will corrode in no time.*

Chapter five

Mo went quiet after that. Bernard had been Mo's best hope. The mayor and Milton saw she was thoughtful and left her alone. Milton took long walks up Soaring Magpie Mountain, and the mayor busied himself with seasonal things such as washing sheets and worming the goats.

Mo spent days in the hammock mulling Bernard over, pointing out to the man in her head what he could have done – so easily – and hadn't. But then, why pull a finger out when there's nothing in it for you? He didn't think much of women and their not-a-hope-in-hell ideas. Or of women full stop.

Mo had known that all along, really.

Because she'd known Bernard all her life. And she'd heard the stories from *before* she was born from her mother. Sue had told her all about Bernard after they'd left Selwyn, in that phase when she was sleeping badly and taking so many pills she couldn't keep track. She told Mo everything, poured it out, hunched on the sofa with the telly on mute, convinced she was dying – which she wasn't, not yet – and that she'd go before anyone knew what had really happened.

Bernard had been the friend that Selwyn had turned to when he met 'a nice young lady, sweet face,' on his way to visit Vanessa. Bernard had said, 'Is she beddable?'

'Highly.'

'Biddable?'

'I would think so.'

'Sounds like marriage material to me. Overall marks out of ten?' and Selwyn had given Sue eight – and nine if she got rid of the ponytail. He later told Sue this, when she'd been to Vidal Sassoon's for a nice short cut to look like Petula Clark for the wedding.

Sue told Mo that Selwyn had given her his number that day at the cemetery and had said to ring, if she felt like a chat, if she fancied a drink – but only *if*, and he'd understand if she didn't.

It was that 'if' that had made the difference. It was the way she could so easily *not* call that had made her want to ring him.

Their first date had been in Selwyn and Bernard's favourite pub – the Horse & Trap – a Toby-jugs-and-brasses place with all-week Sunday lunch and a view onto the moors. The landlord knew Selwyn and didn't bat an eye at his lady-friend. He just reached for two glasses, a pint and a half, and they sat in the snug while the jukebox played the Beatles' 'From Me to You'.

What she saw was a ring finger that had no mark. And that evening, and for a while after, he had a listening ear that he tilted towards her, with his first silver hairs just showing. He didn't boast. He didn't mention the factory. It was all about *her*. Sue had never felt so visible, so understood. She knew she could tell Selwyn anything. And she felt duty-bound to clear the air, to explain about the Lost Child and how, exactly, it'd been lost. And Selwyn had listened and sipped through foam, and at the end, said, 'I am, strictly speaking, against such things – it being Life, and the Law of the Land, and such like.' But there were special circumstances, so it was O.K. with him. She need never mention it again – 'though you can, if it helps, if you want to – but only *if*.'

For a while, they'd sat and watched the sheep chew gorse. Then Selwyn got himself another pint and handed her a shandy. He said, 'I'm very glad to have met you, Sue.'

'Actually, it's Susannah.'

'But Sue for me?'

'I prefer my real name.'

'But think how much time I'll save calling you Sue.'

Did that mean he'd be calling?

'Over the years.'

Was that a proposal?

What Selwyn saw was a woman in a hopsack tunic and a ponytail that could do with undoing. Lips that told him things he had a right to hear, with just a touch of lippy, and that he could imagine kissing. A woman whose confidence had taken a knock, and no harm in that.

Selwyn did it the traditional way and asked Sue's father's permission to marry. Jack had agreed straight away. He was happy that a man of Selwyn's standing would take his daughter – given what had happened – and he hoped she could still have a family, that there was no lasting damage.

Bernard had been Selwyn's best man. He'd given a speech that was so long, people were chewing on leftover crusts and nipping outside to smoke – apart from Jack, who smoked in the corner because it was January and cold and he was sick with cancer at the time.

It'd been a church wedding. Selwyn's choice. He didn't believe in God, not one hundred percent, but he liked to hedge his bets. Also because he'd married his first wife, Vanessa, in a registry office with Glenn Miller and his Orchestra, and this was going to be different. No re-runs. But the main thing that had to be different was: Sue wasn't going to die. Whatever she did, she wasn't going to leave him.

Sue wore white. Everything was as white as possible, even though nothing about that wedding was, in fact, white. Jack, who could hardly walk, held onto his daughter and they went down the aisle to Selwyn. 'There you go, son,' he said. He was glad to be able to deliver her into what looked like a safe pair of hands.

Sue was happy to be given away because she was so glad to be taken. She'd been bowled over by the speed of events, at how quickly a drink in a pub could turn into something as solid and enduring as marriage.

They left the church to 'Jesu, Joy of Man's Desiring', played again at her father's funeral. Jack's choice. It was only five months after their wedding, but as the conveyor belt started up and his coffin was carried through the curtains, to Sue weddings and funerals already seemed one of a kind.

They gathered on the church steps for the photos. Bernard flitted about arranging the ensemble and cracking mother-in-law jokes to get people smiling. And everyone did – apart from her new mother-in-law. Nanastan knew Sue's story and had been against the marriage from the start. She looked into the cameras with that crosshatched face of hers, like a game of noughts and crosses that she never managed to win. And her husband, Stanley, hadn't smiled since Ypres.

Then out of nowhere, Sue told Mo, it'd started to snow. There was confetti and snowflakes and the flashes of cameras, and it'd felt so magical you'd have thought it'd last forever.

Which, at the time, she *did* think.

So did Selwyn. He kissed her lips and said, 'I'm happy as a sandboy and will be till the end of my days.'

After the reception, they drove in Stanley's Jag with cans tied to the bumper to the gates of the not-quite-finished Quality Home of Character. Selwyn lifted his new wife out and carried her down the garden path because the lawn was late being delivered and he didn't want mud on her train. He stepped over the threshold and said: 'You don't need to work now, love.' Sue was Manager of Housing Allocations. 'You don't want to go making homes for the Council. *Priorities*. Make a home for those closest to you.'

By which he meant himself.

'Don't even work your notice. I'll have a word.' Because Selwyn could fix anything in that town. He set his wife down at the kitchen table. And they started their marriage as if they'd been married all their lives. He said, 'I'm parched as hell. Fix us a cup of tea, love.' So Sue made tea, and they drank it from their wedding-present china, and Selwyn said, 'I'm glad we're being sensible and not rushing off on a honeymoon. We're not kids anymore, are we?' Because he had important things to do with O'Shea & Sons and she had things to do with the house. Sue spent an hour or two flicking through swatches of cloth for the curtains, while Selwyn paced the Quality Home, re-taking the measure of it. Later, they sat on the sofa – his side, her side – set that evening for the rest of time, holding hands and watching *The Avengers*. Then Selwyn had a bath and Sue knelt on the bathmat and did his back with the loofah. It must have been the play of the light, but he looked swollen, as if he'd swallowed water. She thought: that's what he'll look like in ten years' time when he's proper middle-aged and putting on a belly. She thought: where will his fat go when he's on top of me then? Did fat go down the sides?

Then Sue had a bath, and put on a nightie, then they got into bed and Selwyn took it off again. They were new sheets, smelling of the packaging, the fold lines still in them. He rolled on his side and said, 'Well, hello Mrs O'Shea.'

'Please, call me Sue.'

She'd given up on Susannah months ago.

The sheets were brown. She and Selwyn were pink. He said, 'We look good together, don't we?'

Remembering it two decades later, Sue thought they looked like two cold slabs of ham. But that was after. At the time, she said, 'Kiss me, Selwyn.'

And he'd taken her hand and kissed the double-rope gold ring from the jewellers in Hatton Garden, and he'd squeezed her fingers. 'My *wife*,' he said. '*My* wife.' He pressed so hard the ring caught skin. In the morning she had a blood blister.

Sue stood at the window that would soon have cream curtains, and stared over the garden that would soon have lawn, and she rubbed the blister and thought of Vanessa.

She thought: Selwyn had held that tight because of her.

* * *

Just before the start of Golden Week – a seven-day holiday for the whole of China – a letter arrived at the Palace. It was another brown envelope from England. Mo knew as she opened it what it would say *Dear Ms Moore*, and then a polite, long-winded rendering of 'Thanks but no thanks…'

Only this one wasn't:

> *Hi!*
>
> *We are* Psst! *an international collective challenging androcentric heteronormativity and hegemonic gender binaries and supporting grassroots sustainable fair-trade initiatives!*

Mo read it again looking for the 'no'.

She read it again looking for a comma.

Then she skimmed on down, but still could find neither the refusal nor the point. She was about to screw the letter up and aim for the bin when numbers caught her eye:

> *We would love to dispatch an order of 2,000 to each of our global outlets in London, New York, Tokyo, Sydney and Rio! Would an order for 10,000 work for you?*
>
> *Please ring to discuss.*

Mo ran to the mayor's house, waving the piece of paper as if she'd just averted war. The mayor wasn't in, but his door was unlocked, and she dashed straight to the phone.

A voice said, '*Psst!*'

'Hello?'

'Please identify yourself in whatever way you feel comfortable.'

'Pardon?'

'Who's calling?'

And Mo explained. She said, 'But how did you hear about us?'

A sample had arrived in the post with a handwritten note, the voice said, and read it out:

> *This might be right up your street. If so, contact a Miss Moore, Pingdi, China, no more to the address than that. A nice young lady, speaks good English.*

'No signature. No name.'

Mo said, 'I know who that is. It's Bernard.'

'We nearly didn't get in touch. At *Psst!* we reject the terms "Miss" and "lady". But we so loved your product, and the collective discussed it and decided that someone who goes to China and makes something as cool as this would reject those labels too. You do, don't you?'

'What?'

'Agree with us.'

An order was hanging on this conversation, whatever it was about, so Mo said yes.

'I know what you're going to say. That "psst!" is a label. Wrong. It is, in fact, an interjection. An attention-seeking signal, vowel-less, and so in terms of the main sound system of English, a nonword. A phonological anomaly. A monomorphemic invitation.'

'Mmm.'

'Exactly.'

'We reject labels. We are not gay or straight. Our sexuality is what we *do*, not who we *are*. We reject the terms "female" and "male". We just *are*. What's in your underpants?'

Mo glanced down. When did she last change them? She was fond of her knickers, a bag of eight in grey flannel, Elephant Brand, from the Dadu store. '*I* am?'

'Exactly. Any more detail is simply not relevant.'

For a moment, silence. Mo glanced into the backyard, where an animal she used to think of as a goat was eating hay as if this was any other day.

The voice said, 'Over-sharing perhaps, excuse me, but I am a penis-possessor.'

'Does that mean you're a man?'

A pause. Was that the intake of breath that preceded a lecture?

Mo said, 'I mean, man-*ish*. Or man-*esque*?'

'Did I mention that word? It means I am a Penis-Possessor,' capitalised this time. 'Take, for instance, what you make. They aren't "sex aids," or "penis substitutes," or "dildos" even.' The voice leaned into the inverted commas. 'They *are* what they *are*.'

'What are they?'

A sound like the suck on the inside of cheeks. 'Orifice-manipulators. Whose orifice? Anyone's. Which orifice? Who cares?' A pause. 'Or maybe even that's claiming too much. Who are we to prescribe? Couldn't it also be a dinner-table centrepiece? A toy for the dog to chew?'

And it went on like that. In code. For ages. Mo hooked the phone under an ear and let the voice unravel. She thought: I'm sorry, Bernard. I take back all those things I said. I hope the soundwaves didn't somehow reach the other side of the world. Thank you for doing this for me – though you probably did it for Selwyn, or his memory, which would be O.K. too, in the circumstances.

Mo thought: ten thousand dildos. It was ten times what the factory produced in a month. Mo spread her fingers. It was such an appealing number: easy to handle. It moved everything on a place. It was the number of green bottles hanging on the wall, of commandments, of a starter for, of people in the bed when the little one said...

'And delivery by Christmas guaranteed?'

Mo had stopped listening ages ago, so she just repeated the last thing she heard: 'Guaranteed,' she said.

In the classifieds of *ATIT* there was a two-page spread for a company in Hong Kong – an outfitter for the trade: 'No order too large, no product too queer' – that could make the extra moulds Mo needed. Kowloon Billy was manager of Love Vogue Hardware Manufacturers and 'extra-fast turnaround no problem,' he told her on the phone. So, that evening and all night, Milton drove Mo in the *Happiness* van all the way to Hong Kong. And as the sun poured its first gold over the border, she waved him goodbye, walked out of China, and took the bus into town.

The Adult Mansions Wholesale Market was a high-rise among high-rises. A sign said UNDER 18S NOT ADMITTED, and a child in nappies was learning to walk, staggering between crates of Vaseline. Shop assistants, full of carried-over boredom, filed curves into their nails and bent over mirrors, fine-tuning their first face of the day.

Mo took the lift to the twentieth floor.

Kowloon Billy swivelled on a swivel chair, his feet just short of the ground. He shook her hand – warm and slick from breakfast. He said he'd heard things were changing over there, but didn't know how fast. 'You are good for business. I am extra-happy to see you.'

Mo sat.

Behind Billy's head, a clutch of inflatable dolls, a host of naked angels, their fingerless hands delivering him to this meeting. On his desk, a packet of Lucky Strike and a marble-yellow model of female genitalia. Billy flicked the cigarettes in Mo's direction. Was that thing an ashtray?

He said, 'Your factory employs how many people?'

Mo wasn't entirely sure. 'The whole village is on the books.'

'Only village?' Billy sucked hard on his cigarette and watched the tip burn. 'I outfit factories the size of *towns*.' He showed Mo the photographs. Thousands of women in uniform were pegged along conveyor belts and fingered electronics under explosions of neon light. They wore mouth masks and numbers, and their plaits zigzagged down their backs like black, broken spines.

Billy reached for an order form. He held a biro in a fist and dug *BESPOKE MOULD – MOORE PINGDI #1.*

Mo handed him the template from which he was going to work. It was the Pink Jade Original, carved by Old Mang when Mr Su had first set up the factory. Old Mang was the last survivor from Pingdi's days as supplier to the Imperial bedroom. He was eighteen when the Empire fell but had never forgotten the craft.

Not that Billy saw craft. He saw a job specification. He flicked through product codes and jotted them onto the order form. Mo watched him do what he must do all day, it was all so automatic. Every so often he answered the phone and took orders in Cantonese, English and German. '*Extra groß?*' he said to Hamburg. '*Na, klar, megagroß haben wir auch.*' He worked his way down Mo's order form, asking questions that thought of everything, the biro poised over the answer he knew was coming.

She thought: she'd been in this situation before, only on Billy's side of the desk, filling in the Deceased Removal Form at Eden House: Name; Age; Date; Time; NOK. Sundays were always busy. And the week after Christmas was known as the Annual Extinction Event. It was as if, when nothing was going on – no Sit-Fit classes and the canteen frying leftovers – souls just got bored and decided to move on. Or, maybe, because it was the time people took stock of the year and what was coming up, that some decided enough was enough, and left.

Now Billy's hand was at the bottom of the form. 'Last thing: delivery. Anything we should know?'

'It's a long way.' Mo pictured the South Gate. 'How big is your lorry?'

'Extra-large.'

Of course it was.

So Billy said he'd deliver to Dadu bus station, and Mo would sort transport out from there. He punched numbers into his calculator. He gave her a discount for not going door to door, took off VAT, and rounded down because she was the first customer of the day. 'But I add for getting through customs, quite a big sum, let's call it insurance.' He spun the calculator round for Mo to see.

Milton had primed her for this moment: she was to look shocked, walk away, be as ruthless as they were. It was competition. It was dog eat dog. It was all in *Free-Market Economics.*

Mo had lived in China a while now, but barely shopped, let alone bargained. She wanted to say: 'I really appreciate the discounts.' On the other hand, the number he'd just shown her was all that was left in the bank. It was the last of her inheritance. Was she really going to give what remained of her father to a man called Billy whose lighter played 'Big Spender' and whose feet didn't reach the ground?

Word soon spread of Mo's Mass Order. And when the LVHM lorry arrived in Dadu, everyone was there to meet it. Boxes were loaded onto shoulders, oxen and donkeys, horses and bicycles and into the back of the *Happiness* van. And after an hour of chaos, a steaming, braying caravan headed to Pingdi, kicking up clouds of dust.

Within a fortnight, the expansion of *Happiness* was complete. Everyone had done their bit: Tan-the-Acrobat, who as a boy had won a competition to perform for Chairman Mao, climbed the old machinery taking nuts and bolts apart. Now in the Production Hall, rows of new moulds hung like teats from a giant silver cow. Right across the valley, neighbours formed relay teams and took to the hills to tap new sap. The Nasu clan did overtime making cakes of indigo dye. The mayor stayed up all night to write *Happiness Then and Now: an operational guide.* Milton stayed up with him and shortened it.

And then, on the last day of the month, the village gathered at the Palace. In the morning, they'd start production of the Mass Order. Staff from the factory canteen circulated, a peony pinned to their kitchen whites. They served the best food the valley could offer: Rainbow Fantails with edible clover that bloomed at night in the forest; heart of roe deer, killed by a bachelor and served with the arrow still in it; Sweet Pillow mushrooms that billowed like clouds and tasted of toasted marshmallow.

The mayor's nephew showed *Jurassic Park*, pirated from Hong Kong and projected onto a sheet pinned between two trees. Children piled into the hammock to watch. They sat in Old Mang's lap and fingered his leathery hands. They gazed at his marble-pink eyes roaming the flicker of light; studied his saliva nests, his clawed feet, his nails yellow and stony.

And then, Mo spotted a car passing through the North Gate, a silver shimmer going too fast for Pingdi.

'It is Doctor Long,' Milton said. 'He has just moved from Shanghai. He runs the new health-check clinic at Dadu hospital.'

Doctor Long rode the bumps in the track, his headlights sparking on the Palace glass. Mo opened the gate and he careened in, scattering the dogs and setting off the toddlers who were milling in the drive.

Milton said, 'Doctor Long put in a bid for the *Happiness* factory.'

The silent engine stopped.

'He wanted to use a government grant to buy it. But money like that has to come all the way from Beijing, and often it never arrives.'

Doctor Long checked his face in the rear-view mirror.

'Also he pushed too hard, as if of course he was the best possible person. But you represent the outside world. Mrs Su said *that* is where the future of the factory lies.'

Mo and Milton waited.

They waited as long as it would take for a fanfare to sound, and then the driver's door clicked open. Polished shoes got out and took the ground as if they owned it. Doctor Long stood for a moment, stiff and in profile – like a statue on an undersized pedestal and so slightly larger than life. His eyes were soaking up the lights of the factory with a look Mo hadn't yet learned to read. And then, when he was finished, he came over to shake her hand. It was a cool grip, the contact brief. 'First, let me say, congratulations on your Mass Order. Second, let me say, I am glad the future of *Happiness* is secure. Mr Su was not the best businessman. But one man's loss is another man's gain.'

'I'm a woman.'

He laughed at that. Then he circled his face across the horizon. 'I think you find it backward here. It *is* backward here. It is classed by the Ministry for Development as a Grade One Backwards Region. But you see that peak?' Mo followed his finger to the glint of snow on Soaring Magpie Mountain. 'One day soon, the authorities will take it down, stone by stone. Instead will be your airport. It happens to mountains all over China. You will have a factory hangar, and from there your goods will fly around the globe.' Doctor Long's gaze swept over the crowd as he described the future of China in primary colours and large round numbers. Then his eyes landed on the drinks. He signalled a waiter over. Doctor Long took a mug of Moonshine and held it under his nose. He rolled a sip over his tongue as if more used to vintage wine. Was he about to spit?

He swallowed and turned to Mo. 'You have heard of the famous Alfred Kinsey? Well, a good friend of mine is China's Kinsey. Dr Shu has collected statistics on marital unhappiness and reported them to the Communist Party. He has shown that family life is unstable, and therefore society is unstable, and then what for the Party?' Doctor Long rocked to and fro on his heels. '*Three-quarters* of all couples are not happy. They rate their private life as "only so-so". Why? They do not know the basics of reproductive anatomy. They are ignorant of the whys and wheres of husband-and-wife techniques. And think of all the cities, towns, villages in this vast country.' He held up his mug and dotted the air with geography. 'Can you imagine the sum of unhappiness? But here *you* are: owner of *Happiness* and with your first Mass Order.' He moved closer to Mo, close enough to smell the aftershave and hair gel, the cocktail of urban habits that hadn't yet washed off. 'My friend, China's Kinsey, would agree with me: your timing is perfect.' He raised his mug and clinked hers – tin mugs, the ring thin.

Just before midnight, the Palace gong sounded. The crowds gathered around the patio, and a hush fell. The mayor stepped onto the stage, into the footlights of tallow torches. He said, 'We have already proven that Pingdi is a bold place, and tonight we take another bold step. We are proud of our reputation as the Bilingual Village. We now have a new honour as the "Village of Good Relations". Our factory will bring *Happiness* to spouses, lovers, admirers and other bed-sharers on five continents. With our Mass Order we serve the people of the world!'

Rockets fizzed pink into the darkness. Whistles sounded. The crowd roared – all except for Old Mang, who seemed alarmed and whispered, 'I see ghosts.'

Mo said, 'That's just reflections in the windows.'

'I see flames.'

'Those are candles.'

'I smell danger.'

Looking back, Mo often thought of that moment, how she didn't pay him any attention. Yet this was the man who'd warned the village of the Hungry Moths of '65, the Rice Blight of '76, and the Great Storm of '87. Mo took Mang's hand and held it, the way she used to in Eden House if residents were afraid on Guy Fawkes Night. 'That smell is fireworks, Mang, not the future.'

The mayor signalled for quiet. 'The day about to begin, the first of November, is All Saints' Day. Religious people honour their saints, both known and unknown. I, as mayor of Pingdi, honour all of *you* – for your efforts and your courage in making the Mass Order possible. You are all saints, all heroes, in your own way; livers of life, which for no-one is easy.'

He got murmurs of thanks for that.

'With our Mass Order, the factory earns, we are paid, we can eat, we can raise our children, we look forward to a bright future.' He raised an arm to the factory lights, and everyone turned to look. 'The word *Happiness* is more than just our name. It is also our beacon, our ray of hope and candle in the wind. In this era of getting rich and famous, we must not forget the happiness of our family, neighbours, friends and strangers, of *all* our human bondage. They say it is a rich man's world. We know it is also a poor man's world. In the depths of night, when we look up into the null and void, this word reminds us that although money makes us happy, people will always make us happier.'

Chapter six

From the Opening Ceremony onwards, *Happiness* went into overdrive. The factory ran three shifts and village Lights Out was a thing of the past. Before long, news of the Mass Order reached the migrants who'd left Pingdi and gone to the east coast to work. As soon as they could, they each packed their bag, drew the curtain one last time across their bunkbed and said goodbye to the room-mates of years.

Every day, parents ran through the South Gate and swept children into their arms that had grown older and stranger, and searched their doubting eyes for recognition. Stories flowed of life in the city. Tears were held back. From their bags, souvenirs from the years in the factory: Christmas crackers, a Barbie doll, Nike shoes. Dogs gave up barking at strangers. The cockerels didn't know when to crow.

Then the *South China Echo* came to the village and interviewed the mayor. They ran a story calling Pingdi the 'Village of Family Reunions.' The mayor greeted every returnee with a long handshake and, as they turned away, an even longer sigh. Mo watched him, his face wistful. He was hoping, she could tell, for a woman who'd heard the news and seen the name, a woman who looked like him but also not like him, to come up to him and say '*Ba*.'

'*Dan? Shi ni ma?*'

Both of them ready for that moment because they'd rehearsed it for years – they just hadn't made it happen, or *let* it happen, maybe.

And then, shortly before Christmas, there was another family reunion. Doctor Long's son was home from school and they were going to celebrate. He sent Mo a card, a festive tree hung with IUDs and sold in aid of Family Planning:

My son is with us for the holidays! Please do us the honour of a visit. Perhaps for tea on Christmas Eve? My wife makes mince pies.

Your friend,

Doctor Long and family

Mo thought: that's very nice, mince pies.

Later, when she looked back on the invitation, she realised she hadn't thought: that's very nice, Doctor Long and his family. Because deep down, at the Opening Ceremony, she'd sniffed him out already.

So, on Christmas Eve, Milton drove Mo from Pingdi to Dadu, where the Longs had a flat in Golden Dawn Gardens. At the sound of the engine, the sentry rose in the sentry box and saluted them through the gate. Milton pulled up on landscaped grounds that foamed with flowers the colours of sunrise. Poised in the gap between golf-course hills, a pagoda in poured concrete. This was Dadu's only tower block. The glass entrance was cut in a semi-circle, the lobby lit with an amber glow, so that from here, from the honeysuckle and the slip-road down to Parking, it looked as though dawn were breaking.

Mo gave her name to a woman at reception, who signed her in with an all-day smile and a boiled sweet from a bowl. Behind her head, a back-lit map of the world. There had been, the digital counter said, twenty-four hours of sunshine in the last twenty-four hours, because at Golden Dawn Gardens they took the global view.

The Longs lived on the top floor and theirs was the only flat. The front door was open and Doctor Long was waiting. He was in a pale linen suit, creased at the crotch, like the symbol on a map for a panoramic view. Behind him, Mrs Long slipped in and out of the kitchen. She wore a one-piece of silver-grey silk that flowed with understatement, and slippers that shimmered close to the ground. Mo swapped her steel-toe boots from the hardware store for slippers from the shoe rack and slid behind Mrs Long into the lounge. It had stripped floorboards and bamboo blinds, white walls, hard chairs and low lighting. 'Less is more,' she said. 'It is the slogan of the Family Planning Commission and the fashion we have brought from Shanghai.'

On the wall, an unframed mirror, and in its centre what Mo now looked like. Her hair was cut these days by the mayor and a fringe queried its way across her forehead. She looked dried by the sun, aerated by the air, fed by the fields, and older. Not tired-older or even wiser-older; just lived-older. Mo thought she looked alive.

Doctor Long said, 'You are not what you thought? My wife also does this. Her face is perfect symmetry. I have measured it. And yet sometimes she looks at the mirror confused, like searching for something, as if she cannot see that she is there.'

Mo turned to Mrs Long, but she'd vanished.

'My wife does duties in the kitchen.'

Mo listened to the sounds of a warming kettle, a telephone, cupboard doors and crockery. 'Should we help?'

'That would be unhelpful.'

Every so often Mrs Long's voice enquired across the hallway if Mo liked Pingdi, and didn't feel too strange here, and do English take sugar in their tea?

Whereas Mo could only do one thing at a time.

She was famous for it. At Eden House, Carol used to check her watch and say, 'Are we in slo-Mo mode? Sweetie, love, we haven't got all day.' Though in fact the residents of Eden House wanted nothing more than to *have* all day, to end the day alive. Whereas Carol could welcome a new resident, freshen up the room of the recently deceased, and sort out her daughter's marriage over the phone, all at the same time. The demands of the day could just dip in and take bits of Carol as if she were a buffet.

Then Mo heard her name. She looked up. 'Her factory is renowned already.' Doctor Long reached for the plate his wife held out. A selection of Christmas motifs had appeared on the table: holly, a pine cone and a plate of mince pies, one of them halved. 'But such things are in the genes. She is the daughter of a famous businessman.'

'The daughter of fame! You have luck!' Mrs Long gave her a long look of envy and a cake fork. 'And your mother?'

The wife of fame. Therefore, eclipsed.

She took the smaller half of the halved mince pie. 'Does your mother bake at Christmas?'

It had been one of her many chores. On their first wedding anniversary, Selwyn had given his wife *The Joy of Baking*. On their second, *The More Joy of Baking*. And Sue had worked through the index alphabetically, diligently, maritally, from Apple Crumble to Yolk. She'd spent several weeks on 'R' because rhubarb crumble was Selwyn's favourite, with Yorkshire rhubarb, the forced type.

Mrs Long said, 'Are you missing home?'

'Pingdi *is* home.'

'I mean your *fumu, gege, didi, jiejie, meimei* et cetera.'

They were all relatives and Mo didn't have any. Either they'd never been born, or were now dead, or else they'd been severed, or had aged and drifted away. Her father had brothers she'd not seen for twenty years. Her mother's sister, Auntie Al, used to run a guesthouse in Blackpool. But they'd not met since Sue's funeral, when she'd leaned on the arm of a lodger who'd never moved out, and had wept that she'd not kept in touch.

'And *your* family?'

By that she meant Mo's children.

But Mo wasn't planning on those. Keeping your own life on track was tricky. But someone else's? Someone who needed you *the whole time*? She'd feel duty-bound, and that would make her feel put-upon, and then she'd feel resentful, and that would make her feel guilty. And then she'd wonder why she wasn't happier, and that would depress her, and then she'd take pills. Which was why she turned to Mrs Long and said, 'I still have plenty of time.'

'Though running out.' Doctor Long ran a finger around his empty plate.

'If you run out,' Mrs Long said, 'you can always adopt, especially here in China. Many foreigners do it. They like the orphanage girls. On Shamian in Guangzhou, it is like a daughter-fête.'

Doctor Long said, 'Adopt is good but genetic is better, and the best age for that is twenty-five.'

'Best for who?'

'The egg.'

Mo still had lots of those. She had most of the eggs she'd been born with: roughly two million, wasn't it? A Birmingham in each ovary.

'Birmingham?' Doctor Long had been there. 'Do not mistake quantity for quality. Your eggs are like all eggs. There are fresh ones and there are spoiled ones that no-one wants to eat.' Doctor Long gestured to a Christmas card. It was inscribed *O come let us adore Him*. It was from a distant cousin, he said, emigrated now, and a believer and a urologist in Washington. 'Jesus is the most famous quality single child in history. When resources are not shared with a sibling, see what they can achieve. Like all nowadays Chinese families, ours is small. By law, we are limited to Lulu. But our government advocates: *Raise the quality of the population! Control its size!* It is the policy of my clinic.'

Doctor Long had just opened the Advanced Family Planning Unit at Dadu hospital. 'Please note,' he said. '*Not* Advanced Planning. We are the Planning Unit for *Advanced* Families.' He was trialling the Pre-Marital Health Check and had been rewarded with a large grant and free supplies of *Selected Mozart*

Classics. His clinic sold it to pregnant mothers as soon as their foetus had ears.

Mrs Long had listened to it with incipient Lulu, could lilt along in unformed Italian to 'Conservati Fedele'.

'I immersed my wife in operas. It is the musical form that best develops auditory range and patience.'

'We spoke only English to my womb. Lulu's first word was "Daddy".'

Doctor Long said his first word had been *fuqin* because his father wanted to be called 'father'. It was a formal upbringing. No diminutives.

Mrs Long said, 'Whereas my first word was *baba*...'

There was no mistaking the pattern, nor the invitation.

Mo said, 'I took a long time to speak.'

Her first word had been 'yes,' according to her mother. But Selwyn had disputed it. He said her first word was 'no'. It had been one of their early arguments, apparently, before her mother had learned not to argue: *it was yes, it was no, oh yes it was, oh no it wasn't*, just like Punch and Judy.

Doctor Long went to the window. Down in the garden, a mini-pagoda. It was the Golden Dawn kindergarten. 'My wife was head-hunted as Pedagogy Expert. This tower block has a very high cultural level. There is a PhD on every floor. The kindergarten wanted advice on Lulu Methodology.'

Mrs Long said, 'Our son studies at The Exceptional School. Usually, candidates offer maths proofs and logic solutions. Lulu was the first pupil ever to be accepted on the basis of a poem. It was a Shelley, *The Mask of Anarchy*, a set text in the Year 12 *Anthology of Authorised English Greats*. It has ninety-two verses of four lines each. He recited it completely from memory. Lulu has exceptional recall.'

So now, from Monday to Friday, Lulu boarded in Yang'an, and came home at the weekend. 'We do not see him so very much because of the burden of homework.' Mrs Long's gaze poured out of the lounge in the direction of her son's room. 'Lu-lu!'

No answer.

And again.

Nothing.

'Lu-lu?' her voice straining and hitting falsetto. She glanced at her husband who had lowered his head and was running a finger along the rods of his iron-work chair. 'In Chinese, we say Lulu does not always *tinghua*. He does not "listen to words".'

Then, with a force Mo hadn't expected: 'Do not ignore your mother!'

And Lulu appeared, alert and alarmed, a brown line drawn in the doorway.

Mrs Long said, 'He is eleven, but already he has the teenage spurt.'

Lulu was unsteady on his feet and looked baffled by his own proportions. 'I have spurted, but still not enough. I lag the average.' He pulled at the waistband of his trousers. 'Everyone in the school is exceptional tall. The girls, they do ballet. The boys, they do *wushu*.' Almost as an afterthought, 'And they hang us upside-down to send blood to the head before class.'

'You can see his healthy complexion?'

All Mo could see was a back-lit boy in a brown tracksuit, and behind him, a wall of books.

Doctor Long said, 'Lulu reads all the time. We like to expose him. What is today's title?'

'*One Flew Over the Cuckoo's Nest*.'

'You see? He is a child of nature. He loves the outdoors. Sometimes it is hard to stay inside and cram him.'

Mo reached out to greet him. 'Hello, Lulu.'

'Hello, Miss Moore. I have waited all my life to meet a foreigner. Can I come with you when you go home?' His skin was dry and dusty, and his handshake ran through her fingers. 'You know, Lulu is not my real name. On my birth certificate, I am Jingming. It means "bright tomorrow".'

Mrs Long said, 'But we call him Lulu. It means "deer".'

Mo said, 'He *is* dear. You *are* dear.'

'The other deer.'

Mrs Long said, '*Both* dears.'

Mo looked at the *Exceptional* logo embroidered onto his pocket. 'Where do the unexceptional children go to school?'

Doctor Long said, 'The truly unexceptional, they do not go at all. Especially the girls. They take care of the home or work in the fields. Average children go to average schools. And my aim – the aim of my clinic – is to make the average *better*. How?'

Lulu answered on automatic, 'Bigger numerator, smaller denominator.'

His father appeared not to hear. 'Genes are a factor. Child-rearing is also a factor. But child-rearing does not come into it if poor-quality types are not born in the first place.'

Mo had a sinking feeling about where this was going, and she really didn't want to go there. But Doctor Long was on a roll. 'The criminals and hooligans and dim-wits and disabled.' An impatient flick of the wrist. 'Who can lead a happy life as a disabled? Who wants to be a burden on society?'

Mo glanced at Lulu who was looking at his shoes.

'They are shunned, abandoned, given away, not registered by their parents. Such people we call *heihaizi* – black children. Officially they do not exist. And if they do not exist, better not to be born in the first place.'

'But isn't that ...' Mo knew exactly what it was, but she found it hard to say the word. '...kind of... eugenics?'

'We call it *yousheng* – superior births. Not long ago, it was forward-thinking in Europe. Now it is forward-thinking in China. Our Minister for Public Health, he said inferior births are serious among ethnic minorities and in the frontier regions. What is Pingdi?'

Mo thought: a lovely village. It was her home. She knew all the children. She thought: Hurrah for the children! Keep your hands off them.

There was silence after that.

Lulu sat on the edge of his chair and swung scuffed eyes from his mother to his father and back. He orbited a mince pie around the lip of his plate.

Mrs Long sensed the change of mood. She reached for the pine cone, held it to her nose and inhaled deep on Christmas. And then she changed the subject: 'So! Snow, churches, queues...' She must have heard her husband's stories many times, because now Doctor Long launched straight into the time he'd spent Christmas in London: how people had placed bets on snow falling, and formed orderly lines for the Boxing Day sales, and fed the homeless in underused churches, and left stockings at the end of the bed.

Mrs Long's voice flowed into pools of wonder. 'What curious customs! Did *you* have a stocking as a child?'

Mo's stocking was a Leeds United sock stuffed with toffees that would keep her quiet till she heard her mother's tread on the stairs. Then she ran down to a bright sea of presents. It was as if a cargo ship had capsized in the sitting room. The O'Sheas measured in packets how satisfied they were, how well things were going. Selwyn made the lists. Sue did the buying. She did the wrapping, even of her own.

Once Nanastan had died, Granddad Stanley always came for Christmas. He had a bed in the orangery for the toilet and no stairs. Selwyn's younger brother drove up from down south, but only for the day. Ted had married Barbara – nice lass, good sense of humour. And they'd had Deborah – nice lass, well-spoken.

Sue cooked for seven.

Selwyn stood with his feet apart and held the knife in both hands as if carving turkey were a martial art.

Everyone had seconds, apart from Sue, who couldn't eat at all. But then, all morning, she'd filled up on trimmings and chit-chat with Barbara and Debs.

They pulled the crackers, and told the jokes, and Selwyn helped whoever had got it to fix the Chinese puzzle.

Then Christmas pudding, the Queen, and silence.

Thank bloody Christ.

The O'Sheas were nappers. Barbara was sparko at the drop of a hat. Debs knelt on the landing and played with her new doll, telling it: 'Excuse me, but people are trying to sleep. Could you keep it down a bit please?' Debs wore school uniform, even on Christmas Day. She had blonde hair that never knotted and white socks that never sank from the knee. Mo had to fight the urge to invite her out to play and arrange a minor incident. She wanted more than anything to dirty Debs.

Then her mother went into the garden – still in her apron and no coat – and she lit a cigarette. She didn't smoke much and she never inhaled. But that one she sucked so hard her cheeks caved in. She ate the smoke for dinner. Then she swung on the swing, gripping hard. She swung higher and higher, her legs straight out, till she could see over the fence of the Quality Home to the hills topped with snow and the other side of Christmas.

All their Christmases were like that, every year the same. In Mo's head they all merged – apart from one: the last Christmas they ever had together.

It was the year Grandad Stanley gave Mo a doll. Maybe it was the sequined dress. Or the name 'Girly Shirley'. Or the fact that Stanley had given it to her, because she didn't actually like her grandfather. But some kind of urgency had taken her. So, Mo went into the orangery where Stanley was coming round from his nap. She cut off the dress with secateurs, wrote the name of the body parts in biro, then dismembered Shirley and laid the bits at his feet. They smelt of Imperial Leather. It was the smell of that soap that stopped Mo from kissing him. She never once let her lips touch Stanley. Or maybe what stopped her were those odd brown eyes, the discarded glances in her direction that never quite got as far as his granddaughter, always a near-miss.

When her father found out, he came up to her bedroom, his fists full of body parts. 'What's the meaning of this?' He waved an arm that said *RIGHT ARM*.

'It's an autopsy.'

'You've killed her.'

'It's plastic.'

'Don't give me silly buggers.'

Mo looked at the carpet. Her mother had managed to keep it cream despite everything she'd spilt on it.

'Look at me.'

Mo looked up.

'What are you going to say?'

'They didn't even give her fingers.'

'Bloody good thing too when you look at what you do with yours.'

Mo looked at her fingers. Biro had come off on them. 'I don't like her. I don't like dolls. I don't like *things*. I don't want stupid *things*.' Mo had never liked stupid things because that was what her father liked. He might have called them antiques or kit or good investments, but really...

'You mean, you don't want stupid *things* like... that new Chopper you pestered me for. Like birthday presents, Christmas presents, like what you've actually got.'

'Stone Age people didn't have things and they survived.'

'No they didn't. They died out. They were taken over by the Bronze Age, which had bronze things, which are better than stones.'

Her father was yelling. 'Do you hear me?'

Mo nodded.

He left her bedroom, slamming the door. Mo picked up the body parts he'd dumped on her bed and wrapped them in her pyjama top. She went to the garden and dug a hole with her fingers in his perfect planted border, and tipped the Girly Shirley bits inside.

Sue saw.

Selwyn saw.

Mo hadn't turned to look, but she knew they both were watching.

Selwyn came down to the garden and covered her with his shadow. He said, quietly now, 'You're a vile child, you know that? How can you be so cruel to your mother?'

'What do you mean?'

'What do you mean "what do you mean?"?'

Mo didn't know yet that the Lost Child was actually the Dead Child. She'd imagined the child had gone missing – lost in the woods or on the moors. Or they'd reached for the wrong hand in the supermarket and been taken away for ever – the way children actually do disappear.

'Come on,' he said in that clipped tone she'd heard him use with dogs.

Who'd have known that Selwyn O'Shea could explode? This was the man who gave money to injured servicemen and rescue animals. Who sponsored the Good Samaritan award. Who visited the Falls Clinic at the hospital because that's where his own mother had died. Mr O'Shea would *never* explode.

And he never did.

At least, not often.

Selwyn led his daughter into the living room, then swept her off her feet with much the same gesture he must have used with his wife the day they married. He placed her on the floor and struck her with his slipper, while Mo breathed in Shake-n-Vac and listened to him grunting.

She thought how old her father was, and that he would soon be dead, and she told herself the slipper stung no more than nettles, which she liked to walk through from time to time, for the bravado of it, and the pain.

Mo had barely touched her mince pie. Doctor Long must have noticed because he said, 'My wife takes great pride in the kitchen. She likes to advance her skills. Perhaps you could give her some traditional mince pie tips.'

Mo took a bite. There was something was odd about it. It looked right – yellow pastry, brown filling – but she couldn't help feeling she was chewing on a mistake.

'What is your opinion?'

Lulu said, 'They are not mince pies. They are mooncakes.' He picked his up and held it at arm's length, placing it in the sky where the moon would rise, 'last quarter, sixty-four percent illumination.' He said, 'The moon is the earth's only natural satellite. It has been walked upon by twelve human beings. All of them were American men. It causes two high tides and two low tides each day. Its atmosphere is toxic. It is moving away from us. Its gravity is one-sixth of that on earth.' He rose from his seat as if weightless and drifted towards the door.

Doctor Long brandished his cake fork like a trident. '*That* is his memory. You see why The Exceptional School took him?'

'You can stay, Lulu, if you want to.' Mrs Long made a grab, but only of the space her son had vacated. 'Please stay and enjoy the conversation. You have only just come *home*.' Her voice lingered over the word. Then her hand fell heavy, her silvery sleeve hanging like a cloud about to rain.

But Lulu had homework to do. 'I am sorry, Miss Moore, that time is so short. But the Headmaster, he says: there is no after-life. There is no Heaven. We come from earth, we return to earth. It is here that we must shine.'

'Merry Christmas, Lulu. I hope Santa brings you what you dream of.'

'I used to believe in Santa. I sent him a letter once, many years ago.' He stood dulled in the doorway in his mud-brown uniform. 'But when I started at the school, I found out Santa Claus is a myth. The first Saint Nicholas was Greek and became bishop of Myra in Turkey. In original depictions, his cloak was green. His red cloak was established in 1931 in an advertisement for Coca-Cola. My school maxim is "*shishi qui shi*. Seek Truth from Facts." It is a quote from Mao Zedong.' Mo watched the back of his tracksuit merge with the shadow of the hallway, and Mrs Long following, sucked into the gulf her son had made.

Then Doctor Long beckoned Mo to the window. Outside, it was already dark. Thin threads of electric street lamps mapped the town. In the distance, Pingdi: clusters of light, the prickle of bare bulbs like the flicker of distant stars. And against the black, the word *HAPPINESS* shone red like a cosmic message.

'And yet, so much *un*happiness,' Doctor Long said. 'Think of all the left-behind wives with their husband in the city. Think of all the spouses sharing a bed and confusing what to do.'

But those weren't really instructions to picture the scene. Doctor Long was lecturing his reflection in the window. 'Where can people go for help? In this, we Chinese lag very badly.' A click of his tongue. '*So* much need and *so* unmet.' With a finger, he traced the horizon. It would be marked, Mo thought, with mooncake grease till Mrs Long next cleaned. 'Not high-rise yet, but Reform and Opening is not to be stopped. Soon all of this will be towers of light.' He pressed a fingertip to the glass, obscuring the Dadu hospital. 'There, on the seventh floor, is my clinic. I am responsible for the health and family futures of every woman below us. As far as the eye can see, she will visit me. I will know her, her family, her child – personally, internally, inside-out. And on the top floor is my office. I call it The Cube. It has an outlook to every direction. I look outwards towards space and forwards into time. The Cube is my crystal ball.' In the reflection in the window, his eyes rested on Mo's. 'China is homeland to one in five of all mankind. It has a Mass Population and a Mass Market. And you can deliver Mass Orders. I foresee partnership between us. *You* have the product; *I* have the women. We have each other's.'

Mo listened for sounds of Mrs Long. From the kitchen, the rhythmic clink of washing up and trumpet blasts from the eighteenth-century. Was that a Mozart classic?

'We are win-win, cannot lose. Like bread and butter both sides.' He went back to the table. 'I propose to give my patients their share of *Happiness*.' He picked up the knife. 'I make you an offer.' He angled it over the last mooncake and tilted his head, judging where the blade should fall.

He cut two halves, closer than his wife, but not quite even. A pad of a finger rounded up the crumbs. 'Deng Xiaoping said, "Let some of the people get rich first." Later on, other people will also get rich, but Mo: the first to get rich will get richest.'

Chapter seven

It was the first of January. Mo woke to a brilliant start to the new year. She lay on her pallet in the smell of straw, staring up to a sky so thick and blue she could chew on it. Usually, on New Year's Day, she thought forwards to what was coming. Today, she thought back – to how, so unexpectedly, and thanks to Bernard and *Psst!*, the factory had been given a new lease of life. She'd signed off the Mass Order in time for Christmas. The down payment was already in her bank and the balance coming at the end of the month. And now, Mo was exhausted. Today, she'd lie in bed disintegrating and stay there till it hurt. It'd be a pyjama day, even though she didn't wear pyjamas. She lay naked in the warmth of a January sun, watching a money spider clamber through the hairs on her legs – long hairs, short legs, though endless to the spider.

Mo listened to the rush of the Menglang and to birds sounding like the snip of scissors cutting the ribbon on the year. And then, the distant sound of an engine. There was only one vehicle in the village, and this wasn't the hack of the *Happiness* van. She heard the car draw nearer, wide tyres churning up the track. Mo went downstairs to a kitchen choked with tobacco and Moonshine, and with gas from the leak she still hadn't managed to find. The floor was scattered with debris – glasses drunk from and forgotten about; bottles skittled in the corner; dry-roasted peanuts and dried squid – the packets left gaping and now even drier.

The car pulled up in the yard, the sun dropping asterisks in the knocks in the bodywork. Then the driver's door broke open and a man stepped out. He came bow-legged over to Mo as if instead of a four-wheel drive, he'd just got off a horse. He stared untroubled into the sun and said hello in English.

'Happy New Year!'

'Is it not too early to say?' He shook Mo's hand with fingers that were chafed and used to gripping, and he gave his name as Gu. She took in the leatherette jacket, the beige trousers, the narrow belt with the over-sized beeper, the loafers. Something was missing.

And then he blinked.

'You're here on business?'

'Business.'

'Retail? Wholesale?'

'Any sale, every sale. We are interested in the whole works.' An arm lassooed the Palace, the factory, the day.

Mo said, 'You know the factory's not open? I can show you the whole works, but no-one works on a holiday.'

Then a tussle with the passenger door and feet fell onto the gravel. A middle-aged man levered himself upright and caught his breath against the car. Similar outfit, bigger sizes. He said his name was Li, 'Our work unit second-in-command, and how are you, Miss?' His lungs laboured under heat and age and unfamiliar English.

'I'm well, thank you.' Mo's eyes floated over the honeysuckle to the roof of the factory. 'And happy.' The name was so bright in the sunlight, the word looked almost sticky. 'How did you hear about us?'

Gu said, 'Who has not heard of the adventures of the English lady?'

Was that a book?

She said, 'Well, if we go to my office, I can make us some English tea.'

They took the car from the Palace to the factory. Mo sat in the passenger seat, dented by Li and still warm. It was the first time she'd had a lift to work. It was an odd sensation, but it seemed to fit a viable business that actually had a future.

Gu said, 'We are right, you *are* Miss Moore, also Ms Moore, also Mo, also Momo?'

But the last only to the mayor.

'We want to be exactly sure we speak with...' and he sliced her up, letter by letter: S-I-M-O-N-E-M-O-O-R-E.

There were no other Western women in the county. 'Who else would I be?'

'Your sister visiting. Your friend.'

Mo had invited friends to visit. Spud had promised to come when the kids were old enough, but given she was still pregnant with the second, that would be years. And Carol had said she'd absolutely love to *but...* She'd written on a postcard. It was of the Bull Ring, Birmingham, her writing tiny, the news spilling over the centre line:

> *Our luck changed when you left. Sorry to have to tell you, but the winter flu took Eden below viable. HQ scattered the remainers and sold the property off. Mr Nash took the coach down to see Gladys a couple of times, and that's what did for him, poor lamb. Buried beside her now. Larry took voluntary. I've got the same kind of post up here, only your shift, doing nights. Love you loads, Carol. PS: Don't worry, Mum's safe, brought her with me to Brum.*

Mo led Gu and Li to her office. She filled the kettle. Li settled in to watch it boil, his mouth ajar as if used to the feel of a bit. Gu's eyes found the picture that Kowloon Billy had sent as a thank you for Mo's order. A couple lounged in an ornamental garden, he with a large jade dildo and she with a look of imperturbability. Billy had attached a note:

> *This picture is from Ming Dynasty. We call it 'spring palace picture'. At LVHM we sell cutting-edge, end-of-millennium technology, but good not to forget that sex aids, even over there, they have long long history.*
>
> *Till next time,*
>
> *Billy.*

She knew what was coming next. Gu would give her a leery smile and ask something like how many words she knew for 'penis'. And she'd say, 'How many have you got?'

But instead, 'Billy what surname?'

Billy didn't have a surname. Mo found the *LVHM* order sheet, signed *Billy* to prove it.

Gu said, 'You *do* have proper paperwork?'

Yes, Mo had shelves and shelves of it – A4 pads, directories, ledgers for this and that.

'I mean, to show everything is correct with your product.'

Yes, she had those papers too. Here was the *LVHM* delivery note, which Milton had checked and signed off. Here was the Sales Order Book, the Receipts Book and Other Books she'd bought because she loved the smell of paper.

The kettle boiled and switched itself off. Li's doleful eyes swung from the kettle to Mo. She found three mugs and the Twinings sent by Carol.

'And the certificates, allowances, registrations, et cetera?'

'Yes, of course...' And then Mo thought: *No*, actually. What certificates?

'You understand we need to be sure your goods are legal.'

She reached into a drawer and retrieved her Samples Box. It was a magnificent box, Mo thought, lined with silver silk and crafted by Mu-the-Woodsman. He could name every tree just from the feel of its bark. She turned it to face her customers. 'How could this *not* be legal?'

Mo undid the catch.

Gu craned forward. 'They are purple.'

'Indigo.'

He reached for Extra Large and looked along its length. He turned it in his palm, weighing it like a firearm.

He passed the box to Li.

'I am sorry, I do not know. They do not look like an anything.' He ran the box under his nose. 'The scent, it is of...' and his gaze dropped to the floor, trying to place it.

Gu felt around with an index finger as if for a trigger. 'Where is the button? The on-off?'

There was no button.

'So where is the power?'

'The self.' Mo took a sip of tea. 'Or other.'

'Other what?'

Li said, 'I think the smell is fortune cookie?'

Gu fingered the lid of the box, where Mu had carved double happiness. 'This is exactly what we have come for.' He reached inside his jacket and pulled out a plastic wallet.

'It's cash only,' Mo said. 'I'm afraid we don't take cards.'

Gu flicked the wallet open and said something that sounded like 'inspector'. 'From Yang'an PSB.'

Mo laughed.

And then she stopped. Not *the* PSB?

'We come from the Public Security Bureau. We are the police.'

Afterwards, when she recounted this to the mayor, Mo couldn't remember exactly what happened next. She knew she told them they weren't the police, they couldn't be. She thought she caught sounds from the canteen, heard the echo of voices on the stairwell, as if this were an ordinary day. She remembered looking out and seeing Soaring Magpie Mountain and thinking the mayor would be tuned to Bush House now, listening to dramas sent to him from London.

Mo reached for Gu's ID. She took her time with it, read it both sides. She held the photo up to the light. So that was

Inspector Gu. He looked exactly like the man in front of her: his nostrils flared, lips serrated, adrenalin turning those eyes black. Sergeant Li's ID had sat in a pocket under his weight for years. Even then, however long ago, he'd looked defeated, even by a camera.

Mo placed the ID between them, precisely midway, as if about to bully-off.

The inspector pulled out a newspaper. 'I am sorry you are unlucky with the timing. This happens only one or twice a decade. But at six o'clock this morning, across the whole of China, our Party launched Strike Hard.' He held the paper up. A crisp old man wagged a finger at a hall of rapt people. The headline turned the front page red: *Down with selfish individualism! No to unchecked Western influence!* 'That is why we are checking *you*, Miss Moore.' His eyes were glazed with efficiency. 'Why did you come to Pingdi, a part of China untouched by foreigners? Because you could have more influence here? Spread your Western beliefs, just like the missionaries? Why did you not go to a city where you could feel at home, be with your own?' He held up a single finger. 'You. Alone. Who but a Selfish has a palace all to themselves? How many square meters, how many acres? Just yours, no sharing.'

'Who's supposed to live with me?'

'Your husband, children, father, mother, sisters, brothers and further afield.' His eyes roved the wall behind her, lining up her absent relatives. 'In China we say: without family you do not exist. To come here by yourself shows something not quite usual about personality. A go-it-alone thinking. Such things can be dangerous. If unchecked, also contagious.' A chin towards the window. 'I notice the villagers, the simple, open people of Pingdi. Since your coming, English is spoken before Putonghua, the official language of this country. Foreign culture is enjoyed before national culture. You celebrate religious death cults.'

Did he mean Halloween?

'The village learns rock-and-roll songs and other alien items.' Gu produced a Roneoed sheet. 'Do you know what this is?'

It was 'Away in a Manger' from the village Christmas concert.

'It is feudal superstition.'

Zeal had tipped him to the edge of the bench, offset by the bulk of Li. 'In the kindergarten, the children do not study reality. They are allowed to imagine. But how will they survive in an untrue world? They play Tig as if there is no such thing as AIDS. They sing defeatist songs such as 'Humpty Dumpty'. A boy named Long Jingming spends unhealthy amounts of time here.'

What did Lulu have to do with it? 'It's his school holiday.'

'He climbs trees.'

How did Gu know that?

'It is regressive behaviour. Human beings have evolved to come down from the trees. A Jingming-level person does not play around. He plays chess and piano.' Gu said, 'You come here – a foreigner – and make a little corner of England. Do you know what that is?'

Was it Rupert Brooke?

'Imperialism.'

She looked at Sergeant Li who seemed to be elsewhere, a lip moving to voices in his head. She'd almost forgotten he was there. She didn't know why he *was* there, except policemen came in twos. And Li provided width, roughly that of the door.

'And now, please, no more chit-chat.' Gu produced a tape-recorder. A cassette was already in it, the case labelled *SIMONE MOORE #0001*. He angled the microphone her way. 'From now on, only official talking. Anything said before I use this will not be permissive.'

'You mean as evidence? Am I being charged?'

He pressed the red button and leaned his arms on the table, elbows wide. 'Miss Moore, please speak slow and clear into the tape-machine and tell us why you came to China.'

Why?

Why were 'why' questions so hard to answer? She'd come to China because... because her father had died and a solicitor sent her a large cheque; because it had been written in the stars, according to Carol; because there was a big house and grounds for sale; because she wanted to know what life was like when you didn't live on the Red Corridor. She said into the mic: 'I. Was. Curious.'

Gu checked his nails, used a thumb to smooth something off. 'Do you know the legend of Chang'e? She is the Lady in the Moon. How did she get there, stuck for all time apart from her husband? She. Was. Curious. Like Pandora and the box. Like Eve and the apple.'

Mo stared through him, might even not have heard. Then she leaned forward and addressed the machine: 'I. Am. Keeping. *Happiness*. Going.'

Gu sucked his teeth at that.

She'd had enough already of English as a Slow and Clear Language, so she just let rip: 'Do you know how many families have been reunited because of the factory? Do you know how many people have jobs here now?'

'And do you know how many left their posts unauthorised? You encouraged desertion. You stole labour power.'

Li tipped himself sideways, freeing up a pocket, and found his lighter. He flicked the lid, setting off 'The East is Red'. He lit a cigarette and gave it to Gu. Then he lit another.

Gu smoked without smoking. He didn't inhale. It was just a way of clouding the air. 'These *Psst!* people. You have seen their internet website?'

'We've only just got our phone back.'

'They have an anything-goes psychology, a delusional thinking. They propagandise you can do whatever you want. Be whoever you want.' He blew a mouthful of smoke across to Mo.

She thought: isn't that *good*?

'Their emblem is a rainbow. What is a rainbow? An optical illusion. Not really there.' Gu fingered his tongue and got rid of a thread of tobacco. 'A rainbow is all the colours except black and white, which are the colours of Real Life.'

Mo picked up her Samples Box and ran it under their eyes. 'I am contributing to the Four Modernisations. Look: This is Science and Technology.'

Gu angled forward. 'Please, show me, where exactly is the science?'

Actually, all Mo could see was the craftsmanship, the simplicity of the cast, the perfect finish, the shimmer of the silver lining.

Gu let her silence spool into the tape. In the end, 'The Four Modernisations do not apply to this box. What we have here is the Six Evils.' Mo watched his Adam's apple run like a slip knot up and down the twine of his neck. 'Miss Moore, you come from the West. In the West, you had the nineteen-sixties. You did swinging and long hair and swapping. What did we do? The Cultural Revolution. We sent young people down to the countryside to learn from the peasants. You do not seem to register where you are. In China, sex is an extreme sensitive subject.'

'But there are a *billion* Chinese. You have more sex in this country than anywhere else on the planet.'

'That is to count acts. It is quantity, not quality.' He tutted at such an elementary error.

'You paint sex slogans in every village. There are posters on every street.'

'These promulgate Party policy on child-numbers and only one.' He tapped a finger across Mo's samples, playing them like a xylophone. 'Perhaps such objects are everyday in your country. Here, they are imperial, feudal and obsolete.' He leaned down and sharpened his cigarette on the edge of the waste-bin. 'Your factory ran into trouble and you needed help. Who did you turn to? Did you approach the Ministry of Health? Or apply to the All China Women's Federation? Or present your plans to the Medical Ethics Committee? No. You rang a man called Billy.'

'I had an order of ten thousand to deliver by Christmas.'

'Actually, we know very well of this Billy. He is on our List. He is a rogue, a wheeler-dealer, a pornographic influence on our doorstep. For now, he is safe on *your* land,' as if Mo owned Hong Kong. 'We can do nothing about him for...' Gu knew exactly how many months, weeks and days till Britain handed over the territory and Kowloon Billy.

Mo picked up her mug and sipped at the tartness of cold tea. It was the taste of Eden House at the end of the night shift – tetchy and tired and waiting for Carol to come and take over. If only she'd burst into this office right now with her optimism and lucky charms.

'If you want to live in this country, and if you wish to *stay*, you must fit in with our values and customs, with our way of life.' He drew on his cigarette and released a column of smoke. 'You are a guest, here on a visa due to be renewed really very soon. It can be cancelled, of course, at *any* time.' He reached inside his jacket and placed a sheet on the table, her way up. 'We have identified your Two Gross Deficiencies.' He slid it towards her. It was typed in Chinese and English and headed *Strike Hard Target: Simone Moore*.

Mo read:

> *First Gross Deficiency: Your factory does not conform to local conditions.*
>
> *Second Gross Deficiency: Your household does not conform to local conditions.*

At the bottom, with a space for her signature:

> *I understand the above-stated Deficiencies and guarantee Rectification by one month's time or else my right to be in the People's Republic of China, and to all Capital and Assets on China soil will be rescinded to nothing.*

Gu unscrewed the lid of his ink pen and held it out to her.

But Mo *didn't* understand the deficiencies. 'Conform' was not a word she'd ever really warmed to. Nor 'rectification'. Nor, for that matter, 'gross'.

Gu glanced at his watch. 'The minutes tick, the hours, the days. Soon it will be first of February, and on that date, I must forewarn you, your factory becomes an illegal.'

'And what happens to it?'

'The State takes control.'

'And what happens to me?'

'The State takes control.'

Mo stared at Gu's implacable face. There was nothing he wouldn't do.

'And we apply all applicable laws.' At the end of his cigarette, a long line of ash had curved to breaking point.

'What if I refuse to sign?'

Gu screwed the lid back on and slipped the pen into his pocket. 'Then I cancel your visa with immediate effectiveness, from here and now on.'

He stood.

Li swung heavy legs over the bench. He gave Mo a shrug and shuffled like an apology towards the door.

'We have a long drive to the Yang'an Bureau. But it is on the way to Hong Kong. Over the border-crossing, and you will be home again. As much English tea as you want.'

Mo went to the window. Out of habit, she glanced up for the factory name, but here inside was the one place there was no red glow of *HAPPINESS*. The sky was still blue, though. The pigs still slept in each other's warmth. Chickens chatted under the bamboo. Pingdi looked perfect, struck hard by nothing but pure sunlight.

'I want Mayor Lin as a witness.'

'The mayor is unavailable.'

Mo picked up the phone and dialled his number. She put the receiver to an ear.

Gu raised his chin, making the bones of his neck click while Mo listened to the silence of a line that had just been cut.

Mo watched her visitors head back to their car, Li plodding and Gu with a strut, always one step ahead. They drove off, creeping through the village, which was probably the speed limit, but also an announcement that they had called. They inched through the South Gate, then revved off in a cloud of red dust back under The Mist.

Mo ran to the mayor's house, taking the long route along the Menglang, where ribby cows stood stark on its banks, staring into the abyss of the river. The mayor was at his window looking out for her. He opened the door and stood on the mat, his trousers black with water. He pulled at his flares, detaching them from his shins. 'There was no time to go all the way to the bridge. I walked across the river.'

Because Mayor Lin had been sent on a wild goose chase – called to a village on the other side of the Menglang, where Old Wang, great-great-grandmother and related to most of the valley, was apparently breathing her last. He'd arrived with condolences and white chrysanthemums picked along the way. But instead of dying, he'd found her listening to the national news, keeping up with Strike Hard.

The mayor switched on his radio. Bush House had been turned to static. Instead, the Strike Hard scores wound into the room in a voice Mo knew from Saturday afternoons, from *World of Sport* and the pools: Shenzhen: three hundred and fifty, Guangzhou: *four* hundred; Beijing: two hundred, Shanghai: two hundred and *one*...

The mayor read the Two Gross Deficiencies. He read them again. Then he took off his glasses and rubbed at his eyes. 'I can tell already, Momo. This one is grisly. I have lived through the Five Failures, the Four Don'ts and the Three Disproportions. We lost a Dadu man to the Disproportions. It was a public execution, the whole town summoned, and broadcast through speakers. Even the Middle School pupils, they were lined up in the yard and silenced for the shot.' He paused. In the street, dogs howled at phantoms, spooked by the hush of the village. 'The family, they had to pay for the bullet.'

'I don't have any family.'

'My own nephew disappeared for a while in that one. They accused his video store of disproportionate foreign movies. They checked every last one. It took them many weeks of film-nights and they finished off his popcorn, but in the end they let him go unscathed. He had just one fine to pay, for *Kramer v Kramer*. They did not approve of the divorce.'

The mayor sat next to Mo now and explained the Gross Deficiencies. 'The first one, it means: we do not like what you *do*. The second one, it means: we do not like who you *are*. Which, I think, covers everything.' A glance out of the window to where the sky was vast, but starting to cloud over. 'Did Gu want anything else?'

'He took a set of keys.'

The mayor picked up his glasses and chewed the end of an arm.

'And he said the factory was one of the Six Evils.'

'Oh... Momo... He accuses us of pornography. We need help. And urgently. And not any old help. We need an expert, a *zhuanjia*. Narcotics, gambling, profiting from superstition... such things are easy by comparison.' A hand threw them aside. 'But pornography has a moving-target definition – one day Biology, next day Rolling Stones. Also it has the harshest punishment.' There was no hesitation: 'You know what we do? We turn to Doctor Long. He is knowledgeable on such topics and he believes in the factory. Also, he has two faces. He can see both sides. He is on our side, but he understands the other. I will telephone him and explain all.'

A plan seemed to calm the mayor. He leaned back in his chair and slackened his face to the slant of the midday sun. 'Tomorrow, everything must appear normal. At the factory, it is Business as Usual. If there are any questions, we deny. Why? Because if it comes out we have been struck hard, no-one will dare cross the threshold. Who can risk *Worked for a Struck-Hard Unit* on their file? But how long will this campaign go on? One month? One year? No-one knows. And yet people must eat.'

Then came a knock at the mayor's door. His name called out. Then more banging, louder this time. 'You see, already they are anxious, already the questioning starts.'

It took a while for whoever it was to give up, but when they had, 'Milton is the only one who can know. From now on, he loads up the van, he drives any which way around the county, and after dark, he unloads at my nephew's video store. There the goods are kept under lock and key until this nonsense is over.'

The mayor stood and went to the window. 'This village is crafted from trees felled under the Ming and it has out-lived every ruction, made good of all that fate has thrown at it. But if we give in to Strike Hard, you know what will happen? Pingdi will be a ghost-town in an instant. Everyone of working age will be thin air. They will head again for the East to the building sites and factory workshops, where they will breathe in sulphur and hammer out the sounds of hell-on-earth. They will grow old making Gaming Boys and Marios. Children who have only just learned to stand will take care of grandparents who will never stand again. I have seen it anywhere and everywhere I have been. Pingdi is the only village I can name where three generations still live under one roof. *Happiness*, Momo. We must not let Gu get his hands on it.'

Chapter eight

The next morning, Mo climbed into the *Happiness* van and sat in the smell of a petrol leak while Milton drove her to the meeting with Doctor Long. He'd removed the dildo that swung from the rear-view mirror and covered the windows with copies of *Farming Today*. Mo watched cows on the way to slaughter lipping at the verge as if it were a free lunch. The radio was on, and more bad news rattled out. Milton switched to the tape, and they listened to Boy George sing 'Karma Chameleon' as they drove the five minutes through The Mist and into town.

They pulled up at the Number One People's Hospital. Usually, the wait in Reception was eased with the slip and slide of Kenny G on sax. Today, the national anthem ran on a loop. People queued in silence, fingering dockets and wounds. A figure in a fall-out suit took Vim and a toothbrush to a sign against smoking, swearing and the chewing of gum.

Mo had been given the code for the lift, but she wasn't going to risk it. If Strike Hard could happen – with no warning, just like that – then *anything* could happen: the lift could get stuck; the cable could snap; war could break out between floors. So Mo took the stairs.

Usually, in Dadu, strangers who knew her would wave and say, 'Hello! Hello! Hello!' – always three times – English discharged like a round of friendly fire. Today, though, just the sound of lungs in a fight against gravity and eyes cast down on cracked lino.

The entrance to the Advanced Family Planning Unit opened on automatic to thick red carpet and the sound of a kettle just reaching the boil. Doctor Long's secretary showed Mo to the Waiting Room – though there was no wait.

'Miss Moore, the mayor has explained me everything.' Doctor Long seemed to have grown taller since Christmas Eve, his eyes brighter, his movements more brisk. 'First let me say, I regret your predicament.' He took her hand and held it as if to console her, and she left it there, letting it be consoled. 'Second let me say, working in Family Planning, I deal daily in predicaments.'

Mo went to the window. Down there, Strike Hard was unfolding, claiming victims, adding to its tally. From the hospital to the horizon, houses fluttered red. Flags hung at every window, caught now and then by a fitful breeze.

Doctor Long said, 'They launch Strike Hard "to satisfy the masses". People want to know that as China grows economically, we also grow morally, there is no downside, no cost. So they target gambling and prostitution, gangs and drugs, hooliganism and bourgeois degeneracy. That one is *you*, Miss Moore.'

Her eyes found the road north, tracked it back to where it ended: in mist that hung like a sigh and the lights of *HAPPINESS* pressed hard against the mountains.

Doctor Long towered at Mo's shoulder, his gaze locked far into the distance, seeing things she couldn't. 'You see, China is not England. England is not China. Your factory sign, it says: "Unchecked Western Influence" in bright Broadway lights.' He massaged his fingers, making the knuckles click. 'Strike Hard hurts, I know. But the PSB, they work by quota. They need *one* from the Dadu and Pingdi District.' He reached for two chairs and invited Mo to sit. 'Next to you, I am the most Western thing for many miles around. I have studied in England. I have many international friends. In Shanghai, I used even the World Wide Web. Some of my searches set off alarms. Once or twice I had visits because I put sensitive body parts into the engine.' He rested his chin on a fist. 'The Strike Hard target, it could have been me. I feel a close shave and a duty to help. I know what you are feeling.' He told Mo what she was feeling, and he got it mostly right. He even knew she felt thirsty. He buzzed his secretary and gave an order for tea. Then he put his palms together and pressed them to his lips, as if in primary-school prayer.

In Mo's head: *Our father, which art in Heaven...* She thought: Selwyn, if you're up there, I'm not sure I *am* doing your will. I seem to have made a right bloody balls-up, as you would have said. I have trespassed, apparently. Please let Doctor Long deliver me from evil Inspector Gu, who just wants power and glory for ever and ever amen.

Mo's head rolled upwards, and when her eyes opened, they came to rest on an air-con breathing empty incantations. Then the brush of small steps on the carpet and his secretary came in with tea.

'It is the Iron Goddess of Mercy. Is it to your liking?'

She held the tea to her nose. It was red, rounded, forgiving.

Doctor Long leaned into the solidity of his chair. 'Contrary to the Deficiencies, I *know* you conform exactly to local conditions. The problem is: Pingdi is *very* local. It has extremely special conditions. Some say it is because of The Mist. It is like a Cloud Nine. But for Inspector Gu, it is mere smog. He is the kind of man who likes clarity, and so we must be clear. We must show we understand him. We must offer something.'

'Not a bribe.'

'We offer understanding. We show that he is right.' Doctor Long inspected his fingernails – squared-off, attended-to. 'Gu looks at your products and asks: where is the peer review? Where are the clinical trials?' He lifted a hand to a wall of portraits – urologists, epidemiologists, sexologists, he said, and he named them all in Chinese. 'And on this wall, we have the famous Alfred Kinsey, William Masters, Virginia Johnson, Beverly Whipple.' He dwelt on her, the G-spot-lady. 'Like you, she sees things on-the-other-hand. Like you, a risky person. What do they all have in common?'

Mo scanned faces with wry corners and cool eyes beyond surprise, eyes that had seen everything.

'They are all ologists. They have *science* in common. And that is what *you* must have.'

Mo had O-level Biology, and had scraped O-level Maths, which she'd needed to get into Elderly Care. And, actually, it'd turned out useful. She was always doing long division with pills, converting Celsius back to Fahrenheit, cutting the 360 degrees of a birthday cake by the number of residents left alive to eat it.

Doctor Long held up both index fingers, like two little dickie birds, Peter and Paul.

'Two Gross Deficiencies. We take them logically in order: the First one first.'

That was fly away Peter.

'The Second one second.'

That was fly away Paul.

'We take your factory. What must we do? We must correct it – the untested, unscientific, uncertified, nature of it.'

That was come back Peter.

'Tomorrow, I take you to a *xing baojian zhongxin*. In English: sexual healthcare centre. For short: sex shop. It is China's first one ever. It is already certified by the Chinese Sexology Committee. We see the standard, the technological level. Then we make necessary corrections and *we* get the approval too.' He stood. 'But the first step in correcting your factory is correcting the title of its manager.'

'You mean call me "Ms"?'

'Doctor.' He signalled to Mo to stand by the window, and in the flatness of the light, his eyes took the measure of her. 'You are small for clothing?'

Large was always comfier.

He put his face round to reception, and a few moments later, his secretary came back with a lab coat. Doctor Long took it from the hanger and slipped it onto Mo's shoulders. 'There. Already less deficiency.' He took a step back to gauge the effect, then held out his hand. 'Pleased to meet you, Mo *Yisheng*.' A firm grip, no consoling this time. 'So, *Doctor* Mo.

'Isn't this lying?'

'It is suggesting something, but only to the suggestible. And is that not *their* error?'

Mo wasn't good at lying. It gave her vertigo – that fear of falling into the chasm between fact and what she was actually saying. The feeling of teetering on the edge of being found out. She said, 'I don't think this is legal.'

'It is customary. It is what everyone does. And if everyone does it, all is fair, no?'

'But then, how can you trust anyone?'

'You trust your instincts on who you can trust.' He reached for her lab coat, turning down the collar and straightening the sleeves. 'So, tell me, how do you feel?'

She felt like a fraud.

'And please do not tell me you feel a fraud. We mean "Doctor" in the catch-all sense.'

'But what if someone asks to see my credentials?'

'When did anyone ever ask to see the credentials of a lab coat?'

The plane to Shanghai carried businessmen and bureaucrats. The window seats were empty – these people had seen it all before. Instead, they read reports and newspapers, their arms spread wide into the aisle as they cruised 35,000 feet above Strike Hard. Front pages were full of photos of people with shaven heads and in prison scrubs. The flight attendants took small steps in stiff orange outfits. Halfway across China, they placed silver-foiled meals in front of men who didn't notice, then shuffled back in the other direction and took them away untouched. Mo watched as they pleased the aisle with smiles that were thin but unbreakable, offering drinks, magazines, Rolex watches.

Doctor Long said, 'Shanghai is time itself. It is already the future. It is the fourth dimension. I was born there.' He leaned towards the window. 'The owner of the sexual healthcare centre, she is forward-thinking, but still she might say things that surprise you. If we have a crash of cultures, do not worry. I will catch the ball. She said to me when I rang, "The future will be Chinese, but the present is still English." She is happy to compare and contrast. She hasn't had contact with London since the day she left.'

And that was where Doctor Long had met her. They'd both had a year at the School of Hygiene and Epidemiology. She was working on methods of mass decontamination, had spent her time in quarantine, in a windowless basement that rattled with the Piccadilly Line. Doctor Long was researching male-male sexual contact in urban public spaces. He'd applied to study Hampstead Heath, of course. But then everyone had. Instead, he was allocated Russell Square. 'A disappointment at first because less data, but in the end, I grew fond.' He took notes from the same wooden bench, and passed the time with the grey squirrels and a quarter pound of chewing nuts. He'd met all kinds of people in London, he said, even *Psst!*-types. 'They helped me to see Russell Square not as a small Camden Council park but as a "performance space for infinite identities".' It's what he'd put in his article, and it was accepted by the *Journal of Genders and Sexualities*. He'd published his statistics on covert sex-acts in *Forensic Psychiatry* in Chinese.

Then the plane tipped, and through the clouds, the city burst into view. Doctor Long put a finger to the window. 'Across the Huangpu River there is Pudong. Ten years ago, just marsh and vegetable plots. See how we Shanghainese profit from time.' Now the horizon fizzed like a sweet shop. The Oriental Pearl TV Tower launched strawberry bonbons into the sky. Neon lights sputtered sherbet across the river. The Jinmao Tower looked as if it had been poured from a pot of syrup and crystallised into the world's third tallest building as it was decanted from the clouds.

Somewhere down there, Mo thought, was China's first official sex shop. Though not, according to Doctor Long, the first *ever* sex shop. There were dozens of them in the big cities now, down small backstreets. 'They do not exist, of course. Just like pornography. Because it is illegal it does not exist, but it *does* exist. Just like prostitution. Because it is illegal it does not exist, but it *does* exist. Just like concubines. Because they are illegal they do not exist, but they *do* exist.' The glance of his chin towards the rest of the cabin. 'Some of the men on this aeroplane, they fly between wives.' He sat back, enjoying the softness of his seat. 'China! Ah, rules and recklessness... pointing fingers and blind eyes... closed doors and open secrets... In my country, nothing is allowed and everything is possible. I am so happy to be Chinese.'

The Tree of Knowledge sexual healthcare centre was housed in Hospital Number Eight. Doctor Tang's office was a suite in Gynaecology, and her door opened the second it was knocked. She wore a champagne-coloured lab coat with the collar turned up and her stethoscope as costume jewellery. Monogrammed on the breast pocket: *SHE*, as if Hygiene and Epidemiology were a luxury brand. Doctor Long presented two business cards – his own and one for Mo. He must have had it printed overnight. Doctor Tang took them, her head inclined, both hands, releasing from her sleeve the scent of something honeyed. She read both cards attentively, first his, then hers. 'It is not easy, Doctor Mo, what you try, to come here as a foreigner and do what is sensitive even for a Chinese. I am admiring of you,' and she reached for Mo's hand and patted it. 'It is for sure you need approval.' She pointed behind her desk, to the certificate from the Chinese Sexology Committee – *Tree of Knowledge* gold-lettered, the paper puckered under the Committee's seal. 'You know about "The 1990 Decision Regarding the Punishment of Criminals who Smuggle, Produce, Traffic in and Disseminate Pornographic Articles"?'

Doctor Tang delivered that in one breath.

'It outlaws obscene tools. The CSC must approve your products as scientific, not pornographic. Otherwise, the law hangs over you. Actually, it *always* hangs over you, but less heavy.'

The CSC had inspected her premises, she said, for hygiene and protection of youth. She'd sanitised every surface – every last corner, every printed page. Then she'd gone to Beijing and taken the CSC test on sexual science. She named the five professors on the panel, said it wouldn't last more than a couple of hours, and to look out for the trick questions. She reached into a drawer and pulled out a thick book: *The Statistical Manual of Sexual Disorders*. 'In here are all possible dysfunctions. All you must do is memorise this.' Doctor Tang had prepared for two months and passed on the first attempt. 'You have only one month, which is half the time, but you are half as old, therefore no problem.' She gave the book to Mo. The *Disorders* weighed heavy. Inscribed on the title page:

May you soon be certified!

Your friend,

糖医生

Doctor Tang

Mo had her doubts about sexual dysfunctions. Her own mother was supposed to have had one. She'd told Mo the story – how Selwyn had booked her in at a private clinic, a knowledgeable chap, and he knew the consultant from various county events. Selwyn drove Sue into Leeds, dropped her off, said he hoped it went well, love, and they find out what was up with her hormones, and not to worry because you can always take pills for them, and he'd wait for her in Wetherspoon's.

Sue wanted to know what was up with her hormones too, because she loved Selwyn. She was his wife, anyway, and sex was what wives did, they both knew that. And marriage was for life, and they were so near the start of it – although, as it turned out, near the end – and she wanted it to go back to how it was. She *wanted* to want sex with Selwyn; she just didn't actually want it. Surely there was something you could take for that?

In the waiting room, leather chairs and help-yourself teas and cellophaned vanilla-tongue biscuits. She watched the fish in the aquarium flit past each other, glassy-eyed, gaping now and then at their chests of useless treasure, and mouthing at the shipwrecks that littered the bottom of their lives.

Then a door opened and a deep voice said, 'Do come in Mrs O'Shea.' The consultant sat tall in front of his library and tidied the tip of his tie. He talked about what a fine man she'd married, about how much he admired Selwyn. And Sue listened, and nodded, and let her eyes drift along his reference books: *The Veterinary Annual, Stockley's Drug Interactions, Wisden*, and she couldn't help wondering how animal-loving cricketers ended up sorting out women's sex lives.

He ran through her bloods, a steady release of numbers, like the bubbles in the fish tank. A little anaemic, but nothing to worry about. Hormonally, well, there are always fluctuations, what with the cycle et cetera, but you are, Mrs O'Shea, perfectly within the normal range.

He made suggestions: treat yourself to a make-over, Mrs O'Shea. His wife knew a smart place in Mayfair.

Or a pleasant perfume, Mrs O'Shea?

He kept calling her that. Not Susannah, or even Sue, even though they'd met in passing. He kept reminding her of her reason for being there: she was married to Selwyn, and he was paying.

Or a low-cut top?

Sue looked at her knees. She felt the pressure behind her eyes.

'Mrs O' Shea?' Sue looked up. The consultant was cupping his hands in front of his chest. 'Why don't you make yourself a bit more *a-go-go*?'

Sue apologised. She pulled the tissue from the cuff of her jumper – used, but only in the car on the way here. Sue liked ribbed jumpers, especially polos. She wasn't fond of her neck, not now it was starting to go. And she liked the feel of it. Because the truth of it was that she'd much rather be hugged by wool from the House of Fraser than by Selwyn Roderick O'Shea.

Doctor Tang led the way through a bamboo curtain and past a sign banning children, dogs and lack of hygiene, and with a grand sweep of her arm, threw open a door. Mo had seen troupes of women make moves like that in Dadu People's Park – their backs set square, angling fans, describing perfect circles with their plimsolled toes. The Tree of Knowledge was misted with classical music. A butterfly mobile fluttered with the breeze. Mo caught the hint of probably tea tree underscored with bleach. Over the counter, a banner said: *Move Towards Scientific Sex!* 'My patients, *they* move towards it.' A dozen men stood fixed at glass displays. It was like a museum with one man at each, taking it in turns to decipher the gadgetry. 'All walks of life come here: workers, peasants, soldiers, entrepreneurs...'

Mo glanced around. There were no children, dogs or dirty people. 'There are no women.'

Doctor Tang said, 'The women go to Family Planning. They do not come to a place like this because of two thousand years of feudal thinking.'

Mo scanned the men for signs of feudal thinking. She found looks she knew from Eden House when Carol wheeled round the Sunday desserts, and the gaze of residents followed her, their faces both hopeful and horrified, their eyes grey with cataracts, their skin tinged pink with guilt and desire, and the look of alarm when their favourite pudding was offered to somebody else.

Doctor Tang's mouth opened a fraction to a ring of bright teeth and a stainless tongue. In a whisper: 'This particular gentleman, he comes here every day.' An elderly man was chewing his cheeks and clinging to the waistband of his hospital pyjamas. He didn't know where to put his feet without looking at the ground. 'He is widowed.' She pointed to the Advice Desk with its First Aid tin and blood pressure gauge. 'He is lonely. He likes to chat with me about his wife.' Mo took in Doctor Tang – her kindly face, her skin marshmallow-dusty. Her perm was thinning and, caught by the neons, it framed her like spun sugar. And that's when Mo saw how soft the doctor was. She thought, if she hugged her, she could squeeze until she felt her own fingers. In the Tree of Knowledge, she had the same effect as the butterflies and piped music. She was here to soothe, cushion, sweeten.

Then the music stopped. 'Can you name the piece?'

Was that a starter for ten? Mo's mind went blank. But Doctor Long landed straight on the buzzer. 'Symphony Number Six from Beethoven.'

'Exactly correct. The *Pastoral Symphony*. We play a tape called *Nature's Greatest Classical Hits*. *The Lark Ascending*, for instance. *The Rite of Spring*, for instance. With our natural atmosphere, we show our patients that sex is part of life, it is biological.'

Doctor Tang put a hand to Mo's elbow and moved across to *Bioelectronics*. The men shuffled on a place. 'I have heard about your product called Dildo. This is your first error. You must choose a name that says what it is on the tin. In Chinese, we call it *jianweiqi*. It means: Health. Consolation. Machine,' said like that, mouthed and weighty. 'It consoles the not-yet-married woman. It keeps her healthy in time for wedding.' Doctor Tang felt in a pocket for keys and unlocked the cabinet. Mo noticed the wedding ring, the fit tight, the shine dulled by the years.

She reached for a box that said *jianweiqi*. 'Now I show you your second error. Notice the difference with Dildo,' and she lifted the lid. Inside, a pink figure lay draped in gauze under a vaulted Perspex lid. 'Observe he is human-coloured.'

'Aren't humans lots of colours?'

A nod at that. 'But none of them indigo.'

Mo peered closer. It was as if Action Man had died and been laid in state. 'Who is it?'

'We call him Mister Mode. He is the missing husband, but will be introduced to her sometime soon. It is the name of our brand. He is the result of scientific averages. We did much study. We surveyed all the statistics. We found the average length of vagina, the average width of vagina, we made him average good-looking.' The tip of Doctor Tang's finger hovered over his head, tracing the features. A pearly nail tracked the eyes, nose, the line of the hair, the way expert fingers did on *The Antiques Roadshow*.

Then Doctor Tang removed the lid and lifted Mister Mode out of his casket and placed him on the counter. In the bottom of the box, a chemistry set. 'This one, we have it everywhere in the hospital. It kills dead all known germs,' and a puff of aerosol – heady, almost alcohol – that Mo knew from Eden House, from wiping down surfaces after the Co-op had been for the body.

'But the lubricant, *that* took effort. Too much, and the vagina is like catching eels. Too little, and it is sea urchin. We studied average vaginal discharge across all ages, both quantity and quality. And this...' She released a drop onto Mister Mode's forehead, baptising him with it. '...is the perfect co-efficient of friction for national average intercourse.'

Doctor Tang folded back the gauze cover, unsheathing the shaft and revealing at the base the kind of control panel that comes with a Scalextric. 'Your third and most important error is: Dildo has no technicality. It leaves all to the imagination. This allows unscientific things to occur.' She put a finger to a dial and Mister Mode trembled till his features blurred. She turned another and he writhed and twisted, creeping round, leaving a trail of lubricant like the wake of a giant snail. 'At peak output, it takes exactly one minute to turn a full circle.'

Which made it perfect for timing an egg.

Doctor Tang tipped the box and the instruction manual fell into her hand.

In fact, it was a book: *The Natural Science of Sex*. She ran a finger down the contents: Human Physiology (Normal and Abnormal); Health Benefits of Regular Sexual Intercourse; Excitement-Plateau-Orgasm-Resolution and How to Perform the Cycle; Climactic synchronisation.'

Doctor Tang checked her watch. 'Men are average two minutes. Women are average twelve.'

Doctor Long glanced at his.

Mo didn't wear a watch. Could you actually calculate an average, she wondered, when there were so many cases of Never, when the time lag was infinite, or at least till you gave up and made a cup of tea?

'And at twelve minutes...' Then a woman's voice, breathy and strained, fell into Doctor Tang's palm. 'She says *"Kuai dianr! kuai dianr! Wo shufu! Shufu!"* Mister Mode offers suggestions, hints what to say, such as "Quicker! Quicker! Oh, comfortable! Comfortable!"' Doctor Tang turned to Doctor Long. 'Is that a correct translation?' And then to Mo: 'Is that what *English* people say?'

What *did* English people say?

Her Diploma Dave had been chatty. He used to say, 'Hello!' as if they'd only just met and they'd been wrestling empty sheets up till then. He'd say, 'Happy Sunday!' because it usually was, because that was their best opportunity when it was Dave's turn to travel. Sundays was when the preacher came from the Gospel Group, and for an hour it was relatively quiet on the Red Corridor. There were fewer attempts outside her door to put names to faces people saw every day, fewer conversations with wives long since dead.

Dave and Mo shared her single bed. It had wheels that shunted them across the room and a waterproof cover that rattled so loud you could hear it outside the door. When they were done, as Dave used to say, they lay head-to-toe, smoke rising at Mo's feet from his roll-up. His feet never smelt, and he had straight, flat-topped toes like the keys on a manual typewriter. Mo used to wonder what English would be like if it only had ten letters. Good for quiet types, probably, because there'd be so much less to say, and all the while, Dave talked through his cigarette, telling her all the things he wanted to do, and all the places he wanted to go with her. Then he folded the end of his cigarette over, came down to her end of the bed, and put his lips to an earlobe. Sometimes he even nibbled. '*Say* something to me.'

From the lounge, messages in multi-faith boomed over the deafness of the residents.

'*Tell* me things,' he said.

'Which category?' She meant Entertainment, History, Sport and Leisure... Dave was keen on *Trivial Pursuit*.

'*You* things.'

It wasn't a category Mo talked much about.

'So, *us* things, then.'

That one even less.

So then they got up, and Dave put on his boxers and shifted the waistband up and then down, working out which side of his belly to put it. He stood on his toes in front of the half-mirror, trying to see all of himself. He said to Mo, 'How do I look?'

He looked like a man about to turn thirty and worried about his belly. He looked ordinary and pale and harmless, and that's what she loved about him.

When Mo went up to Dave's place, he cooked them a meal and put a candle on the table in a wine bottle kept from their first date, the billowing robes of wax like something Roman Catholic.

Dave was lapsed. But still he smelt of incense. Lined up along his bathroom shelf, the whole range of Body Shop for Men.

When he got undressed, he folded his clothes on the back of the chair then got into bed and wrapped himself around her, a perfect fit. Spoons, he called it. He was tidy with cutlery too.

But if she woke in the night, Dave had always turned and was asleep on his back. You wouldn't know he was breathing. Sometimes she leaned over to check. He looked peaceful – and medieval, like the graves of knights with their hands in prayer and their feet cocked for pigeons to sit on.

On the counter of the Tree of Knowledge, Mister Mode slept and had possibly died. Looking at him closely now, Mo thought he was a bit like Diploma Dave. It was the page-boy haircut and the spread of the nose. And Dave had been Mister Average: average height, average build, medium brown hair, bloke-type face. And he'd been averagely taken by Mo. He hadn't fallen head over heels. He'd strolled in at walking pace, stayed a while, and didn't seem to mind walking out again.

But he *had* been uncommonly understanding. He didn't mind her foibles such as earplugs and snacking on crackers in the night. He was exceptionally willing to see her point of view, to compromise. Was that a good thing?

Maybe at the UN.

But at the General Assembly of their relationship, convened in the morning over coffee and toast, it was...

'You think I'm boring, don't you?'

Mo took a bite and chewed that over. There *was* something margarine, something easy-spread straight from the fridge, about Dave. She said, 'You think I'm frigid don't you.'

'Only your feet.'

That was another unusual thing about him. Dave let her warm her feet between his thighs.

Also, he drew hearts and stuck them around her room. He left her post-it notes saying *Love You!*

Mo wrote messages back: *I don't know what you mean. Please be more specific.*

And he actually was.

Her room at Eden House had been plastered with Dave's precise kindnesses, till the central heating had peeled them off. They kept it hot for the residents and, in the end, his messages had dropped to the carpet and curled up like flies and died.

Mo looked now at Mister Mode – willing but stilled – and thought: maybe she *did* miss Dave.

Or something like him.

Or something like those notes.

Chapter nine

Mo and Doctor Long stepped out of the Tree of Knowledge and straight into the rush hour. Doctor Long flagged a hand, bagging a taxi stuck in the distance. Mo watched women work the jam, beating out a sales pitch to drivers going nowhere for feather dusters and laminated maps of the world. A bus drew up and nurses leaned into each other's backs until something gave and there was room to get on.

Doctor Long said, 'Doctor Tang has shown us what we must do. Only we do it better. We take a name that suits this time of Strike Hard: not personal-individual like "Mister" and not Western-fashion like "Mode". The taxi crept into the kerb. 'I think: *Scientific Universal Vibrator*.'

But that would make it the SUV.

'And we apply technology. We give it power. Rocket Power. Super power.

And that made it sound like the Arms Race.

The taxi made its way across town on an elevated highway that tracked the waistline of the city. Planters strapped to its side draped flowers over the road. Shanghai wore it like a diamante belt. They pulled up at the Coming Century Tower. The lobby was all commotion, people hurrying to catch up with whatever had left them behind. TV screens had rolling market coverage, flashing red and green as fortunes were lost and made. Disco balls spun each other's sparkle. Digital clocks told the time to the tenth of a second. In Sydney, it would soon be tomorrow. 'You see how hectic the future will be?' Doctor Long said. 'This is what we must be part of.'

At the lift, a bellboy Mo had never seen before was dressed like a flight attendant and greeted them both by name. He pressed the top button, then settled his gaze downwards and studied the shine on his shoes. It was a slow, smooth cruise with 'The Blue Danube' to the top of the tower. Doctor Long said, 'When you meet with the Chinese Sexology Committee, you will make a presentation about Marriage Bonds. You will explain how the correct application of the SUV binds husband and wife together.'

Mo glanced at the bellboy, wondering if he spoke English. But he was glued to his own reflection and humming Strauss under his breath. The lift sighed to a halt at the 88th floor. A bell pinged. The bellboy saluted them, his eyes shielded by the length of his teenage lashes, and they stepped onto red carpet and into ionised air. They went to Mo's room. Doctor Long drew the curtains and switched on a lamp. A circle of yellow light stained the spotless carpet. 'It is best for you to stay here till we meet again tomorrow. Shanghai is not Pingdi. It is the future, and the future is glorious but also dangerous. As we say: *Zhuyi anquan!* Pay attention to safety!' And he went around the room explaining the security features. 'This is how you double-lock the door. Here is the safe box.' The bathroom seemed to know they were coming, lit their way, offered water, blew them hot air. The sink and the toilet wore *SANITISED* sashes. 'In this room, A is OK.' He paused. 'But just in case...' He flicked open The Coming Century directory. 'Here are emergency numbers. Here is Reception. If the telephone rings, please pick it up and listen for who. It might be me. But if a woman asks if you have everything you need – or even if a man does – tell them you are sleeping already and put the phone down. *Do* you have everything you need? For instance, food: please order your evening meal from Room Service. There is international choice.' He turned to a page of double-decker burgers and pastel-shaded shakes. He picked up the remote and switched on the TV. He tapped through the channels. 'Usually this one is BBC, but in Strike Hard only snowstorm.' He stopped at Chinese news in English, where a grey-faced couple sat in front of a wall of watery screens looking as though they were broadcasting from a diving bell. Over a shoulder, John Major was marble-eyed and mouthing things on mute.

He turned the telly off. 'It is better for you to profit from Time. You have much to absorb and much to prepare. Tomorrow, I introduce you to China's Kinsey, my friend Doctor Shu. He has the statistics on what, where, when, why and how of sex in this city.' He cast around the room for sources of disturbance, turning down the thermostat and adjusting the curtains to cut out a sliver of light. 'Sleep well. You must wake with an open mind and an excellent memory.'

When Doctor Long had gone, Mo picked up the *Statistical Manual*. It was bi-lingual and littered with diagnostic codes. It listed Sexual Dysfunctions, Paraphilias and Gender Identity Disorders. There were subtypes: Lifelong and Acquired, Generalised and Situational. They could be due to a General Medical Condition, or Substance-Induced, or Combined Factors, and was she really supposed to memorise all this?

Mo rested the *Manual* in the palms of her hands like you do with Weigh-the-Cake. Three pounds? A little more? She took it to the bathroom and weighed it on the scales: 1.5 kilos. If this was the Eden House summer fête, she'd have taken the *Statistical Manual* home.

Mo felt the shine of the paper, sniffed the binding, and began the Introduction by the Chinese Sexology Committee about intervening in sexual disorders for the good of the socialist order. Her eyes ran over the lines, but she wasn't really reading. She was remembering, thinking back to her first ever sex shop – the Peep Hole shop, as it was known, because the blacked-out window had a spyhole for adults, or anyone over five feet tall. She'd been carried past it hundreds of times. She'd toddled and skipped and run past it. And then one day, she'd just slowed her pace and stopped. It was raining, of course. It rained every time she and her mother took the bus to Leeds. Behind them, shoppers didn't give them a second glance. They'd folded up their faces into tight grey packages against rain that was falling in dirty, crumpled sheets over their weekend.

It seemed so unhaveable at the time. But then, all the best things seem out of reach when you're nine years old. Mo said, 'What exactly do they sell in there?'

'I don't know.'

It sounded like the truth. It sounded as though her mother hadn't been in, even though she was old enough.

'Don't they sell sex in a sex shop?'

Her mother sniffed.

Mo sniffed. The air smelt of wet concrete and candyfloss from the shop next door.

Her mother said, 'Are you hungry?'

'Don't you *want* to know?'

'Let's get candyfloss.' A tug on Mo's hand.

'*Do* they sell sex in a sex shop?'

Mo felt her hand let go. 'More like aids.'

'Like First Aid?' Mo pictured plasters, bandages, Savlon, and adults slugging it out, bruising each other, inflicting wounds, while they did whatever it was they did when they made love.

Then a man brushed past, cap dripping, hands in his pockets, and a shoulder shoved open the door. Thanks to the rain, he spent a while wiping his feet on the STEP INSIDE, LOVE mat. Thanks to the rain, Mo got to see a red light and a young woman with dark eyeshadow leaning a careless face into a hand.

And then the door crept shut.

They bought candyfloss and ate it in front of the Peep Hole shop. Her mother's face was printed on the glass. Mo tried to read it. Perhaps she was thinking about Selwyn. But then, probably not Selwyn. He was in the factory, even though it was a Saturday, sorting out something important, looking forward to coming home to his tea.

Mo tore off clumps of candyfloss as big as her mouth and big enough to choke her, and felt it dissolve to nothing on her tongue. It was like coming up for air in the swimming pool. It was like falling over and feeling the pain ebb away. And it was like her thoughts sometimes. They dissolved too, especially on Mondays, when they had a mental arithmetic test. Or when her father whispered to her mother, and her mother's face went serious and she didn't whisper back.

Mo stood where the two shops joined, one foot in front of each, one foot either side of the line of age and permission. She knew which she liked more. She was sure sex would be better than candyfloss, and that's where she wanted to spend her pocket money. She wanted to give her one pound fifty to the woman with the heavy eyes in exchange for one of her Aids.

In the morning, Doctor Long picked Mo up and led her across the People's Square for brunch in the Scottish-themed café, Yaldi! He opened the door to the low moan of bagpipes and wallpaper checked in midnight blue. At a corner table, deep in the gloom, a lone figure. Doctor Shu was the café's only customer. 'Normally, the café is packed and heaving, but with...' He seemed afraid to say the words 'Strike Hard'. His anxious eyes flicked to the waitress who watched them from the counter without blinking.

Doctor Long gave her a nod, indicating that he was going and she'd have one fewer problems to solve.

'Doctor Long, *please* do stay.' It came out bleated, more beseech than invitation.

'You know what they say: two is company...'

'But I *like* a crowd. I come here because usually it *is* so crowded.'

Doctor Shu also came here, it turned out, when he wanted to remember Scotland. He'd spent time in Glasgow investigating the effects of divorce on life expectancy. 'People in Glasgow, they live short. I hypothesised that marriage breakdown is a factor.' Does divorce make you ill, he wanted to know. Does it reduce life expectancy, and if so by how many years? He got a grant from the Sino-Scottish Friendship Society, and spent six months in The Calton, lodging in the spare room of a family undertakers, and analysing the life history of every death they handled. And as a thank-you, once a week, he cooked them sweet-and-sour. And what Doctor Shu discovered was: yes, divorce and morbidity were correlated. But not as strongly as deep-fried Mars Bars and Irn-Bru.

When Doctor Long had gone, the waitress emerged from the shadows with a large pad and doughy fingers wrapped around a Saltire pen. She looked displeased to see them, and took the order from several feet away.

Mo glanced down the menu. 'I'll take the haggis and chips, please.'

She shook her head. 'It has to be cooked.'

'Then... the chicken tikka masala?'

The waitress jutted her chin to the back of the café where the kitchen door was chained shut and the cook was off.

So, for starters, Mo chose the honeydew melon.

Doctor Shu said, 'I have the same.'

'And the Scotch egg and salad.'

'I have the same.'

'And for afters, the sliced peaches.'

'Everything the same. The same is always best. The modal average is safest. Statistics show this.'

Mo took in his profile, the ovine slide from forehead to nose to chin buried in a thick wool scarf.

Then Doctor Shu cast a palm across the blue-green check of the table. 'Do you know which tartan this is? It is Johnson. As in Virginia Johnson. As in Masters and Johnson. As in H.S.R.C.'

He seemed to think Mo would know what he was talking about, but all that came to mind was her HSBC credit card and long waits on the phone to Coventry.

Doctor Shu gestured towards a red shimmer in the middle of the café. 'Usually, I sit there, at the MacDougall table. My host-family in Glasgow was MacDougall. I like it also because red is a happy colour. But today I choose this table because today we discuss the Human Sexual Response Cycle, and especially, I explain you: *orgasm*.' He pressed his palms against the tartan. 'Orgasm is like marriage adhesive. It binds couples together. This is what you must tell them at your exam in Beijing. Your SUVs release natural fluid glue.'

And still his hands were stuck to the table.

'Orgasm is the peak. In Chinese we say *"xing gao chao"*. It means "sex high tide".' Doctor Shu moved aside the vase with the thistle to whisper. 'Important to say it clearly, not confusing with "xin *gao chao*". That is "*new* high tide", a campaign against criminals. Like a Strike Hard, only worse.'

Then the melon arrived, a slice of honeydew placed flat on the plate and offered like a down-turned mouth. Doctor Shu must have seen it too because he spun his plate 180 degrees and looked happier after that.

Mo picked up her spoon and ate.

Doctor Shu picked up his spoon and talked. 'The man, he ejaculates. We say *shejing*. He shoots sperm. It makes him relax. It prevents the build-up of tension to a point where he gets blootered and whoring, as Mr MacDougall liked to say. Men, they ejaculate. Women, they do not. Or some say they *do*. I also heard this in Glasgow.' He put his spoon to the fruit, found it unripe, juiceless. 'But at least the wife has vaginal secretions. And that makes the glue. It is like a chemical formula: semen plus secretions equals marriage cement.'

Mo finished off her melon. She ran a tongue around her mouth, a tart taste gathering.

'In China, we like to summarise things with sayings such as: *nanqiang nüruo*. It means "men are strong and women are weak". Also *nankuai nüman*. It means "men are quick and women are slow". There is a time lag. Like England lags behind

China, so women lag behind men. Except...' He picked up his spoon, but only to wave it at her and make his point. 'Women *can* be quick. I have discovered this through experiments on my wife, with straight-out legs and hyperventilation.'

'Oh God, *please*...' That was really too much information. 'Please eat,' Mo said.

But Dr Shu had more to tell her. 'Husband-and-wife life cannot take for ever. People must also sleep. They must be in time for work. Perhaps they share their room with the in-laws just the other side of the curtain. There is a housing shortage in Shanghai. Many people, they cannot afford privacy. They cannot afford foreplay items such as scent and silky underclothes. So, best for the woman to be as quick as the man.'

Mo nodded at his plate, encouraging him to eat.

He nodded back. And they nodded together in synchronised misunderstanding.

'If the wife can be accelerated with a machine such as yours, there is a better chance for *xing tongbu*. Sexual synchronisation. There are six permutations for orgasm.' He held up five fingers and his spoon. 'Husband then wife; wife then husband; husband first, wife not at all; wife first, husband not at all; no orgasm...'

The waitress interrupted to clear their plates, then leaned across the table, flipping a damp cloth back and forth and leaving a streak of something sour.

'But the best,' and he patted the air with the back of his spoon, 'is same-time simultaneous. Same is *always* best. And so we see the vast and even the *socialist* importance of your SUVs: same-time simultaneous equals happy couples, equals happy families, equals happy society, equals happy China.'

The waitress reappeared with the Scotch eggs rolling around the lip of the plate. She'd halved a tomato with a serrated knife and it had bled red, like a damaged organ.

Doctor Shu reached between his knees and pulled a document from a briefcase: *Quantity and Quality of Orgasm – a dialectical approach.* 'A successful orgasm is when a man, unimpeded by his wife's body, expels semen between 30 to 60 centimetres. That is the ideal strength of propulsion.'

Doctor Shu had written marginal notes in soft lead pencil. They were smudged and spotted with a selection from the Yaldi! menu. 'For a wife, a successful orgasm is when she has ten contractions, one every 0.8 seconds.'

'How is she supposed to keep count?'

Doctor Shu looked puzzled. 'It is not difficult maths. It is only one to ten. Do you know how many types of female orgasm there are?'

Mo thought: sex in China involves an awful lot of counting.

'Thirty-eight.'

That seemed random. 'Is it a lucky number?'

'Not *especially* lucky.' Doctor Shu thought about it. He chewed at the crust of his Scotch egg. Then he came up with something. 'Thirty-eight is three-eight! It is March the eighth. It is International Women's Day!' He said, 'The Chair of the Chinese Sexology Committee discovered *all* the types.'

'What's her name?'

'He is a professor. His work in this area cost him much effort. You can imagine!' He poured salt into his palm and cast it over his food like confetti. 'You will meet the Chair at your exam in Beijing, so you must know about his findings,' and he recited some of the orgasm-types: 'the "passage of electric current type," the "temporary cessation of breathing type," the "temporary body paralysis type," the "as if drunk and stupid type"...'

'Have you finished?' The waitress was at the table picking up Mo's empty plate. She'd eaten too quickly and was feeling sick. Doctor Shu held onto his, but still didn't eat. 'Lack of orgasm is a threat to marriage. But I have proved that a bigger threat...' He lugged a box-file onto the table and pulled out *Divorce – statistically significant risks*. '...the *biggest* threat of all, is lack of child.'

Mo's eyes slid away from the document and came to a halt on the lid of the ketchup that had leaked and browned and hardened.

'Doctor Long told me you are childless.'

Had he?

'This is risky.'

'I'm not married.'

'It is a huge risk,' and his arms measured the length of it – as long as the tartan table, black at the corners where a cloth had never reached. 'If a wife does not have a baby, people think she is strange. They laugh at her. Mock her. The pressure, it comes from all sides: parents, in-laws, husband, neighbours, friends, colleagues. Also *self*. Therefore, I conclude: best to be normal. Safest to be a mother.'

Mo let her gaze drift over Doctor Shu's shoulder. Outside, it was a wet-mouthed kind of day – thin, clammy, ever-so-slightly acid. Pollarded trees hung their stumps over the road. Children at the Little Eton kindergarten slugged at each other behind iron gates.

'After I did the Cox proportional hazard model, I found that a son has a high protective effect on marriage. But with a girl or no baby, the risk is about the same. It means having a daughter is like having no baby at all.'

Mo wanted to grab him and say: *Hello! I am female and I exist!* She wanted to jump up and down with the waitress shouting: *Look, daughters!* And Doctor Shu would have been mortified: 'I didn't mean *you*. My statistics are not *personal*.'

Which was always the trouble with stats.

Mo's gaze went back towards the window. On the other side of the street, the Western Foodstuffs Restaurant had a scattering of white faces. She said, 'What percentage of the Shanghai population is foreign?' Because Inspector Gu had told her she'd feel more at home in a city.

'You are most welcome! Also, if homesick, you can try Chaoyang district in Beijing because of the foreign embassies and associated cuisines. Also Shamian Island in Guangzhou.' He said it was a popular thing to adopt a Chinese child and the U.S. consulate was there. People stayed at the White Swan, and ate steaks and drank beer, and signed off the paperwork. 'Mostly unwanted girls because of the One-Child Policy.' A ruffle of his coat, the tail-end of a shrug. 'A girl causes parents to argue. But a boy, he carries the name. He takes the family to the next generation. At least in China.'

Also, Mo thought, when it came to the O'Sheas.

'So Doctor Long is lucky.'

Or perhaps he just made his luck. Mo had heard how some of the rich got their sons: by having the scan and paying for the op. Illegal so it does not exist, but it does exist, as Doctor Long himself would have said.

Doctor Shu asked, 'Have you met Jingming?'

'Lulu?' He came to the Palace when he was home from school and whenever he was allowed. He cycled from Dadu, said hello to Mo, then disappeared into the undergrowth. He'd built himself a hideout, and he stayed there for hours in the company of wildlife, watching how it just *was*, and not trying all the time to be better. He ate from the trees and day-dreamed till the light faded and he had to get back to Golden Dawn Gardens.

'An exceptional talented boy. Top marks at everything he touches. And for his parents, he is a protective factor. Whereas I have a daughter. Although, with regard to Lily, my wife and I are a statistical anomaly. We see eye to eye on her. We even agreed about Rocky.' He was the fiancé with the PhD that Lily had let emigrate to Connecticut. 'She did not pay him enough interest and he called it off and lives in Stamford now, working for very big pharma.' As if reminded, he reached into a pocket for a pill to aid digestion. 'That is how it is in China: PhD men marry MA women. MA men marry BA women. BA men marry High School women. Some people do not get married at all. Lily must be careful. Her MA is a risk to her marriage prospects. Many Old Maids have MAs.'

'Did she like him?'

'She thought he was so-so. He had a PhD, but a hard-boiled heart.' Doctor Shu tampered with the remains of his Scotch egg but seemed reluctant to finish it. 'And Rocky was not discreet. Their petting-relations were noticed, and Lily was summoned to a Morality Hearing. The Chairman, he said: "Petting anytime you want leads to intercourse anytime you want, and that is no different from animals. But you are *not* a beast of the field. You are one of China's best minds. If you show no restraint, what are you? A slut and screw-around. What do you get? Bastards." He did not say those terms exactly. I learned those words in Glasgow.'

Doctor Shu riffled his folder. 'Before she could leave the Morality Hearing, Lily had to sign this.' Against a backdrop of ice-clear water, and in a script that ran down the page, the East Coast Normal University's Purity Pledge:

> *I commit to loving the Motherland*
>
> *And caring for her people;*
>
> *To treasure each moment of life,*
>
> *And build a safe future;*
>
> *To handle my studies*
>
> *With rigorous science*
>
> *And be pure in thought and deed.*

'I thought The Pledge could be useful for your factory. Print it on a banner and hang it over the entrance so workers are reminded at the start of each day. Except instead of "my studies" put "SUVs". What do you think?'

Mo thought she'd never have survived growing up in China. There was Lily, old enough to do an MA and banned from kissing on campus. And when Mo was twelve she used to stay over at her friend Chrissy's house and do striptease on the bed, spinning her knickers round a finger and flinging them onto the gerbils, while Chrissy swung her torch across the ceiling and sang 'You Sexy Thing'.

Things like that went on in her class.

There was Julie, who sat next to Nicky. They were best friends and did everything together, including – when Julie's parents took the dogs for a walk – fishing her dad's magazines from under the bed and feeling sick and screaming, because that couldn't be what was really down there.

Then there was Oliver, who played the clarinet and showed his todger to anyone who wanted to see it. There were queues by the trees at the bottom of the playing field. People in the school band even got to touch it because the music room had a lock.

Also, Stewart, who pulled Jackie onto the bank and bounced on top of her, holding her wrists, while chewing a Bazooka Joe. And when he got off, she had grass in her hair and a look like the swim-suit women who come out of the box at the London Palladium, sawn in half and amazed they're still alive.

It was their first year at secondary school, 1976, that hot summer of undone buttons, the ladybird plague and 'You to Me are Everything'.

Doctor Shu put his knife and fork together. He'd given up on his egg. And perhaps the thought of eggs led to the thought of sperm because: '*Your* parents had a girl. Are *you* a risk factor? Do your parents fight?'

Mo's parents hadn't fought because Sue knew better than to fight Selwyn over anything. But at some point, fairly early on in the marriage, Sue had started talking about *my* daughter instead of *our* daughter.

Because Sue couldn't change much about her actual situation, but she could change the use of possessives, and in her mind, that changed a lot.

When Mo was born, Selwyn had hesitated when the midwife had asked if he wanted to meet his baby girl.

'A *girl?*' But it was O'Shea & *Sons*. And his mother had told him that Sue's pregnancy showed all the signs of a boy. Nanastan had even chosen her grandson's name. It would begin with an 'S', of course, and she'd settled on 'Simon' because Selwyn's favourite game had been 'Simon Says' with himself in the title role. Sue had gone along with it because she liked Simon and Garfunkel. She'd often sung 'The Sound of Silence' in the last days of her marriage.

So, Selwyn went into the delivery room, and pecked his wife's cheek, and bent over his child's face and said, 'You wouldn't know if you weren't told, would you?' He ran a hand over her head. 'I didn't know they came out with hair. It's *my* colour, isn't it.' He fingered her fingers, said how alive she was, and tiny, and *his*. 'We'll just add a letter,' he said to his wife.

And so Mo became Simon-with-an-e; the Simon who wasn't; the next in line of O'Shea & Sons; the boy who turned out to be a girl.

They had photos taken together: Sue holding Mo; Selwyn holding Sue holding Mo; and after much fumbling, of Selwyn holding Mo. He clasped her in front of his chest as if she had handles and this was a trophy, the flash went, then he gave her back. And he never really took her again.

Now the peaches arrived, frayed at the edges. Doctor Shu counted his segments. He counted Mo's. 'You have less.' He paused. 'But countable peaches, therefore you have fewer. But anyway, better the same. Always best the same,' and he spooned fruit from his to hers until the bowls were even.

Mo ate. She frowned. The peaches tasted of the tin they'd come from. Doctor Shu was frowning too, but not because of dessert. 'Except there *is* an exception. If a wife has the *same money* as the husband, this is risky for marriage. She is easy to go, not bound to stay.'

Thank God.

And thank Sue's Uncle Bill. Because when he died, Sue came into some money of her own. Not much, because there weren't many takers for a back-to-back terrace in Burnley with no garden, a coke boiler and the railway rattling the windows. But when the cheque arrived in the post, she thought she wouldn't mention it to Selwyn. He'd never met her uncle anyway, had never really registered he existed. So she went to the Halifax and opened an account in her own name. She didn't know what she'd do with the money. Not exactly. But she'd spend it on herself. On something she really wanted.

And then Christmas came, what turned out to be the last O'Shea Christmas – though Sue didn't know it at the time. On Boxing Day, Selwyn drove his father home, and put on the heating and sorted him out with a cup of tea. And while Selwyn was gone, Sue arranged the house so it was theirs again, and put Stanley's sheets in to wash and plugged in the Airwick. She made Selwyn a nice turkey-bubble, and put her hair up, and matched the necklace he'd given her for Christmas with one of his favourite blouses. And after he'd eaten and was soft with a Jameson's and a laugh at *Morecambe and Wise*, she said: 'Selwyn, love, I've been thinking, perhaps it's time for a break. Just three nights, staying with Al.' She said it with the tone of a weather forecaster who tells you tomorrow will be pleasantly sunny with a warm, light breeze. 'She invited me up, and she's not been so well, and I...' She wasn't going to say 'want a few days to myself – just a taste, just a reminder.' She knew not even to say: 'think it would do me some good.' Good would be counterproductive.

'Oh aye?' He lowered his tumbler onto the armrest, the whisky stirring gold. 'And how you going to get there, if your chauffeur's not invited?'

'It's not that you're not *invited*. I just didn't think you'd want to come.'

'I don't want to come.'

'So I'll get the train.'

'Oh aye? So I'm paying for your British Rail jollies now, am I?'

Doctor Shu wiped his lips on a napkin. 'So, there we have it: the orgasm,' and he sank back into his chair. He seemed happy, soporific even. Then he reached out a finger and traced patterns in the Johnson tartan. 'The Cycle, it is everywhere you look... Excitement. Plateau. Orgasm. Resolution... The four phases are like the movements of a symphony. Like the acts of a theatre play. Even, perhaps, how your own story will turn out: you are excited to leave England; you plateau in China; you achieve the goal of the Two Gross Deficiencies; you live happily ever after.'

Then the waitress approached, scuffing her heels and totting up the bill in her head.

'Here comes another example: the four phases of our meal – starter, main, dessert. And now we are at Resolution, which is I pay the bill.' He took out his wallet and put a note on the table.

So the tinned peaches were the climax. They were sticky, anyway.

The waitress gave him the change and said thank you for coming and now they were closed.

Doctor Shu emptied his wallet of coins and counted out a tip. Mo watched as he sorted by denomination and arranged them in towers, making patterns with his loose change.

'You look frowning. Is there something you do not understand?'

She didn't understand patterns, or maths, or cycles, or what on earth she was doing here talking to a sexologist who had made sex so unsexy.

'Do not worry. Doctor Long is my friend, and you are his friend, so we are friends, we stick together.' Doctor Shu ran a finger down the sides of the coins, straightening them up. 'What you try here in China is unprecedented. There is an element of unknown, of gamble. But Doctor Long always gets what he wants. What *you* want, *he* wants. Therefore, you will get what you want.'

Doctor Shu's world seemed full of logic like that. So easy. So implausible.

She thought the towers of coins looked like casino chips. And didn't the house always win in the end?

Chapter ten

The Coming Century had felt like a stay in a private hospital, with Doctor Long calling round every so often to make sure all was well and she was enjoying the comforts of the room. But now it was almost eleven and check-out, and Mo would be discharged into the world she knew – a world in which, in fact, she felt more comfortable. Doctor Long had got up early and was already on his way to the train station. He was going to Xiamen, a city, he said, famous for Piano Island, where cars were banned and love of classical music was a must. 'Harmonious now, but not always.' Xiamen had been fought over – by the Portuguese, British, French and Dutch. They'd all been there and left their mark. And today, Doctor Long was going to meet Mr Li, manufacturer of model battleships, fighter-planes, missiles and rockets, and who could supply power-packs for the SUVs of the magnitude the doctor was looking for.

Mo tested her rucksack. It was weighted with Doctor Shu's papers and a corner of the *Statistical Manual* angled into her back. But still there was space for waxed apples for the journey, and the hotel shaving kit, umbrella and loofah as souvenirs for the mayor. She thumbed the Directory for ways to while away the last few minutes and found calls inland were free. So, Mo picked up the phone and dialled the mayor's number. *Would you like anything else from the future*? she'd ask him. Something plastic-wrapped, perfumed, throw-away?

But there was no answer.

Then Mo phoned the factory, and still no-one picked up. So she tried the only other number in the village.

Straight away, the sound of the lifted receiver.

Then silence.

Mo said, 'Are you meant to be in my house?'

'Where are you?' It was Lulu.

Mo glanced at the hotel clock. It said 10:57 and bad news was coming, she could tell from the smallness of his voice.

Lulu said, 'Come back quietly.'

Not quickly. But then, no-one ever got to Pingdi quickly. But *quietly*?

'The mayor sleeps.'

Was that a euphemism? In the corridor, Mo heard the dirge of a hoover. Then the rap of knuckles on the neighbour's door.

'He needs rest.'

So alive then.

Lulu said, 'There was a visit from Inspector Gu. The mayor has been Struck Hard.' He told her that he'd been on his way to the Palace to spend some time in her garden, and he'd just gone through the South Gate when he saw a car with a Yang'an plate parked outside the mayor's house. His front door was wide open. Then Lulu heard shouting. 'The mayor was accused of aiding and abetting the BBC.' The inspector had sat at the mayor's desk and taken his time dismantling the radio, the mayor's beloved Shanghai 131, awarded by the PLA for Outstanding Service in Korea. The Shanghai was the size of a small television. Gu had made the mayor watch as he'd taken off the wooden casing, removed the Bakelite dials and the green light that hummed, and as he'd watched, the mayor himself had seemed dismantled. He'd pleaded with Gu to stop: he had no idea what he was doing, how much the radio mattered. But the more he'd pleaded, the more pleasure Gu took in the slow but accurate work of his screwdriver.

When he'd finished, Gu bagged up the parts for Forensics. It was evidence, he said, and every piece had to be logged. Then he pressed the mayor's thumbs onto an inkpad, and the mayor signed a docket to confirm the debris was his. Gu put the evidence into his briefcase, dusted off his hands, got back into his car, and zoomed off.

The mayor had run after Gu, Lulu said, barefoot and in pyjamas. 'I shouted to him to stop, but he just kept running.' So Lulu cycled to the factory, found Milton, and they drove in the van till they caught up with the mayor. He'd got to the last bend before The Mist. 'Even when he could not run, his feet kept running.' Lulu had seen the mayor fall. 'A hard one,' he said. 'His temple was cut and his eyes would not open. We picked up the pieces of his broken glasses. But do not be afraid when you see him. He looks worse than reality. It is just bruises and wounds and confusion.'

But Mo knew what falls could do. They'd been the beginning of the end for so many men at Eden House. Mr Todd, for instance, who'd tripped over his own feet doing keep fit and died the same night. And Mr Willis, who'd reached too far to pick delphiniums and lost his balance and never got up again.

'Are you on your own in the Palace?'

'Old Mang is here talking to the mayor, telling him stories, keeping his mind alive. And the couple from The Usual Place tries to feed him soup.'

'And Milton?'

'He collects Mrs Su. Milton said Inspector Gu has gone to war with us. It is time for reinforcements.'

It was dusk when Mo's bus crept into Dadu station. The poster of Deng Xiaoping welcomed the world over a rim of petunias. Milton was there in the *Happiness* van, napping on the steering wheel. The bus was late, delayed by goats on a hair-pin bend and by police searching for hooligan elements. Then the passenger door of the van swung open and a lithe figure jumped down. 'There you are *at last*!' as if Mrs Su had been looking for her all this time. It was a different woman from the one who'd met her at Hong Kong airport. Improving Mr Su's prison conditions had consumed and transformed her. She was sparky and light on her feet, her hair razored and steely-grey. 'You are not to worry. This Gu-man is the one to be nervous. *I* am here now. I have put the Long March rocket into space. My hair has been singed by fireballs. I can handle dynamite.'

They climbed into the van. Mrs Su breathed deep. She inhaled the fumes that leached from the petrol can and closed her eyes as if appreciating the scent of flowers. Milton started the engine. The windscreen wipers slipped back and forth, marbling the view with insects. Mrs Su wound down the window and rested an elbow outside. 'You know Deng Xiaoping said, "When you Reform and Open the window, some flies will get in."? Well, Gu-man thinks the mayor's radio is a window. He thinks the BBC is flies.'

She spat onto the road.

Milton turned out of the station. He took the way back slowly, headlights on. 'The mayor stays in the Palace, Momo.' It was the first time Milton had ever called her that. 'I hope you do not mind.'

She said, 'Is Lulu upset?' He'd seen the argument with Gu and the mayor and the radio.

Milton didn't answer. He kept his eyes on the road, looking out for pitfalls that appeared from nowhere. He seemed weary, as if night were falling heavier than usual and landing entirely on his shoulders.

Mrs Su said, 'In time he will forget.' She held her breath as they passed through The Mist. 'Though with Lulu's memory, he will *never* forget. But he will put it behind him.' He'd seen things like that before, she said. The Exceptional School was more sticks than carrots. 'Like my husband. He had sticks in prison. They locked him away for months like a dog, and by the time his trial came, he was already crazy, his mind gone simple.' She put a hand on Mo's thigh and squeezed. 'I am sorry I cannot buy this Gu-man off. But all your money has gone. It was not cheap to reduce my husband's jail sentence. It cost much to buy him a glimpse of sunshine and a cooked meal each day.' Because Mr Su, she said, had made the beginner's mistake of telling the truth in court. His defence was that he was a professional actor, and playing the part of Ronaldo – the Portuguese off-shore billionaire – was just another role. And 100,000 yuan? Ronaldo could lose that in a single night at the casino and wouldn't even blink.

Mrs Su had watched the trial from the gallery. She hoped the prosecution lawyer would say, 'My case has been made, your Honour,' and leave for an early lunch. But instead, he told the judge that negotiations were underway for Macau to be returned to China and the Portuguese had to be kept sweet. The last thing they needed was a self-confessed, life-long identity thief impersonating the most famous Portuguese in town. The judge understood the political context. He didn't think much of actors either. He said, 'What kind of a job is it to dress up in costume and recite from a script?' He adjusted his wig and robes, made theatrical moves with a gavel, and sent Mr Su down for thirty years, the first ten in solitary.

Milton swung into the Palace yard and parked under the light that he'd left on. Mrs Su and Mo crept upstairs and nudged the mayor's door open. His eyes were closed, his face mauve and puffy, with the kind of shine to the skin Mo knew from funeral parlours and bodies polished up for viewing. The air was clogged with wax from the candles and sandalwood incense that disguised the chamber-pot. In the corner, a large brown trunk. 'I have brought all known measures against bruising, anxiety and the PSB.' Kitchen-sink smells seeped out: vinegar, ammonia, rubber gloves, and was that alcohol? Mrs Su had everything in there – apart from personal possessions. Her luggage was devoted entirely to the care of the mayor. Then she squatted and lifted out a black case. It was a Shanghai 132, one grade up from the radio the mayor had lost. 'No-one must know, only me, you, Milton and the mayor. But of all possible medicines, a radio is the best cure he can have.'

Mrs Su turned it on and scrolled through static till a voice came out. Mo listened. A woman was speaking, soft and soporific, like a presenter on *Woman's Hour*. At Eden House, Mo used to listen to that at the end of her night shift to put herself to sleep. And then, 'Dan! Dan?' The mayor's hand crept in Mo's direction.

'It's Mo.'

His pyjama sleeves were torn, his thumbs bruised with Gu's ink. '*Shi ni ma?*'

She watched his face, his expression too bent out of shape to read. 'Your Momo.'

'Dan?'

'Tell him yes.'

'But I'm not.'

'But as poetry.'

The mayor's face tipped a fraction in Mo's direction.

'You are the *meaning* of Dan, the *idea* of her.'

And, actually, Mo had held many men's hands at Eden House – and been their wife, daughter, mother, lover – whichever absence their heart at that moment had needed to fill.

The mayor's eyes opened a fraction, just enough to find candlelight blinding. A frown as he tried to focus. Then the gap between his lashes filled with water.

Mrs Su blotted his cheeks with a tissue. She rubbed something onto his thumbs that smelt of Brasso and turned the pads green. 'You see why the mayor *has* to have a radio. He truly believes that his Shanghai will one day bring Dan back to him.' He told himself that one day he'd turn it on and someone at the BBC would say, 'And now, a remarkable story from China: the tale of one young woman who disowned her father in stormy political times, and decades later, found a way back to him.' He believed that because it was the radio that had come between them, Dan would use the radio to find him again.

'But children...' Mrs Su took a swig from a bottle. 'They do not think like that. They do not think rational. They do not even think *ir*rational. They just break your heart and kick aside the pieces. They ravage you. Like a plague. The mayor is plagued by the thought of Dan, who he loves to shreds despite the evidence. His radio-dream is not realistic, but to be a parent is to be unrealistic. It is to be mad. Possessed.'

Another swig.

'It is why I have never had one.'

She wiped a sleeve across the rim of the bottle, then pressed her chin to her breastbone, stifling the burn. 'Also, I am a rocket scientist. I am trained in delivery systems, and I can tell you: with humans, the design is wrong. Where else in nature are there forceps, screaming, ripping open and dying?' Mrs Su went to the window and stared outside. The vastness, blackness, the nothingness of it, seemed to soothe her. 'Twenty years ago, humans sent a message into space hoping aliens would hear it. They aimed at M13.'

Mo thought: of all the aliens in the universe, did we really have to contact ones that lived in a place named after a motorway? Couldn't we aim our pitch at a point in the sky that had some Chinese poetry: the Azure Dragon of the East, for instance, or the Vermillion Bird of the South?

'It will take 25,000 years to reach M13, and 25,000 years for Whoever to call back. And yet they did not realise: the aliens, they have already landed.' Mrs Su turned to Mo. 'Take a child – half mother, half father – you should recognise the parts, no? But you look at them and think: *who are you?* And they look at you and think the same, only with less love. Then they disown you. Then they are gone. Forever.'

Mrs Su went over to the mayor and listened for a while to the rake of his breathing. Mo took a hand, and rubbed a thumb, working at the stain. She imagined the mayor imagining she was Dan: fortyish now, and a wife and mother. And that would mean he had a grandchild. The mayor had family out there somewhere.

Then Mrs Su said, 'You look in trouble.'

Mo *was* troubled.

Because sometimes children *did* disown parents. Because hadn't she disowned Selwyn? She'd refused to see him, had run away from weekly access. And he'd reacted by going to court and claiming permanent custody. His solicitor had told the magistrate: 'My client's daughter is exposed to emotional instability that is impairing her judgement and already hindering her future life chances. The Respondent has furthermore been unable to secure proper employment since leaving the marital home and depends on state support.'

Which was true.

Sue had thought she'd have no trouble finding a job back in Housing Allocations. They knew her there. 'But that was how long ago?' the woman in Personnel said. So Sue had signed up with Kelly Girl. She'd temped all over, one stint in Rent Arrears, sorting out evictions, making arrangements for people to lose their homes.

'We also have reason to believe,' Selwyn's solicitor said, 'that Mrs O'Shea suffers periods of...'

'I'm Ms Moore.'

'Are we correct in thinking you are prescribed medication for mild to moderate depression?'

Anxiety, actually. And how had Selwyn found out about that?

The magistrate had looked thoughtful. But she'd also looked young and newly trained. 'I would like the wishes of the child to be taken into consideration.' And she'd adjourned the case till a report was ready.

On the way out, Selwyn said to his solicitor, and to everyone in earshot, including his estranged wife: 'How does a *child* know what's best for her? That's what parents are *for*.' A hand like a tiller, as he guided his solicitor out of the door. 'And why's Ronny Thorpe not on the bench?' Selwyn liked Ronny. He played the occasional round of golf with him.

Sue got home from court, the salt from dry tears mottling her cheeks, and recited the proceedings verbatim: *he said, I said, oh yes you did, oh no I didn't.* It was back to Punch and Judy. Mo wrote it all down. It would help the police investigation if Selwyn ever got them, and if he didn't, she'd turn it into a book one day and tell the world what he'd done.

Two weeks later, a woman had knocked at Mo and Sue's door – the kind of woman that Selwyn would have called 'a nice girl': neat and petite though she could do without them glasses. Sue showed her into the kitchen. The tea was already in the pot, the Ginger Nuts arranged like petals round the plate. And then Mo's mother disappeared.

She'd told Mo that someone from the court was coming for a chat. She hadn't said it was a Child Psychologist, though, because Mo didn't need psychologising, because running away from your father was perfectly sane, given events.

The Child Psychologist didn't say that's what she was either, just that she was called Flora. She chit-chatted about Mo's new school and her new friends and had she made them, while the roar of *Grandstand* broke through the floor.

'Have you said hello to your neighbours?'

Mister Man didn't say hello. He pretended not to know Mo if he bumped into her at the chute. He just took his time fisting his bags of rubbish. Mister Man didn't like the upstairs neighbours because they were always changing and the kids had heavy feet.

It took Flora a while to get round to Selwyn, by which time her jacket was off, her sleeves pushed up to her elbows, a daisy bangle around her wrist. Mo took that as a good sign. Flora was literal. If Mo told it straight, she'd write it down word for word, and that's what would get back to court.

'Tell me about your father.'

'What about him?'

'What do you most *like* about him?'

'That he's not here.'

Flora looked around, taking the place in. Her eyes wandered through to the living room, across the lino floor with the four dents where a table used to be, and up to a curtain rail with hooks and no curtain. 'Do you have everything you need?'

They'd lived out of a suitcase since the day they'd slipped out of the Quality Home. Sue had said that they'd go back – in a few days, at most a few weeks – and collect the things they'd left. They'd hire a van and a driver. By then Selwyn would have got used to the idea they weren't coming back. He'd have had a chance to calm down, divvy things up, be reasonable.

They had no idea that on the day they left, Selwyn would comb the house for everything Sue owned and take it to the dump and chuck it. Or that he'd change the locks and install an alarm linked straight to the police. Or that when she asked about having one or two of the white goods, he'd say: '*White* goods? They're *my* goods. *I* paid for them. *My* money.'

Several months later, and via her solicitor, Sue wrote to Selwyn: *My client requests access to the property to collect your daughter's personal possessions, in particular clothing and books required for school.*

And a reply came back in Selwyn's block capitals: *THEY ARE THE ONLY REMINDERS I HAVE OF MY DAUGHTER. I NEED THEM MORE THAN SHE DOES, THANK YOU VERY MUCH.*

Flora said, 'Tell me about something *nice* you and your father have done together.'

Mo watched Flora's fingers killing time. Mo thought: *Here's the church and here's the steeple, open the doors and here's the people.* Churches. What were they good for? Marriages and funerals. Life's all-time disasters.

'There must have been *something*.' Flora leaned forward to coax an idea, the V of her neck spotted with freckles and smelling like a vase. 'On holiday? A birthday?'

Mo had just had a birthday. She'd kept his card as evidence. She thought the court might be interested. It'd arrived a day late with a second-class stamp, no news, no enquiry, just the message *Love Dad.*

'He did say *"Love* Dad".'

'But only as an order.' Mo said, 'He's *not* getting me. I'm *not* going to live with him.'

'I know that.'

'So why are you here?'

'I need to hear why.'

Flora's bag was open on the kitchen floor, and in it, a clipboard and a form. She'd fill it in afterwards, back in the car, leaning on the steering wheel and scribbling notes while it was still fresh in her mind. Mo watched her gaze rove the kitchen: the electric stove brown with years; the cupboards black from a chip-pan fire; the walls purple, the grout yellow. A bruised kitchen. Beaten up. Flora's eyes had stopped on the fridge, on the Klingon magnet and take-away menu from the Golden Fortune restaurant. 'What would be the luckiest thing that could happen to you?'

A different father, though it was too late for that.

An address he didn't know about.

Flora held the mug in front of her face and blew mist over her lenses. Then she turned to the window. Outside, a cherry tree, its fruit bloodying the gravel. Mo used to like trees. But that one had branches as good as a ladder – she'd tested, and it could be done – which was why, if they needed air, it was on a chain. It was why at night they double-locked everything and double-checked.

'You run away from access every time.'

Mo and her mother had escaped from Selwyn once, and now Mo had to do it again, every single Saturday.

'Why's that?'

'There are some dangerous people in the world, aren't there?'

'Of course there are.'

'And some of them are fathers.'

'Some of them.'

'Well one of them is mine.' Because by this time, Selwyn had told them the bully boys of Leeds were onto them. He'd told them the price on their heads. Sue had taken out life insurance. She kept a hammer beside the bed.

Mrs Su tiptoed away from the sleeping mayor and led Mo through to the next room. She'd set herself up here to be close to him, but also to be close to her husband. It had been Mr Su's favourite room and he'd spent days in here, dreaming and smoking. She could still smell him, she said. It had a view down to the patio, like a Lord's Room at the Globe. He used to lean on the windowsill and imagine all the plays. 'The theatre was his life. His life was theatre. But then, he never could tell where the stage ended and the world began.'

This room had a mirror, bought from the Central Ballet Troupe, encrusted with rust and drilled across the middle where the bar had been. 'All the plays, they contain a mirror.' Mrs Su looked at herself, straightened her back, raised her chin. 'But, it was "to be or not to be", and it turned out the latter.' She cast her eyes over Mo's reflection – the Mao jacket from the General Store and haircut from the mayor. 'Except for the years, I think we could be twins. You know there are several twins in Shakespeare.'

But weren't twins with an age gap just mother and daughter?

'When he is released, we could always perform. I think, *What You Will*.'

'Will I?'

They didn't do Shakespeare at Mo's school because, according to her English teacher, there were things that spoke more directly to our daily experience, as she dished out copies of *Waiting for the Barbarians*. The irony was that the school was on the Shakespeare Estate. And when the Council finally moved Mo and her mother out of the flat above Mister Man, they got a permanent place on Ophelia Drive. Mo's bedroom looked over Titus Way, a dank little cul-de-sac that stank of dead meat and ended at the Bickerstaff sausage plant.

Mrs Su was pacing the room now as if it were a stage, testing the acoustics with 'Tomorrow and tomorrow and tomorrow,' and tilting an ear at the echo. 'The room is just as I remember it.' She filled her chest with familiar air. And then, with unexpected drama, 'You make me so proud!' Mrs Su pulled Mo close, as if she really had been looking for her all this time. Mo could smell the White Cat washing powder and feel the heat of her cheek. 'I am truly sorry for your trouble. But think how you have made Pingdi famous, and that makes *you* famous. And you speak so Chinese-sounding Chinese. And you will be amazing in Beijing. You will blow the professors' brains out.' Mo felt the touch of her hand on the back of her head, finding the bit the mayor's scissors had missed.

Mo said, 'I can't help thinking: if only the mayor had kept his Flying Pigeon. Then he'd have cycled after Gu instead of running, and then he wouldn't have fallen, and then none of this would have happened.'

Mrs Su said, 'In your place, I would think the same. I am in a similar place, but older, and so I can tell you: if the mayor had a bicycle, he would have cycled too fast and still had an accident. That radio meant everything to him. He could not be broken only on the inside. It had to show. He had to be injured on the outside too.' Mrs Su moved her hand up and over the swirl of Mo's hair and, somehow, she knew to leave it there. One warm, hypnotic palm keeping Mo's head on, her thoughts in, stilling her mind, putting her to sleep. It's what her mother had done when Mo used to hear noises in the night, someone creeping about, and she asked her mother to check. Mo curled into the shape her mother had made, while Sue slipped on slippers and took the hammer into every room of the flat. And then she'd come back, and climb in around Mo, and put her hand exactly where Mrs Su's was now. It was what it felt like when it was safe to go to sleep, when the world wouldn't end tonight.

Chapter eleven

For days, Mo tried to commit the *Statistical Manual* to memory. She asked Mrs Su for help, and she learned techniques from the theatre: reading her lines aloud, copying the *Manual* out, jotting down first letters. She tried reciting the disorders to the mirror and was amazed at the way it stopped her blinking and her lower lip did the talking, like a *Thunderbirds* puppet. She took the *Manual* to bed and wondered what people did if they actually had dysmenorrhea, dysphoria, dyspareunia... She fell asleep and had bad dreams that something hot and heavy was on top of her, and when she woke up the *Manual* was on her face, the pages creased and damp.

Mo had memorised things before – for school exams and at university – but never an entire book. And, mostly, she'd got by on her wits. But for Beijing, that wouldn't work. She had to be thorough, and she had to be exceptionally good.

Which was why she thought of the Longs. It was the weekend, which meant Lulu was home from school. He'd memorised the ninety-two verses of *The Mask of Anarchy* and recited them perfectly for his entrance exam. Could he come to the Palace and teach her how he did it?

Mrs Long listened with small, audible intakes of breath, to show she understood. But when she spoke, it was in a tone so reasonable and with such a calculated use of verbs that Mo knew it would end in a no. 'I *should* help, and I *would* help if I *could* help. Lulu also. But he *must* stay at home for revision. Unfortunately, he has no time to demonstrate The Method.'

A voice from far off: 'He has finished.'

Mo said, 'It's urgent, Mrs Long. I'm taking the exam in...'

'And Lulu has a vital test on *Monday*.'

'But I'm worried. What if I fail? We're talking Strike Hard. The *factory* is at stake!'

'And what if Lulu fails? His future is at stake.' Mrs Long managed to be alarmist with infinite composure. 'I promised my husband I would keep him on track.'

'And your husband promised me all the help that I needed.'

A pause.

Was that almost a sigh?

It sounded a familiar bind.

Lulu must have jumped straight on his bike and pedalled as hard as he could, because the kettle had only just boiled when he dashed through the Palace gate. He looked rained-on and euphoric. He'd cycled straight through puddles, his Exceptional tracksuit striped with mud. The wind would have been in his hair if his school had allowed him to grow it. In his pannier, a box labelled *Upright*. He said in England guests offered fruit or flowers, but Mo had those already in the garden. 'So instead, I bring you Brain Formula.' It was administered at school to every pupil because 'a phial a day keeps the dunces away', the School Nurse said. He unscrewed a bottle and held it under Mo's nose. It was thick and liquorice, the smell of childhood coughs and days off school spent in bed with Horlicks and *Jackie*.

'When you see the memory feat performed, it feels amazing. Like at the circus, as if magic. But, actually, it is a simple skill known already to the Greeks and the Romans. They called it The Method of Loci.' He took a seat at the kitchen table. 'With this method, I guarantee, you will remember *anything*: all the facts you must know for Beijing; every word of Chinese; every flora and fauna in your garden; everything that has ever happened to you. What I will show you has so much power, you will never be able to forget.'

It was the technique that had got him into The Exceptional School, and it was taught to new pupils as their first lesson because then they'd have total recall of their entire Exceptional career. 'Our teacher said we were all born talented and this is a meta-talent. It is like we are born again.'

Lulu took pen and paper and asked Mo to look away because to draw the Memory Palace he had to concentrate. So Mo turned her back and listened to Lulu rock in his chair and mouth things to the page.

Mo imagined his Palace like the one on the wall of the Dadu Bus Station. All day long, the man in the ticket office stared at it, dreaming his way out, till a bus came in and he turned to sell tickets through a rake of iron bars. Mo pictured tiered roofs, their upturned corners clipping the sky, a turquoise moat glinting with carp, stone dragons with a ball in their jaws and a tumble of marble terraces.

Then Lulu said it was OK to look, and he presented Mo with an architect's floorplan. 'This is my home, where you have visited.'

He could draw perfect straight lines without a ruler.

'A Memory Palace must be somewhere you know well, so you can walk in your mind from room to room and see it exactly.'

The Long's flat was much bigger than Mo had realised, with lots of rooms she had no idea existed.

'This is the door where you came in... This room we ate... This here is my father's suite.'

Doctor Long had a *suite*?

'His study, his library, his laboratory, his sauna.' It was where he did 'thinking and calculating and being undisturbed.' Lulu clasped his hands. 'So, this book...' and he leaned forward like a doctor asking after the ailment. 'What title must you memorise?'

Mo couldn't say *The Statistical Manual of Sexual Disorders*. Not to Lulu, aged eleven, however old he seemed. '*Good Housekeeping*,' she said.

He nodded, familiar with the title. 'My mother has memorised it too. Only in China, we call it the *Three Obediences and Four Virtues*,' and he demonstrated with his diagram. In the hallway, he wrote *First Obedience*. 'Why there? Because a woman's First Obedience is to her father, and in our hallway there is a photograph of my mother's father.' In Doctor Long's study, he wrote *Second Obedience*. 'Why there? Because the second obedience is to her husband. And when my parents have a disagreement, my father says "not in front of Lulu," and they go into his study, and when my mother comes out, the argument is over.'

Mo was listening, but only half. She was also thinking about the Second Gross Deficiency because according to that, her household did not conform to local conditions. Was *this* what she was supposed to replicate? Did Gu expect her to have a set-up like the Long's?

Lulu went on allocating Obediences and Virtues to the top floor of Golden Dawn Gardens: wifely speech in the lounge because that was where Mrs Long entertained guests; wifely appearance in the bathroom because that was where she checked her face and removed the faults and tidied up her hair; wifely work in the kitchen because that was where she did domestic duties after getting home from working at the kindergarten. 'And now, when you want to remember the Obediences and Virtues, you just walk in your head from room to room and see what you wrote there.'

'I'm not sure I can do this Lulu.'

'Draw a Palace?'

'Meet the Gross Deficiencies.'

'Do you know what Mao Zedong said?'

Did he have a saying for everything?

'"Investigation may be likened to the long months of pregnancy, and solving a problem, to the day of birth. To investigate a problem is, indeed, to solve it."'

Mo didn't tell him she had no plans to be a mother.

* * *

Mo's Memory Palace was Selwyn's palace. He'd lorded it in the Quality Home, loved to throw open the patio doors, spread himself out on the gold Dralon sofa, and 'peruse the view,' as he used to say – follow the perfect stripes he'd put in the lawn as far as the eye could see. Now Mo drew the lounge: the sofa, the fireplace with the French dogs from Harrogate and the ring of low chairs for when Selwyn had company. She used to watch her father's guests – the smiles that seemed to ache, and the lurch when they laughed at his jokes as if they'd been shot. When new people came, Mo had to wear the Canaries dress, which was where he'd bought it – a frothy, itchy, pink confection – then Selwyn would say, 'This is my Simone, say hello Simone,' and he nodded her into a quiet corner, where she sat, her face pale and long, like an upturned stick of candyfloss.

Mo drew the bathroom, where Sue had changed for visitors. She'd put her hair up, and 'that chain I got you for your birthday, love. Something nice to show off your neck.'

Selwyn had a thing about necks.

Mo drew the cloakroom where her father had kept his slipper. The kitchen, where the end truly started, with the doorframe chipped and the carpet sticky. The spare room with the single bed that her father had hammered to pieces. Mo drew the hallway, with the souvenirs of Civil War, and her mother's scribbled note to Selwyn stuck on the Guest Book, and their two suitcases as they waited for the minicab to take them away.

The driver had got out to help with the luggage. 'You off on holiday at this time of year?'

'I'm visiting my mother.'

'Long visit.'

'She's very unwell.'

Actually, she was dead.

He was quiet after that. He turned the radio on. The weather was the headlines. They'd woken up to drifts of snow. The snow of many winters had fallen on Yorkshire in flakes big enough to eat. Powerlines were down. Villages had been cut off overnight. The gritters hadn't been out and the road slipped under them. Mo's breath condensed on the window and she wrote *The Great Escape* in mirror writing then watched the words gather droplets and stutter down the glass. Her father would be in the office now, on the phone to someone, telling them it was unprecedented, and you can't have it as bad as we have up here, while his secretary hovered in the frosted glass with a steaming cup of tea.

The station car park was deserted. The driver lifted the cases from the boot and gave Sue his card to ring for the lift back home.

Inside, the ticket office pooled melted snow. A sandwich-board said: DUE TO SIBERIAN FREEZING CONDITIONS NO TRAINS SORRY TILL FURTHER NOTICE.

Sue said through the security grille and to an empty chair, 'They can't *all* be cancelled.'

A voice from nowhere: 'Best to go back home and sit it out, love.'

'But I *have* to get away.'

'Don't I know the feeling...'

Sue let out a sound Mo hadn't heard before, from the pit of the stomach, as if she'd been hit.

A moment's pause, then a woman came to the counter reading a timetable covered in crosses as if she'd been playing Battleships. 'Where'd you been looking to go to?'

'What time will it get here?'

There was one train moving in the entire country, 'heading extremely slowly, mind' in the direction of London.

Which was the wrong way for Auntie Al's, but it'd get them out of town. So Sue bought two tickets to King's Cross. She paused by the Waiting Room, where the electric fire was on and Johnny Mathis was singing 'When a Child is Born'. But someone in there was bound to recognise Selwyn's wife and think it good manners to say hello, and chat about the weather, and how was your Christmas, and do give my best to Mr O'Shea.

So they went into the cold and waited at the far end of the platform, by the danger signs and yellow lines and warnings not to cross.

Mo used the edge of her wellies to scrape up snow. She made a snowman and named it Selwyn Roderick. In a few days, she thought, when the weather improved, there would be no trace of him.

Sue took off her mittens, a gift from Selwyn, because 'anything you need doing with fingers, love, I can do for you.' She ripped up the minicab card and nearly did confetti, but couldn't quite bring herself because not littering trumped celebration. Every now and then, she peered through the spin of snowflakes to where the tracks bent out of town, telling the train they didn't have forever.

When it finally arrived, it was standing room only. But her mother must have looked old or disabled or pregnant because a man stood and offered her his seat. Sue sank back and closed her eyes. The carriage was gritty with sweat and sweet with chewing gum and cheap station coffee. She felt in her pocket for a hankie and held it over her nose. After a while, she turned to the window and dabbed at her eyes. They crept through whited-out, flattened England. They stopped at places Mo didn't know existed. And the grey sky, heavy with day-long snow, darkened to an early dusk.

Her mother reached out a hand and said they'd get off at the next one.

'Where is it?'

Sue turned to the window till a place name flicked into view: Stevenage.

Opposite the station, a fish-and-chip shop. They bought an Extra Large and ate it in the Coin-Op, where it was warm and had somewhere to sit. Mo watched the drums turn while Sue churned over her *List of Things to Do*: first thing in the morning, find a call box and ring Mo's school and say she'd be away for a fortnight. A planned absence – unavoidable, yes – and of course Mo would catch up with the classwork, and no, we have no contact details at all, we have completely disappeared.

Two weeks with Auntie Al, that was the plan. It'd give Sue time to get things sorted: go to the Council and tell them they were homeless, go to the Job Centre and tell them she needed a job, go to the doctor and get some pills to help her sleep, go to the Halifax and tell them her personal details were confidential, and not to be conned if Mr O'Shea came in and said, 'Don't be silly, not to a woman's *husband*.' And Mo could... Sue looked at Mo as if only now remembering she was there. She took her daughter's hand, slippy from the chips. Mo sat in the smell of Dreft, while her mother felt the bones of every finger.

Then they walked into town, looking for somewhere to spend the night, keeping pace with cars at a crawl. But Stevenage was shut. At the bus station, they found a municipal map, but when they wiped away the snow, someone had taken a blade to *You Are Here*.

And then they spotted a house, still fairy-lit from Christmas, with a sign that said VACANCY.

An elderly man came to the door bringing with him the smell of burnt toast. 'It's what it says: *a* vacancy. Not *cies*.'

He had a stoop and white hair and could have been Santa who'd kicked off his boots after a long day in the Grotto.

'We'll manage.'

'One bed, the both of you?'

'Just the one night.'

The man took them in – a hard look with clouded eyes. Then 'I see,' and he shuffled back towards the kitchen leaving the front door open. Over his shoulder he said to sign in.

'It's cash. I'm paying cash.'

'So I can call you by your name.'

So Sue took the pen and scribbled *Sue&Mo* in the Guest Book, and then wished she hadn't because Selwyn would be home by now and ringing round and reporting them missing, and she hadn't written illegibly enough.

They lay end to end in the single bed, hanging onto each other's ankles. The curtains didn't meet and the light outside the window frosted the ceiling white. The storage heater was off. The room was freezing and smelt of clothes that had taken too long to dry. Mo turned her face to the wall. The chips in the woodchip paper looked like the sperm in her Biology book. The whole room was covered in it. Mo tried to count them. She didn't know her mother wasn't asleep till she felt something warm trickle round her ankle. Mo said not to worry. It would stop snowing soon, and this was a new life, an adventure, and everything would be all right. Probably, she thought, it would.

Then her mother's voice came sieved through the nylon sheet: she could imagine Selwyn finding the note – written in a hurry on the pad she used for shopping. Because it wasn't fair, was it, just to vanish; it was a Thursday, after all, Sainsbury's night. Selwyn would get home and change into slippers and have a wash and check the telly, and it could be teatime and nothing on the table before he noticed that anything was missing.

The note was in Sue's hand, but the letters rushing forward, anxious to be gone:

SELWYN

Did twelve years. No blame.

Just snow too thick to see through.

Not lost. Don't look. Sue.

Which read more like a haiku than a note ending a marriage.

Mo had no idea how long Lulu had been gone. She didn't hear him come back into the kitchen, just out of nowhere: 'You sit in darkness, Mo.'

She looked up. How late was it? Soon he'd have to head home. He'd cycle to Golden Dawn Gardens, then ring to say he was safely back and she'd say: 'Night, night. Sleep tight.'

'Greetings from my parents.'

'And don't let the bugs bite.'

Because that's what her mother used to say till they left Selwyn and had real things to worry about.

Now Lulu lit a candle and put it beside her. 'You look exhausted.'

Why did children always tell the truth?

'You look a long way away.'

'I was in England.'

He'd brought them Noodles #2 from The Usual Place. Lulu sat beside her and took her drawing, walking in his head around the Quality Home. 'Your childhood house has many rooms. Your parents could have had several children. In England, parents do.'

'I think it depends how well they get on.'

'When you were born, the average was 2.93.'

Probably, that was the kind of thing you picked up if you grew up with Doctor Long – casual teatime chat about global fertility rates.

But then, Mo's family hadn't been average. And imagine, her mother had once told her, what Selwyn would have said if she'd had another girl. And if they'd had a boy, imagine the triumphalism. So, no. Mo was all she'd needed, and she'd taken the pill to make sure of it. Selwyn had made a big thing of that in court. '*My* wife,' he told the magistrate, 'planned *my* family without deigning to tell me. What does that make her?'

'In charge of her body,' Sue's solicitor said. It had all turned nasty. Sue had a solicitor and Legal Aid, and Selwyn had an injunction not to go near them.

Lulu said, 'My father would like to fill our home with his children, but he can't. By law, he is limited to me. By law, *I* am limited to me. And it is not so easy to be a singleton, is it? We carry all the expectation.'

Mo looked at those bright, unscuffed eyes, and thought how at odds they were with the things he said, how old Lulu seemed.

His face followed the first bats that skidded across the sky. 'Did you know they are mammals and give birth to singletons? They suckle their young with milk. It is everywhere like that in China. We all must have one-but-only-one. Will *you* have a child, Mo?'

The men at Eden House used to ask her that, when they'd had a midnight chat and a handful from the Roses tin, and she'd helped them off with their slippers, and tucked them back into bed. And she'd say, 'It's the oldies I like. *They're* my favourite.'

Which was true.

But also a way of not saying that she'd mothered once already.

Because that was how it had felt.

It'd begun with her mother's headaches, crippling ones she was sure were due to a tumour. So Mo had felt all over her head, telling her she was fine and wondering if those bumps were cancer or just the shape of her skull. Then her mother went to the doctor and asked for a scan.

'When did the headaches start?'

'When I left my husband.' Though not, actually, when they'd left. It was when they'd been rehoused a five-minute drive from the Quality Home. 'I don't feel safe,' her mother had told the Council. 'He can smell us from here.'

The doctor put his pen down. 'Well, then. The headaches are psychosomatic. Meaning...'

'I know what it means.'

'Meaning the quickest way to get rid of them is to go back to Selwyn.'

The doctor was on first name terms with her estranged husband.

'Do you know what he's *done* to us?'

'I'm aware of what he's done *for* you.'

Because what he'd done had got into Sue's head, went round and round and bothered her all night long. Sometimes she had a glass of wine to go off; sometimes she took a Diaz; sometimes both. When that happened, she overslept. If she went into work, it was noted down as a Lateness. So, usually, she phoned in sick, and in the end, Kelly Girl dropped her. The manager said, 'Mrs O'Shea, we cannot afford to keep you on our books.'

She was still Mrs O'Shea. Selwyn was contesting the divorce.

'You're giving the company a bad name.'

'But I got a hundred per cent in the entrance test.' Her mother was the only Girl in years who'd done that, who could work out compound interest and knew 'bookkeeping' had two 'k's.

So Sue stayed at home and watched daytime telly. She won *Countdown* several times from the sofa, and wondered how her life would have turned out if she'd married Richard Whiteley instead of Selwyn. When Mo got home from school, she collected the cereal bowls lined up on the floor. She opened the post – letters from his solicitor, letters from hers, red bills, blue bills, three-bags-full bills. She leaned over her mother and kissed her on the forehead the way you do when someone has died, and said, 'Have you done your teeth today?'

One time, her mother went into hospital – the Heart Unit – because Selwyn had 'trampled all over it, he didn't care,' according to Auntie Al; chronic hyperventilation leading to cardiac exhaustion, according to the doctor. 'We'll put your mother to sleep,' he said, which is what you did to sick pets, and she stayed asleep for weeks. If she came round because the pills were wearing off, Mo would tell her mother what day it was, where she was, who she was. It was the summer of the Moscow Olympics. Mo spent that summer in the smell of bedside vases that reeked of blocked drains, listening to all the sounds a troubled heart can make, while on the ward telly, the world's fittest broke records for endurance, strength and speed.

Mo listened to the sound of Mrs Su dropping things upstairs and the blur of the radio from the mayor's room. She said to Lulu: 'You weren't too upset by the mayor's injuries?'

'I have seen bruises before.' He pulled up a trouser leg and showed Mo his. Except it was more than that. A chunk had been taken out of him.

'I fell off a horse.'

Mo thought he was joking.

'We have started Polo at school.' He picked at a triangular scab. It was the width of his shin.

'Doesn't that hurt?'

'That is the point. I am practising.'

'For what?'

'For worse.' He said, 'You know in Nazi times, a brown triangle was the sign of a gypsy-man.'

'We're not in Nazi times.'

He worked off a corner, revealing wet. 'I am going to tell you something I have not told to anyone, and especially not my father.'

And then he said nothing.

Lulu finished his noodles. He went to the window and angled himself against the sill. Said to the glass, 'I am *not* going to have a child. A child is mine to have or not to have. And my father, he will *not* have it.' His see-through reflection was burnt by the flicker of the candle. 'He has no argument. You know Four Horsemen and an Apocalypse are coming? There will be Great Fires. Crops will turn to desert. I have done the maths. I have drawn the graphs.' An outstretched arm traced a line to the top corner of the window, to a damp patch Mo hadn't noticed where the rain was getting in, to where the next century ended and the world had gone into meltdown.

Dear Lulu. He needed more light. Mo found the box of candles and lined them up on the sill. The orange flames multiplied in the window. The whole Palace could have been ablaze.

'Some people think they are special, that when The End comes, they will survive it.' He put a finger to where a moth, drawn by the light, beat its body against the glass. 'But the only survivors will be such things. Insects. Perhaps also billionaires. But they will live underground, buried alive, like the emperor's concubines. My father says we must populate earth with special minds and talents who can solve the problem of The End. It is why I am at The Exceptional School. My classmates and I, we are supposed to be Saviours of the World.'

Standing there with his back to her, his hunched shoulders could have been angel wings.

'And for my father, that makes him a God.' Then he licked two fingers and went along the candles, snuffing them out with the sizzle of spit and a smell that made Mo think of birthday wishes. He looked up at the night sky. 'There. Thanks to the darkness, the moon shines brighter now.'

Mo said, 'Tell me things, Lulu.'

'What kind of things?'

'Moon things.'

'I already have. You tell *me* moon things.'

And so Mo said that in England the moon was made of blue cheese, and that dogs howl at it, and that when she worked at Eden House she used to sit with The Wakeful singing 'Moon River' and drinking hot chocolate, and it made them happy – Mr Nash especially, because the Man in the Moon looked just like him, he said. It was like staring into a mirror.

Outside, a moon that was very nearly full spilled second-hand sunlight over the Palace garden, frosting it, turning pools of rain to ice. 'You have a heavenly garden, Mo. It is paradise on earth. I love it in all weathers.' Lulu spoke over his shoulder, his profile just like his father's – the same bones, but the slighter version, or maybe the slighted one. He told her how, when the sun was out, the crickets made the grass move as if a breeze were blowing and the whole garden sounded like a tambourine. He loved the talk of the goldfinches, like water running on porcelain. And when it rained, he listened to sparrows washing in the gutter. He loved the rain, the way the leaves kept dripping, and the trees kept raining, long after the clouds had gone. He loved the way that fine rain turned cobwebs into crystals and hung lace across the garden. And the Menglang. Always the sound of the Menglang. The sound of water on the loose, broken free from its own skin.

Chapter twelve

Something had happened to Doctor Long while he'd been away in Xiamen. He'd returned looking buoyant and bullet-proof. Maybe it was the sea air, or a week with Mr Li talking about military hardware. Whatever it was, it had done him a power of good. Or, at least, it had done him a power. He came into the Palace as if he owned it, forgetting to knock, failing to take off his shoes, and stamping his tracks from the morning's rain across the kitchen floor.

'Mr Li is a man who truly understands me,' said as if this were rare, an intellectual feat. 'He grasped the SUV instantly. And what is more, he is an action man. Already the prototype is under construction.'

The grey hairs with which Doctor Long had gone to Xiamen had vanished. And his hands, all animation as he talked, looked tended. Had his nails been seen to too?

'We discussed plans for the factory, future products, where the market goes from here.'

'Without me?'

'And how has your homework been coming along?' But before Mo could answer, he raised a traffic-warden palm to stop her. 'Which dysfunction is a persistent failure of orgasm following a normal sexual arousal phase of a woman?'

'Anorgasmia.'

'In Chinese?

'*Xing gaochao quefa zheng*.'

'Diagnostic code?

'444.01'

Doctor Long looked impressed. 'What is persistent involuntary spasm of the entrance of the vagina, stopping penetration and interfering with the man's intercourse?'

'Vaginismus. *Xing tengtong.* 444.04'

Doctor Long clapped. 'It is like a miracle.' Then a deep, satisfied sigh. 'There you are: a young English woman. The only one in the world, maybe, who can say *xing tengtong* so perfect. You know, Deng Xiaoping said, "It does not matter if the cat is black or white, so long as it catches mice." Means: it does not matter if you are man or woman, Chinese or English, so long as you can recite the disorders.' He leaned against the kitchen sink as if steadying himself for more miracles. 'Female Gender Identity Disorder is...'

'Insistence on wearing typical masculine clothing. Assertion of no interest in feminine markers such as breasts or menstru—'

'Exactly!'

'But only thanks to Lulu. I couldn't have done it without him.'

'I mean: that is my *point*, exactly.'

Doctor Long had lost her. A pause while Mo replayed what they'd just said.

'I mean your boots from the builders. Your trousers worn by soldiers. Typical men's clothing.'

'It's typical *my* clothing.'

'And your vests.'

Mo loved her vests. They were grey and came in bags of three from the cheap men's shelf. 'I haven't got anything else.'

'*Exactly.* That is my point. It is what we have to change.' He stood full-square to Mo. If the sun had been shining, he'd have cast a long shadow. 'You are doing great guns with the memorising. We will make more mock-tests, and if you keep up like this you will pass. I will book your exam with the Sexology Committee. But for the professors, you must dress properly. They do not like lack of clarity – not in answers, not in the person answering. You must remember: Pingdi is not Beijing.

The men on the Panel are not the mayor. How is the mayor, by the way?'

He was out of bed now and reciting the shipping forecast on the hour, which was when it would have been broadcast if the signal hadn't been jammed. Mo said, 'When I went to Shanghai I was allowed to dress as myself. And the mayor is improving, thank you for the afterthought, by the way.'

'That is because in Shanghai, you met only Doctor Tang and Doctor Shu. They have both spent time in London. They have seen the sex-blur, the long hair on men, the short hair on women, the trousers all over, even men in frocks. But the *Panel* men...'

'What will they be wearing?'

'Suits. And possibly medals. The Chairman was decorated for the Paracels and Family Planning.'

'And I'll have my lab coat.'

'Naturally.'

'So I can wear whatever I like underneath it. No-one can tell.'

'Oh, but the Panel men can. They have had many years of looking under lab coats.'

Mo needed some air. She went to the door that Doctor Long had left open. In the trees, a family of jays was falling out. Sparrows were brawling. 'Well then, I had better not detain you, since I have so much to amend.'

Doctor Long came to the door but didn't go through it. 'Mo, do not shoo the messenger. I still have things to explain you. *I* am not the norms. You need a Clarification, but it will not be for ever. It is only for Beijing.'

Wasn't that Scientology? Didn't John Travolta have one of those?

'I propose I drive you and my wife to the Rising East Plaza. She can help you buy clothes. And do not worry. I will pay. Any price is worth it for the factory to succeed. But you must meet the Panel men's expectations.' His eyes swept from her unmade face, to her unkempt hair, to her unpainted nails. 'My wife can advise. For the Panel men, you must look clearly like something they recognise. Like a wife, like a mother.'

'But I'm not.'

Doctor Long was still. He turned to his shoes, polished leather even here in the countryside, and he seemed to be counting. Mo counted too. When she got to ten, Doctor Long said to his own bright shine: 'You need signage, Mo. You need female markings. Please, at least try to look like a woman.'

Mo dawdled on her Flying Pigeon to Golden Dawn Gardens. She'd show willing about this shopping trip, but not very. When she got to the Longs' flat, they were in the hallway and both were fretting: Doctor Long because Mo had kept him waiting, and Mrs Long because of her husband. Also, because they'd planned to let Mo borrow any outfits she wanted from Mrs Long's wardrobe, and now it was too late.

'For what?' There was no appointment. All they were doing was going into town.

'We are late for the appointed time to leave,' Doctor Long said.

Mrs Long put a hand to the door of her walk-in wardrobe. 'But it is good to be economical with money?'

'Also with my time.' Doctor Long beat out a rhythm with the keys in his pocket. 'You know our Chinese saying?'

Mrs Long cut in: 'Men are quick and women...like to browse. Can she browse? Yes she can browse. Yes you can browse. But quickly, please.'

Doctor Long checked his watch.

And Mo went inside and shut the door.

It was a studio-flat of a wardrobe – carpeted, with a two-seater sofa, a mirrored wall and a dressing table. There was air-con, speakers and a small fridge. Did Mrs Long spend whole days in here? Mo thought: if women browse, then that's what she'd do, and she made herself at home. It took a while to get her bearings and take stock. But Mrs Long, she discovered, could dress many parts – all of them clearly female. She had Exemplary-Mother clothes that didn't show sick or stains or cleavage. Also kindergarten outfits in poster-paint colours. There was an entire wall of garments Mo couldn't name, with missing sleeves and slits where you didn't need them, for appearing on the arm of Doctor Long. The locked drawer of the dressing table might have been Mrs Long as Lover. And all the while, through the wall, came something like the sound of a church, the monotone chant of prayer, which was Lulu memorising.

When Mo re-emerged, Doctor Long had given up and had gone down to wait in the car. Mrs Long said, 'I hope you found something?'

Mo had found a screwdriver in the fuse-box, which she'd put in her back pocket. She made a show of tugging at her waistband. 'I'm afraid nothing fits.'

Mrs Long's face fell. 'I am too thin. I am sorry.' She flapped her dress putting air where flesh would be. Then she put her head round the wardrobe door. 'If we had more time, I am sure I could find you something.' She reached inside and grabbed at the nearest rail.

'What is it?'

'An anything. We take anything down to the car.'

Mo and Mrs Long sat in the back and put on safety-belts. Doctor Long put on shades and swung out of the underground garage, too fast to acknowledge the guard's salute. He swung out of the compound and out of Dadu, throwing the steering wheel from hand to hand. As soon as he'd swung onto the highway, he pressed his foot to the floor and watched as the dials on the dashboard swung to the right and off the scale.

Doctor Long jumped a red light and swerved to avoid the on-coming traffic. A lorry driver leaned on his horn. Doctor Long leaned on his, only longer.

'Doctor Long? That light was red.'

'It was not.'

Mrs Long turned to Mo. 'Red is a happy colour.'

'That was dangerous.'

'*I* am driving.'

Mrs Long said, 'It was *pale* red. It was pink. Pink is my favourite colour. What is it your favourite colour?'

At that moment, it was black.

Mrs Long took a deep breath. Her fingers drifted upwards and pulled on the strap as if it were a handbrake. Outside the window, rural China was one long blur. Then she pushed against the hold of the seat belt to say: 'Perhaps, honey, a little slower?'

'*Honey*? You do not even like honey.'

She leaned back.

Mo thought: the Three Obediences and Four Virtues. Look where they got you: strapped by child-size seat belts in the back of a speeding car. She turned her face to the glass. Already they were at the Yang'an Technological Development Zone. At regular intervals they passed regular sculptures, as if an urban planner had sat an exam in solid geometry and set the solutions down by the side of the road. They reached the city centre in silence. It was a bright Saturday and everyone was out and about. Invitations to spend money straddled the street. Messages of success, real and proposed, ran the height of offices and the width of shopping malls. The traffic slowed, then stopped. Doctor Long wound down his window, letting in a slug of exhaust. Rap music from nowhere measured how long the wait. He yelled at a cyclist for the simple fact of moving.

'I think from here we walk to the Rising East,' Mrs Long said. 'With blood in the brain we make excellent purchases.'

'I give you an hour, then find you at the entrance.' A glance in the rear-view mirror. 'Or do you need two?'

They took the route along the bank of the river. Mrs Long made small talk about the weather. Mo listened to the pitter-patter of her voice and to the plaintive horns of ships, to the cries of hawkers and the tinkle of their wind-up toys as they circled on the pavement.

Mo said, 'I'm sorry to take up your Saturday, Mrs Long. Your day off. Your day with Lulu.'

'No sorry. I am happy to help. If my husband is happy, then *I* am happy. His star sign is dragon. You have seen, such people can be fiery, not so realistic.'

Which meant today's mood was ordained by the stars, all part of the natural order.

'Dragons need calmness to balance them. Ideally, they marry a rooster.'

'What are you?'

'I am a sheep, which is not a rooster. I was born two years early, but sheep do have helpful traits.' And Mrs Long listed them: to be gentle and mild and just and enduring and ready to sacrifice and...

But Mo had stopped listening. Something had caught her eye. She slowed her pace.

Mrs Long slowed hers.

Glimpsed over a high wall, what looked like a barracks: dark-brick dormitory blocks laid out in rows, the doorways numbered, the windows barred. Or was it a prison?

'It is relevant,' Mrs Long said, 'to our business today. She dropped her voice. 'It is where the *Psst!*-people go.' Doctor Long must have passed the term on. It was a hospital, she said, where the yin males and the yang females, the homosexuals and lesbians and et ceteras got medical help. 'They dispose of the muddle.'

Dispose? Mo thought of canary-yellow bins and the safe disposal of clinical waste.

'They get cured here. Not one hundred per cent success. Not every case. It depends how unclear they are and how well they co-operate. But treated, anyway.'

'Treated how?' Through iron bars, people queued blankly at the hospital shop for toilet paper, Rejoice shampoo and bruised apples, for Fanta and Double Happiness cigarettes.

'There is aversion therapy. That means they avert their unwanted behaviour. Also comprehension therapy. That means they comprehend the nature of their illness. Also marital therapy. That means they get married.' She said, 'Some *tongzhi*, they marry a normal woman. His wife moves into his house. They have a child, best a son. They look after their elderly parents, which is the law. And through exposure, he comes to realise that this is the natural way, a normal household, and this makes him happy.'

In a corner of the grounds, a platoon of in-patients in tartan uniforms shuffled about to a half-shared rhythm, filling their locked-up lungs with morning air. In the distance, a line of dark firs, the shape of upturned hearts.

'But a few *tongzhi*,' she said, 'they do not take a normal-woman wife. They make contact with a *lala*. It is *huxiang bangzhu* – mutual help. They both go through marriage-and-parent motions. Neither is cured, but society is not disturbed either.'

In upstairs windows, watery light hung in naked bulbs and the shadows of people in pyjamas were washed up against the glass.

Mrs Long turned to Mo. 'You look depressing.'

It *was* depressing. In their own way, all these people had been Struck Hard. They were trying to meet the Second Gross Deficiency by changing who they were and making a household that conformed to local conditions.

Mrs Long stared up at the window too. 'It is not their fault. Their mothers did not take enough care when they were pregnant. Their hormones were shaken up and out of order.' She put an arm through Mo's. 'So you see, it is best not to be a *Psst!*-person. Best to clarify of your own free will, not in such a place.' She meant by shopping at the Rising East. '*I* am clear, look.'

Mo did look. She saw a clear complexion, a clear conscience, a woman who clearly wanted to please her husband.

'It is best to show your feminine side.'

Mo leaned in close and spoke into an ear the way you do with something intimate, when you have a secret to share. 'Mrs Long? This *is* my feminine side.'

Outside the Plaza, a sign said NO DOGS, NO FOOD, NO DRESSED IN RAGS. A man with shades and a buzz cut sat in a carpet of fur – snappy little dogs with cartoon faces, trotting around on their cut-short legs and restricted by local law to 35 cm. He exchanged pets for tokens and for a couple of yuan kept them safe till the shopping was done. Mrs Long pushed open the door to air that was powdery and peachy – the smell of women's handbags gaping open at a sink. They rose on an escalator through a mist of Richard Clayderman's piano. He was working his way through carols left over from Christmas.

Across the atrium, the sort of red banner you usually saw on schools and factories urging the message of the moment: *Study Hard! Work Hard!* and right now *Strike Hard!* Mo looked more closely: *Protect the Organ that Feeds the Future!*

The Rising East was hosting a Bra Festival.

A troupe of plastic torsos stood shoulder to shoulder, their conical breasts offered to visitors. Chairs were filling for a talk on 'The Political Work of the Breast'. Mrs Long said, 'It is funded by the All-China Women's Federation. It is propaganda work. The bras might even be given away for free.'

Then an assistant cantered up to them in platform shoes she couldn't quite control. Her head was large, features small, her face mostly empty. She spoke to Mrs Long in fast, local Chinese.

'Where is your friend visiting from?'

'I'm not visiting.'

'She can speak?'

'I'm from England.'

The assistant scanned Mo's face with eyes narrowed by mascara. 'Margaret Thatcher. Iron Lady.'

'Not any more.'

'Margaret Thatcher came to China. She bought pearls from the Red Bridge Market. She wears iron bras.'

'I think that's Madonna.'

The assistant looked wistful. 'You come from a very developed country.' She turned her face to the glass roof where the sky stretched from here all the way to England. England was always 'very developed' and Mo never knew how to respond. Today, she said, 'England's very small.' She could hardly remember it. It seemed like a tiny speck of self-importance on the far side of the world.

'England is a rich country,' and she quoted the exchange rate Renminbi to Sterling. 'You are rich. You can buy anything you want.' An arm offered up the whole of the Women's Department. 'What *do* you want?'

'My friend has an important meeting. We've come to buy clothes to impress professors.'

'Professor Ru is a professor. She's from the Federation.' On the podium, a woman in a two-piece was arranging her notes and testing the mic with 'breast, breast.'

The assistant said, 'Breasts are an outward sign of female beauty.'

Mo glanced at the woman's chest. Two hard spheres loomed from under her blouse. Were they beautiful? Mo thought they looked hoisted. Did she want to grab them? She wanted to lob them with a tennis racquet back over the net.

The assistant said, 'Western women have big ones, much bigger than ours.' She gestured around the festival. Stragglers to the lecture strayed among the torsos, weighing the silk in their fingertips, feeling the catch of the lace. 'I've seen them in films. *The Fugitive, True Lies, Forrest Gump.* Huge breasts, right out here,' and she cupped her hands in front of her chest in ballet first position. Then she paused. She was short despite her shoes, and it was close to a child's face that she tilted up to Mo. 'Yours aren't big. Why aren't yours big?'

Mrs Long put an arm through Mo's. 'My friend has lived in China for quite some time.'

The assistant searched Mo's chest, as if by looking harder she might, after all, uncover them.

'They *were* big once,' Mo said. 'My breasts used to be enormous. Comparatively enormous.'

Mo was ten at the time. It'd started with pin-point hardening, and soreness, and angles that cast a first shadow on her clothes. Then, over the months, they stiffened into pyramids. Pyramids, Mo discovered, if she bobbed up and down on her toes, spin like Catherine Wheels. For a while, they were part of her morning routine: knickers, socks, Catherine Wheels! vest, T-shirt, jumper, trews.

Then the pyramids softened into curves, and they swelled until she had the biggest breasts in school. It was a distinction that would last no more than a year, but until they were outgrown, they were common property. Everyone claimed a stake in their well-being. Especially Julie, who sat next to Mo, which gave her privileged access. 'You know they're drooping.'

'Only because you're looking down at them. It's the angle. Perspective.'

'If you let them stretch they'll not bounce back. I asked my dad.' Julie's father was a mechanical engineer. He worked for Vickers and knew about springs.

Mo thought: were other people's fathers really talking about her breasts? Her own father was, but that was different. He found them distracting. Just the fact of them disturbed him. One Sunday lunch, when his wife was clearing the table, he'd said, 'They put me off my food. They're like two little Chihuahuas barking at me. Get her a bra for God's sake.'

'Selwyn, love, she hasn't got any breasts to speak of.'

'*I* speak of them.'

Mo thought: who to? She knew men in the street noticed them and said things to themselves – how young she was for breasts, maybe, or how grown up; or what they'd do with them, if it were legal, whatever it was men did.

'She lets all and sundry stare at them.'

Mo said, 'I don't want a bra. I don't care if they droop.' She thought probably she didn't – though it would depend how far. She didn't want them hitting the carrier bags as she lugged the shopping home.

Her mother took the vanilla blancmange from the fridge and set three bowls on the table.

Her father checked the wobble. 'You *will* care. You'll be sorry.' He cut in with his spoon, and said through a mouthful: 'She's taking the mickey.' And then to Mo's chest: 'You're taking the mickey. I'm buying you a bra in the morning.'

After lunch, when her father had had his nap and had settled down to Bob Monkhouse and *Celebrity Squares*, Mo wrote her mother a note. She put it in her handbag: *Can you buy it instead?*

The next day, when Mo got home from school, a bra had appeared on her bed. The box said it was one hundred percent cotton and size 34A. What did that mean? How many letters were there? Did her chest lead the entire alphabet? She imagined 34Z breasts dragging on the floor. *The Co-operative Store*, the label said.

Mo put the bra on the way she'd seen her mother do it: clasp at the front, swivel to the back, left strap, right strap, rearrange.

She looked in the mirror. She saw a face suspended between the sexes. An overgrown child. An undergrown adult. The ghost of one person, the sketch of the next. Her geometry all mixed up – the lines and angles, cusps and curves – depending how you looked.

Her gaze moved down.

There.

Would that do?

Restrained. Co-operating. Would her father be happy as a sandboy now?

Professor Ru had spotted Mo and come over. She offered a cool, bloodless hand. 'In my lecture, I will explain the Five Musts for breast care.' The professor wore a red worsted suit, which meant she wanted to look happy but also nerdy. 'Why? Because healthy breasts are a sign of a healthy body. A healthy body produces a healthy child. Healthy children will make China strong.' At every 'healthy' she dipped her head, pressing out a double chin and making her hang-dog features swing. She invited Mo to listen to the talk, perhaps say a few words afterwards? To endorse the friendship between our two countries? Then a curious look as if something about Mo had struck her. 'You're not *alone* in China?'

Mrs Long said, 'My friend is with *me*.'

'Where is your husband?'

Mo waved a vague hand towards a rack of girdles. They were discounted, she saw, and in flamingo pink and stood like a gathering of migrating birds. 'Somewhere in the future.'

'In the *near* future,' Mrs Long said.

'So you're engaged!' She checked Mo's hands looking for a ring, and instead found ragged nails. 'What work do you do?'

'She works for my husband.' Mrs Long paused. 'Also, *he* works for *her*. They work together. It is a joint venture.'

'I run a factory.'

'I think it must be demanding work. My advice to you is: wear gloves. Also, use both sides of your body equally. It is best for the breasts. Otherwise it can affect symmetry. Even if you're just talking on the telephone, change hands often.' She demonstrated, swinging an imaginary receiver from ear to ear. 'Change hands whenever you pause for breath.'

She paused for breath.

'Also when sitting. Don't cross your legs. Keep your back straight. No slouching. In the short term, round shoulders give you a cleavage. In the long term, your breasts stick together.'

She narrowed her eyes to check Mo's chest, scanned the T-shirt, which, now Mo looked, was fraying at the seams. She possibly saw the line of the men's-shelf vest. 'I think you should pay more attention to your breasts.'

The truth was Mo rarely thought about them. And if they crossed her mind, they were on a par with her navel, or her coccyx, or appendix: what were they *for*, exactly?

'Are you actually wearing a bra?'

'I don't own a bra.'

Mrs Long laughed as if that were a joke, just strange Western humour.

'But you *must* wear a bra to avoid shapeless-hang. Even small ones do that. It stops the blood flow and that causes all sorts of problems...' She rattled off medical terms on the edge of Mo's vocabulary. Did she just say 'frost bite'?

At some point, though, Mo knew she'd have to keep an eye on her breasts. No-one ever said it, but breasts were actually bombs. They were explosives strapped to your chest, waiting to detonate cancer.

'Also, they don't look very nice. Of the four kinds of breast, they are the least attractive.'

'There are *precisely* four types of breast?'

Mrs Long wafted a hand at the number. 'Four is such an inexact concept.'

'The four types are: shapeless-hang, like-a-bell, spherical and conical. Conical are the best. It has to do with right-angles and Greeks.' She stood back and raised a finger to Mrs Long's chest, triangulating like a surveyor. 'Yours are perfect cones.'

Mrs Long blushed.

The professor turned to Mo. 'You don't have right-angles. You don't have any angles. You have more an airport runway.'

Mrs Long breathed into Mo's ear. 'I've always loved airports. I find them exciting places.'

'But the important thing is to make the most of whatever we have.' She was about to list female body-parts, but something about Mo's face was troubling her. 'Is that a disease?'

'They're freckles.'

'In China we have a saying: hide the ugly, show the beautiful. You can remove them with....'

'I like my freckles.'

Mrs Long said, 'Freckles are a Western sign of beauty.'

Dear Mrs Long. She didn't have to say that.

'My advice is: wear make-up.'

'I don't have any make-up.'

'You should wear nicer clothes. Some red or pink. Women's colours.'

Mo turned her face to her builder's boots.

'And grow your hair.'

'My friend doesn't have time.'

'Or part it. Stick it flat.'

Mo used to have long hair, but she'd had it cut off as soon as they'd left Selwyn. The school nurse noticed, told her it didn't suit her. She asked Mo if she'd rather have been born a boy, if she felt trapped – like a boy in a girl's body. But Mo didn't even feel like a girl in a girl's body: she felt like an animal hunted by her father.

Mo raised her head and spoke so firmly that nearby faces turned: 'I *like* my hair. I *like* my clothes. I *never* wear make-up. I *like* the way I look.'

A long pause while they listened in silence to 'Silent Night.' Then the professor excused herself. She went to the podium, taking small steps, her shoulders back, her head perfectly level. Mo thought she could balance any amount of prejudice on that.

Mrs Long checked her watch. They'd been shopping for nearly an hour and best not to be late. 'Also not empty-handed.' She reached into the bin of festival give-aways and held it out to Mo.

'I don't need a bra.'

'It is not a bra. It is a gesture.'

It was in the Federation's red and white. The logo was over the nipple, and not unlike the emblem of Hong Kong. Which meant that in a couple of years, the UK would relinquish control of Mo's chest. Maybe the Queen would be there to see it. Cannon-fire. The national anthem. The lowering of the flag.

'Please take it for my husband.'

That was the last thing she would do.

'Then, please, Momo, take it for me.'

Mo stuffed the bra into her back pocket, wedging it next to the screwdriver. Then they stood on the escalator and were carried down through a fug of perfume so thick you could taste it, and they went out into the sun to wait.

Mrs Long stood feet together, arms straight, her handbag dangling against her shins as if all she had in there was pocket money and innocence. She arranged her face, placid and plausible. 'For sure he will make us wait. I estimate ten minutes.'

Mo said, 'If he's going to be late, I could always go back and buy something.' They didn't have a lot to show for an hour's shopping. One Federation bra.

'I got *much* from the hour, the most I have ever got from the Women's Department.'

'A Plaza carrier bag at least?'

'I will explain him.' Mrs Long glanced both ways, checking for her husband. 'When he comes, he will say very brightly: "So, do we know who we are? Know where we stand? Are we all clear now?" I will tell him you are the clearest unclear person I know.' She swapped hands with her handbag.

'He won't like that.'

'No. So for a while, he will not like my cooking, my clothes, my weight. And then it will pass. It always does.'

It was hot in the sun. Mrs Long checked her watch. Mo took out her bottle of water. Dog-Man took out his. He poured an inch into a bowl and a pack of tiny dogs fought over it. He tugged so hard on their leashes that they bared their teeth. He said to himself but so they both could hear: 'Not to worry. In my experience...' A shove of a foot to part them. '...the owner might take ages, but he always comes back in the end.'

Chapter thirteen

So, this was it: the First Gross Deficiency, make or break. Mo sat in the lobby of the Army Hospital and waited for her name to be called. This hospital was where the Chinese Sexology Committee had its headquarters, and today she was going to take their exam. She watched tides of theatre orderlies wheel trolleys of bloody sheets to and fro. Patients in pyjamas studied their scars and prescriptions. The corridors were lined with gilded mirrors – baroque and insistent reminders of the mishaps and wars that had brought people here. A banner quoted Chairman Mao: *In waking a tiger, use a long stick.*

Doctor Long had seen Mo and Mrs Su onto the hard sleeper at Yang'an station and then taken the plane to Beijing. He had business to attend to, he said. Groundwork to lay. He'd meet them again in the capital when the train arrived in a couple of days. He gave Mo a crib sheet, a summary of the awards and distinguishing features of the five men on the Examining Panel. They were facts to memorise en route and to drop into the conversation – casually and complimentarily – on the day of the exam.

They had the bottom bunks. Mrs Su laid out food supplies for the journey: damp sponge-cake and dried duck. Then she inserted ear plugs, boxed her pillow into shape and started snoring. Mo had felt too sick to eat and too awake to sleep. What if, in the exam, her mind went blank and she forgot everything she knew? What if she didn't get approval from the Chinese Sexology Committee? What if she failed the Gross Deficiency and Gu confiscated the factory? It took her breath away. Mo was anxious even though Mrs Su was with her and ready to breathe fire; even though the mayor had hung his luckiest charm around her neck; even though Doctor Long had tested her on the *Sexual Disorders* and she'd answered every question correctly.

So, Mo had stood in the sway between carriages and watched hour after hour of flat China go by. Every so often, they reached the wrecked edge of a city – a bracelet of junk, graffiti and half-dressed children. Then the train slowed into the station. Billboards advertised real estate – *Regent on the River, Home of Tycoons* – and dark men from the fields were perched underneath them on nylon bags stuffed square with all they owned.

Mo wondered what sexual disorders they might have: work-so-hard-all-I-want-to-do-is-sleep disease. Haven't-been-home-in-years syndrome.

Then a few minutes of slamming doors and breathlessness, and they were off again. The bell curve of the city fell away, dissolving into shacks with roofs held on with bricks, and rubbish tips and people crawling through them.

All day, Mo answered questions from passing passengers, always the same: which country are you from? How much do you earn? What's the tax rate in England? 'England is very developed,' they said. 'What are you doing in China?'

'I run a factory.'

At night she heard whispering in the upper bunks: the Foreign Boss had amazing Chinese, but was it a man or a woman?

Mo was summoned to her exam on the dot of eleven. She opened the Conference Room door to five men in lab coats and air that curled with cigarette smoke. The windows were tall, and the brown crud of ages sieved the winter light. Outside, the charcoal outline of the Fragrant Hills and the reach of trees tipped with dead berries.

The Chairman of the Panel got out of his seat to shake her hand, and fixed her with his odd, asymmetrical gaze. This was the man who had observed the thirty-eight types of orgasm, one way or another. His late middle age was smoothed away by good cheer and the good offices of low lighting. She knew he was the Chairman because of the medals, but mainly because of the glass eye. He'd served in the Navy and lost an eye near Dragon Hole in the South China Sea.

The man each side of him had a medal too. They could have been twins. Mo followed the thick line of their eyebrows strung across their forehead, their ageing features hanging from them like damp laundry. Under their lab coats, an Army uniform and an Air Force one. They'd fought in India and the Soviet Union in wars Mo had never heard of, till primed by Doctor Long. They'd been injured in service, hospitalised, and repaired in Urology, sewn back together with implants and prostheses. It was in this very hospital that they'd found a new vocation, something that was meaningful and personal. And here they sat, decorated for courage in battle, and now two of China's leading sexologists.

'We have heard everything about you.' The Chairman's voice was regional and tarry, the sound of a small-town smoker. 'We know all the facts. Long Dayan has told us of your contribution to Socialism with Chinese characteristics.'

Mo had never heard anyone use Doctor Long's first name, not even his wife.

'Dayan told us you have brought an Expert Witness.'

Mrs Su was in the toilets now, putting finishing touches to her presentation and changing into her outfit.

'First, however...' He turned serious. 'We Test You. We Assess Your Scientific Knowledge,' delivered like that, weighty and impossibly hard.

Mo's mind emptied.

'Are you ready?'

She felt sick.

'Involuntary spasm of the entrance to the vagina is called...?'

'Pardon?' because she actually knew that one.

He repeated the question and Mo got it right.

The Professor of Army Sports, an old man in greying trainers, was keeping her score. He spoke through his nose, sounding like Wimbledon.

The Chairman said, 'What is the diagnostic code for anorgasmia?'

Mo knew that one too.

The six permutations for orgasm?

And that one. Next he'd ask... something about the H.S.R.C.?

'What are the stages of the Human Sexual Response Cycle?'

Was that what Doctor Long had been doing here in Beijing? Laying the groundwork for the test, softening up the Chair, making sure all she had to do was go through the motions?

Mo looked at him with a question.

Was that a nod back?

She wiped the sweat from her palms. Her breathing calmed. Now that the fog of panic had lifted, she could glance around the room. On the windowsill, a calendar, a cactus and a plastic model of female genitals. At some point, an orange ovary had been removed, and now it lay gathering dust against the thirty-one days of January.

'There are how many types of orgasm?'

The Professor of Morality lengthened his neck. He was the only civilian and the man who'd filled the entire room with smoke.

'Please list as many as you can.'

In front of Morality, a reused coffee jar full of green tea. From where Mo sat, his unmoved face rested on it as if commemorating himself on a plinth of Nescafé.

In her head, Mo entered her Memory Palace. She went into the kitchen of the Quality Home, reached up to open the cupboard and ran her eyes along the top shelf: Angel Delight, Babycham, Tabasco, Sherbet Fountain, pickled onions, Marmite...

Thanks to Lulu, she could name all thirty-eight types.

The Chairman rose to his feet to applaud that, startling the Army and Air Force whose eyelids were beginning to close. There were more questions, and Mo knew the answers, and the Chair knew she'd know the answers, and at the end Army Sports announced a perfect score.

The Chair said, 'That most successfully concludes Part One. Anything from the Panel?'

The Professor of Morality put up his hand. He seemed a long way off across the length of a table. He looked at Mo and held her gaze to ask: 'Is she married?'

Was she married? What had Doctor Long told them? What was she to do? Truth or lies? Behind her, the hum of a fan and a water dispenser booming softly.

'Only she doesn't look married.' He fingered the folds under his eyes.

How did he *know*? Had he seen under her lab coat, just as Doctor Long had warned? Had he seen she wasn't wearing women's colours? That she wasn't even wearing a bra? The souvenir from the All-China Women's Federation was on her kitchen windowsill, the padded cups now growing cress. 'What makes you say that?' Mo said.

'I *have* a wife.'

'We *all* have wives! Of course she's a wife.' The Chairman laughed, his good eye bright, his glass one landing slightly beside the point.

So, Mo was married. But then, who was her husband?

The Chairman said, 'Her husband's a journalist. He works for the *Evening Star*. It has regular coverage of sex issues. They'll publish my research when Doctor Mo goes back. Soon, England will hear of the thirty-eight types.'

Was she going back to England? What had Doctor Long been telling him? But before she could make even roundabout enquiries, the Chairman was checking his watch and calling for the Expert Witness.

Mrs Su entered and gave the Chair a military salute. She introduced herself as Senior Master Sergeant Su, retired.

'At ease.'

She shuffled her feet in the mayor's loaned boots. In fact, the whole outfit was his. She'd come to the Panel dressed for Korea.

Then Mrs Su laid out her credentials: she had worked at Base 27, the space centre in the mountains of Xichang. She had led the team that developed the Long March rocket. She was present on 24 April 1970 when her rocket had launched The East Is Red satellite into space.

The Air Force man said, 'I saw it! The whole university gathered at the television set. I watched the moment through binoculars.'

'Mao Zedong said "Women hold up half the sky."' Mrs Su's short arms mimed the feat. 'But they also hold up half of space.'

The Panel applauded that.

Then she turned to her boots and paused. She waited for stillness to return to the room. Then she raised her head and gazed just above and beyond the Chairman's shoulder. When she spoke, it was quieter and with a wistfulness Mo had never heard from her before. 'Space. The final frontier. Our mission: to explore strange new worlds, to seek out new life and new civilizations, to take China into uncharted realms.' Mrs Su talked, and the men on the Panel followed her hands as they described the orbit of celestial bodies, the twists and turns of outer space. And she must have bent time out of shape because when Mo glanced at the clock, twenty minutes had gone by. The smell of frying was coming from the hospital canteen. Mo was starving. If only she'd had some breakfast. But the Panel-men had no hunger. They were transfixed.

Mrs Su said, 'I ask you, learned professors: What *is* space?'

The Professor of Morality looked thoughtful at that because the conversation was finally turning philosophical. He reached into a pocket and tapped out a cigarette.

'Is space not mysterious, manifold, curved, silent, dark, yin?'

His eyes narrowed as they focussed on the lighter.

'And what is the female form? Is it not mysterious, manifold, curved, silent, dark, yin?'

He blew smoke through his nostrils.

'Doctor Mo has developed technology that will boldly go where no man has gone before. Honoured professors, may I present the Scientific Universal Vibrator.' And from the pocket on her trouser leg, she produced a miniature rocket.

The Panel gasped. The Air Force man coughed, dislodging his teeth. But a hand was ready to catch them and he reinserted his look of astonishment.

'This model is named the Long March in honour of our country's space-age achievements.'

They all got out of their seats and hobbled round to view it. Admire the Chinese flag on it. Touch it. Prod it. Spar with it.

'Gentlemen, please, hold it in your firm grasp.' They took it in turns to press stiff fingers to the shaft. Mo knew that action from Eden House, when the residents in Physio put all their life-force into cheap rubber balls, squeezing with bones so riddled with age that they could break at any time.

'Notice the shaft is supple. Why? Because it is sheathed in latex.' Mrs Su said things like *vulcanisation*, *polymer chains*, *Young's modulus*, and the professors chewed their lips and made sounds of distant recognition.

'The vibrator expands, it contracts, it expands, it contracts. It expands to fill the space available.'

Wasn't that Sod's Law?

'It fits all bodies, of all shapes and sizes. And that is why it is truly the Scientific *Universal* Vibrator. It serves *all* the people.'

'Hear hear!' the Chairman said.

Mrs Su invited the Panel back to their seats. She gave them time to settle, to sniff their fingers, confer in whispers. She waited till their voices had subsided. 'When people contemplate space, often they are moved to poetry. So too, in physical love.

So too in the sensations of conjoined bodies, the penetration of one being by another.'

Mo watched the men's faces, found them both expectant and blank, except for the Professor of Morality, who'd erased himself with cigarette smoke.

'As one great cosmologist-poet said...' Mrs Su pressed a button on the SUV and a voice echoed from deep inside her palm: 'The sensation of depth is overwhelming. The darkness is immortal. The blackness itself is pure and blazing and fierce.'

Silence.

Just the hum of the electric fan and the Air Force man's laboured breathing. The professors had turned pensive. Their eyes had dropped, their gaze fixed now on the faux grain of the table, its twists and turns like the spin of far-off galaxies.

'The universe,' Mrs Su said, 'pulses with galactic cosmic radiation, the nuclei of atoms, stripped of their electrons and accelerated by the magnetic fields of the remains of supernovae.' A pause to let that sink in. Then, quieter: 'I offer, as a parallel, the clitoris.'

The professors glanced up – puzzled, Mo thought.

'It too pulses with energy, with electrical signals channelled through eight thousand nerve fibres, more than anywhere else in the body.'

The Professor of Army Sports waved an arm to query that. But Mrs Su wasn't taking questions.

'I take you back, gentlemen, to March 16 1966, to when Gemini 8, under the command of Neil Armstrong, docked with the Agena Target Vehicle.' Grunts from the Panel. They seemed to remember that. 'It was the first docking of two craft in space.' Then Mrs Su reached into a pocket and brought out something that could have come from a bicycle store – the kind of clip that keeps trousers from catching. At arm's length she pressed it onto the vibrator. 'Thus dock the Clitoral Probe and the SUV.'

She turned a dial and the probe began to hum. Another turn, and the pitch rose till it harmonised with the fan. At maximum, the attachment blurred. 'With what event did the universe begin?'

'The Big Bang!' It was a five-man chorus.

'Professor Chairman,' she said. 'I give you the thirty-ninth type.'

The Chairman applauded. He said how thrilled he was and thanked her for expanding his taxonomy.

Mrs Su blushed. Then she protested. 'Please, don't thank me. I have merely presented the end result. This was all Doctor Mo's work.'

Which everyone knew was untrue.

But it didn't matter.

The Chairman took Mo's hand. 'I endorse you and your factory, unanimously, on behalf of the Panel.' Then he added, because he was still in the rush of excitement at witnessing the advance of science: 'With Distinction. And for Life.'

When Mo got back to her hotel room, she knew the cleaners had been in. All traces of her had been erased – the towels fresh, sheets creaseless, bins emptied, sprays sprayed. But Doctor Long, apparently, had been in too, because propped against the pillows and on hotel notepaper:

> *Congratulations! You have done well. I will*
> *telephone Inspector Gu and tell him the result.*
> *Rest now. You will need it.*

Beside the note, a certificate from the Chinese Sexology Committee. In bold, gold characters:

> *The Happiness Factory, Pingdi, P.R.C. is a model*
> *work unit. It conforms to local conditions, serves*
> *the interests of the Chinese people and is a major*
> *contribution to science and the stability of the*
> *nation.*

It was framed and signed by the Chairman and dated today.

Doctor Long seemed to be everywhere, and one step ahead. And Mo had only just missed him, apparently, because when she went to make a cup of tea, the kettle was still warm, and when she went to the loo, she caught the tail-end of his aftershave.

A small and remote part of her brain told her that was odd. But most of her brain told her how tired she was and how glad that was over, and that at least Doctor Long had a plan and knew where they were going.

She kicked off her shoes and fell onto the bed. Then she remembered her hunger. She rolled over and reached for the Room Service directory. But before she could even open it, Mo had fallen asleep.

Mo dreamt.

She dreamt that Inspector Gu had failed her. He'd put her on a plane to England and told her there was no food for the entire flight. Then there was a fire in an engine, and Mrs Su, who was suddenly on the plane too, said she could fly a plane – she could fly anything – and she burst into the cockpit and grabbed the controls. And Mo tossed and turned and yelled '333.01!' which was the code for impotence, while Mrs Su dodged mountains and brought them out of a tailspin and alarms rang through the cabin.

Mo woke with a start, then realised her phone was ringing. It was dark in the room, the curtains open, still night outside. The clock on the TV flashed a permanent noon.

Mo picked up the receiver.

'I am sorry to raise you so early.' Doctor Long's voice.

Mo rolled to the edge of the bed, tipped herself upright, found herself already dressed and still in her lab coat. She went to the window. Outside, an old woman dozed in an armchair. Her silver hair looked frosted in this light. Had she been there all night?

'I hope you slept well. I have important information to tell you, and not so much time.'

What time was it? Mo checked her watch – 6.30 on the dot. Doctor Long must have been up a while and waiting for the earliest acceptable moment to call.

'Inspector Gu is a tough one, I am afraid. He said the Chinese Sexology Committee is one thing, but the Party line on Strike Hard is another. We talked the events of yesterday over and over.'

'He can't say I haven't passed.'

'He did not say that. Not once I had played him the tape-recording.'

Mo had no idea the exam had been taped.

'It took all my powers of persuasion. With Gu, it is like playing chess: if this, then that; if that, then the next. All possible scenarios. He thinks many moves ahead.'

Mo had no idea about chess.

'You were the Queen, by the way.'

Was that good or bad?

'It was a battle of wits.'

But she knew there was a King.

'In the end, Inspector Gu conceded. You have met the First Gross Deficiency.'

Mo flopped on the bed with relief. 'Thank God for that.' She picked up her certificate and flicked moonlight across it, making the lettering flash.

'No thanks needed. It is only what I promised to do.'

Mo said, 'And *I* didn't meet the Gross Deficiency. We *both* did.' From giving her the lab coat to helping out with this certificate, Doctor Long had been there.

He said, 'But, please do not forget, *you* were the one Struck Hard.'

That was true.

Mo went back to the window. Down in the street, cleaners in red overalls scratched at the kerb with brooms. An orange team rubbed shine into the bus stop. The green team picked up litter.

'So!' Doctor Long sounded brisk. 'Your next task is the other one.'

'You mean the household-thing?'

'*No*... not "the household-thing". The Second Gross – and I mean *Gross* – Deficiency.'

Did he really have to do that? Emphasise the failing so early in the morning? Mo needed a cup of tea. She reached for the kettle. It didn't have enough water but she put it on anyway. She said, 'Inspector Gu wants me to conform to local conditions? Well, I already *do*. I speak Chinese. I live in the village. I wash my clothes in water from the Menglang. I buy vests from the men's shelf. I avoid the number four and I love the number eight. You can't get more same-as-everyone-else than that.'

No answer from Doctor Long. She fiddled with the buttons on the bedside table. *Do Not Disturb* wasn't working.

Then he said, 'What is the word for household?'

'*Jiating*.'

'What is the word for family members?'

'*Jiaren*.'

'What is the word for family tree?'

'*Jiapu*.'

'What do they have in common?'

'*Jia*.'

He sang it at her down the line – all one note, first tone: *jia, jia, jia*. 'How long have you known that word?'

It was one of the first characters Mo had learned to write. It was a pig under a roof.

'We are not talking about where you live and where you shop and how superstitious you are. We are talking about *who* you live *with*. Blood ties. *Jia*, Mo. You know the weight of this word. The pride evoked by it. The tears shed because of it. The blood spilled over it. When Inspector Gu says your household does not conform to local conditions, he means your *family members* do not conform.'

'He knows why. He knows they're dead.'

'That is not his problem. Nor is it mine.'

'Though, actually,' Mo said, 'they're *not* dead. I'm keeping them alive just by being here. All I am is their genes.' Wasn't that why people had children, after all? To cheat death and carry on walking around in their offspring's shoes?

'Do you know how little time you have left to meet the Second Gross Deficiency?'

'It can't be *that* gross or you'd have done something about it by now.' Mo listened to the kettle give up and switch itself off. 'Wouldn't you?'

For a long time, neither said anything. In the end, 'Do you play chess, Mo?'

It was one of those games that clever people played to remind themselves how clever they were. David Dave had played it, but only with himself, and in the newspaper. When they had tea in bed on a Sunday morning, he'd do the chess in his Dire Straits T-shirt, and she'd stroke Lovecat and catch up with the obituaries.

Doctor Long said, 'What is *your* next move, Mo?'

'Why did you tell the Chairman I'm going to England?'

'What is the date today?'

Mo didn't want to think about that. She glanced out of the window. Red plastic bags had caught in the wind and snagged in the trees like unlit lanterns. *Jia, jia, jia*. Mo ran the sound through her head. She tried it in all the tones: fourth tone and it meant 'quarrel'. She felt suddenly quarrelsome. 'So, what do you propose I do?'

'In China, if we are in trouble, we turn to family. It is what I would do: turn to my parents, to my wife, to my son in certain circumstances.'

But that was the whole point. How could she turn to family about not having family? It was illogical. A head-fuck. A fuck-up. Actually, from Doctor Long right now, it felt like an up-yours.

Mo stood. Outside, Beijing was just beginning to move. Heavy-lidded men, indifferent to another morning, were in slippers and overcoats and on their first cigarette of the day.

She said, 'What happens in chess if you're running out of moves?'

'You buy time – which you do not have – and hope your opponent makes a false move, which he will not.' Down the phone-line, the belt of a distant horn. 'Or you resign.'

'And in the end?'

'One person wins. The other one loses. And that is chess, Mo. That is life.' Then his voice addressed to someone else.

'Where are you, Doctor Long?'

'On the way to the Ministry of Aviation. I plan to build the airport. I will move Soaring Magpie Mountain.'

Or that's what it sounded like. But he couldn't have said that – it was ridiculous. His voice was starting to wobble now, though, and the line break up.

'*Please*, Doctor Long. I can't do this alone. I need your help.'

'I am in a car.'

'*And* on the phone?'

'Mobile telephony has not yet reached Pingdi, but that is something I also intend to change. The factory must have the most modern communications. The Long March will be flying off the shelves.' He listed his schedule of imminent meetings. 'For the foreseeable future, I am in Ministries. I am unavailable. I am sorry.'

Then a sound like a lit fuse fizzed along the line.

'Hello? Doctor Long? Are you still there?'

'I am going into a tunnel.' His voice was loud, pressed over electrical noise. Then something struck her about the way he'd spoken, and it wasn't the volume or the buzz on the line. It was the word 'the'. He hadn't said, '*your* factory' or '*your* shelves'.

In his mind, he was detaching her. Doctor Long was letting her go.

Chapter fourteen

When Mo and Mrs Su returned from Beijing, the mayor was well enough to be out of bed. They found him in the hammock and someone's sheep shearing the lawn. *Just a Minute* was on. Clement Freud lowed at the mayor's feet. Life felt for a moment how it should be, how it always used to be, before Inspector Gu turned up. The mayor squinted at Mrs Su. She was still in his battle fatigues. 'Not back from Korea already?'

'The war is not over yet.'

And Mo explained about the Second Gross Deficiency.

The mayor didn't seem worried. Doctor Long in a tunnel? There was bound to be light at the end of it. And Mo needed a family? Her dead relatives were alive, if she kept them alive – with mementoes, he said, with photos. The mayor had portraits of his dead family by his front door, and he talked to them every time he went out and came back in – kept them up to date with the goings-on in the village. The details of their faces had been swallowed by the years. Just their eyes looked out, dark and alarmed that the world had turned out this way. He liked to name their names: his father's. His mother's. The incantation of his many brothers. His world was pregnant with the dead. And he really did believe in ghosts. The whole country did, he said, even if they didn't. Come Qingming, every person in China swept the graves of their ancestors. It was a nation of gamblers and they all bet on the afterlife.

But Mo didn't have any mementoes of her family: the day she and her mother had left the Quality Home, the last thing they'd wanted was souvenirs of their life with Selwyn. All the black-and-white prints with their royal-icing corners, and all the red-eye, autofocus family blurs that were gummed in place under sheets of cellophane, were left behind in the mahogany cabinet that Sue had made brilliant with Pledge. The only reminder Mo had of her father was a Standing Order that showed up on her bank statements: YORKS P&L, GOLD SERVICE, PLOT 515. It was the maintenance contract with Parks and Leisure that meant once a month, a man in rubber gloves tugged at weeds that had seeded from other Gold plots, and raked litter from her father's gravel.

The day after Mo got back, Doctor Long rang the Palace to report on his ministerial meetings. 'The future is brighter than ever!' There was no 'hello'. 'I have on board good men, businessmen, cool heads, visionaries,' and he recounted his triumphs in bulletpoints. 'One: the village will expand and swallow up Dadu. Two: the mountain will be moved. Three: an expressway will link Yang'an to Jiazhishi.'

Mo had never heard of the place.

'It is the new name of Pingdi. Jiazhishi as in "Value City". It is like your Worthington, only bigger. The ministerial vote was unanimous, of course. Who is drawn to a place called "Flat Ground"? It is like "Level Playing Field". That is for failing to seek advantage on. It is for settling for the same as everyone else on. Where in "Pingdi" is aspiration? Soon there will be an eight-lane expressway for all the hard-workers and risk-takers.' In the background, brash laughter, the sound of someone raising a toast.

'Where are you Doctor Long?'

'In the Friendship Hotel. I am dining with my new friends. *Ganbei!*' said to the table. 'And how are you getting on with your household tasks, Mo?'

She listened to them knock back their *baijiu* and slam their glasses down.

Doctor Long said, 'If nothing to report, it is, perhaps, not going so hopefully.' Then with good cheer: 'To help things along, I have already been in touch with Inspector Gu. I tried to negotiate. I put to him the points you made about conforming already to the Second Gross Deficiency.'

Mo trailed the phone to the window. In the garden, Mrs Su was hanging out the washing – the mayor's clothes, Mo's clothes, her own clothes – the laundry indistinguishable and interchangeable.

'I asked him to be explicit about his requirements. Also, I asked for leniency. *Explicitly*: you need a family: a husband, in-laws, a child. *Leniently*, he will settle for just a husband.'

But Mo didn't want a husband. She'd never wanted one. 'How can I get a husband just like that?'

'You marry a man, just like that.'

Mrs Su hoisted the clothes prop, raising a line of once-white underwear into the sky, a whole washing-line of surrender.

'The mayor is authorised to issue marriage certificates. He can marry you as soon as there is a suitor.'

In the distance, Mo saw clouds were gathering. Mrs Su was always in denial about the weather.

'You will not have to be married for long. Only until your divorce.'

'I've already been divorced.' Mo meant from her father. She'd been through the court hearings, the battles over property, money, maintenance, access. Divorce, she knew, was civil war.

'It is child's play. Our *Marriage Law* permits instant divorce. Chapter Four, Article Twenty-Five: "Complete alienation of mutual affection". You are a foreigner, which we also call "alien". Any marriage *you* make will count as alienation.' The mayor, Doctor Long said, kept records of all the boys born in the valley and all the marriages made. From there, she could deduce likely candidates. China had no shortage of males. They outweighed females 130 to 100 in this part of the country. All she had to do was find an unmarried one, aged at least twenty-two, and not blind or deaf.

'What's that got to do with it?'

'The *Marriage Law* forbids disabled unions.' Then, 'Excuse me for one moment...' Mo heard a thankyou said over his shoulder. Was that for a refill? A compliment? Then a burble of background conversation. Doctor Long had lost interest in Mo by the time he came back on the line. 'Just find a man. We go from there. I ring to check you have one as soon as I am home.'

A few days later, Mo's telephone rang. 'Well?'

She knew it would be him. The phone rang differently, it sounded peevish, whenever Doctor Long called.

'Yes, I *am* well thank you. And how are you?'

He sighed down the line. A tried and tired voice said, 'Have you done *anything* to help yourself?'

Well, yes, she had. Mo had asked the mayor if he knew any bachelors, and he'd said the valley was full of *guanggun* – bare branches. 'But suitable for *you*, Mo? And willing straightaway to divorce?' These men wanted to marry down. And she was not down, though not up either. She was just... not what they had in mind. But, still, he could think of a couple of men who were good-hearted and fine farmers, devoted to their parents and their pigs.

The mayor had set off into the valley with firecrackers that he'd light as soon as there was good news. Mo had seen him off, had watched till he disappeared behind the Pink Pagoda. She'd waited all day for distant explosions, for the mayor to emerge with a husband, or at least a proposal. Instead, when he returned, he'd handed her pigs' trotters, hard and shiny and tied together like ice-skates. 'I told them how lovely you are. But that, they said, had nothing to do with it.' The mayor unbuckled his bag and placed more animal parts on the table, laid out like an autopsy. He'd dabbed at the blood that followed the grain of the wood. No-one had wanted him to return empty-handed.

Now there was an intake of breath down the phone line. Doctor Long said, 'And the Village of Rejects?'

'It's a no-go zone, except for the police.'

On the map, it was called Fengzhisheng – Sound of the Wind. All day, abandoned men sat on their doorsteps working their jaws, and dogs gnawed their own bones. At dusk, the fighting started. Sometimes you could hear them in Pingdi if the wind blew that way.

'So, send an advert to the Head of the village.' Doctor Long sounded impatient. 'Tell him to put it up.'

'You mean like last time?'

Because a few years before, Fengzhisheng had organised a Market to Find Suitable Wives. They'd advertised with the age, height and weight of every bachelor, and the *mu* of land and head of livestock that they owned. The worth of each man was matched by the Village Fund, so that along with marriage went fridges, washing machines, sewing machines. Women had swarmed from miles around. And when the couples had finally settled, the Head of the village married them. It was the eighth of the eighth, 1988. It couldn't have been more auspicious.

'And what exactly would my advert say?' Mo asked him. She thought: *British woman. Struck Hard. Broke. Face like a cricket bat. Chest like a runway. Seeks marriage of convenience and instant divorce.*

'It would say "reward". It would say "recompense".'

Because only days after their wedding, all the wives and their white goods vanished. The event had made national headlines. It was a sign of 'materialist greed and bourgeois tendencies'. It had put Fengzhishi on the map – only now as the Village of Rejects.

'You mean *buy* myself a husband?'

'*Rent* would be more accurate. But, clearly, you are rejecting the Rejects. So. Now. Listen.' Mo heard the irritation. 'I have done *all* I can to persuade Inspector Gu. I have tried everything. And, to my last proposal, in principle he agrees. He compromises, *again.* He gives much ground *again.* He shows very willing, so *you* must show willing too.

'To what?'

'The Pre-Marital Health Check. Inspector Gu is not insisting on a physical-man-husband immediately. Only on the *willingness* to have one.'

A deferred husband? A theoretical one? That didn't sound too bad.

'All want-to-be wives have the Pre-Marital Health Check. It is the law.'

'Did *your* wife have it?'

'We were married before it became law. But even so, yes, we volunteered her.' He said, 'We make sure no HIV, no syphilis, no gonorrhoea.'

Mo loosened her hold on the phone.

'No mental illness in the family. No low intelligence.'

She held the receiver away from her ear. But even so she could hear him.

'No unusual facial features. No unusual body features. Also an inspection of the anus, vulva, vagina and its secretions. The man too, the relevant parts. It is done in a hospital by a qualified doctor.'

'What kind of doctor?'

'The kind you are talking to.'

In the yard, the bleat of ewes as a ram tried to mount them.

He said, 'I have time to see you now, if you would like. The test takes no more than an hour. What do you think? For Inspector Gu, a clean certificate means you are fit to marry. You have marriage in mind at least.'

Silence.

'Is that a yes?'

'No.'

'You mean it is a no, or you mean it is not a yes, you are still thinking of your next move?'

'I told you I do not play chess.'

'And neither should you play the fool.' Doctor Long tutted. 'You have only days left to the deadline. What will you do? Do not even think of running. Do not think of hiding. A white in China?'

Mo let his words circle and eddy. She watched dust spin in the sunlight. In the back of her mind, she was hearing someone's voice.

Doctor Long said, 'There is *nowhere* you can hide.'

Then the sun went in and the dust disappeared.

Mo thanked Doctor Long, said he'd been most helpful.

And she meant it.

Because, actually, there *was* somewhere she could hide. His own wife had mentioned it: Shamian. It was the nearest place to Pingdi where a white-skinned person could vanish. As Mo put the phone down, she heard David Dave: *if in doubt, run*.

That evening, Mo cycled down the village High Street. She didn't have much luggage – a small bag, the kind she always carried. From The Usual Place the smell of frying garlic and songs in two-part harmony. The Twins were celebrating their birthday. Mo slowed as she passed the mayor's house, glanced at his dark window, thought she might have caught his shadow. She pedalled hard through The Mist towards Dadu. The road was unlit, but she knew it off by heart, could navigate it in every season and in all weathers. Except, today it was already different. The Ministry of Construction had sent diggers out to fill the drainage ditches and level the camber. At the edge of Dadu, the hand-painted arrow that had pointed the way to *The Happiness Factory* had gone. In its place, an official green-and-white sign told visitors in Chinese and English that it was five kilometres this way to Jiazhishi.

The Dadu hospital torched the evening sky, Doctor Long's Cube blazing in every direction. Mo headed into town. She reached the bus station as the last departure to Yang'an was starting its motor and coughing black smoke against the wall of the dumpling stand. The man at the ticket office knew Mo well and sold her a return without asking. She said, 'Would you keep this safe for the mayor?' and gave him the Flying Pigeon.

He handed her a blank envelope.

'What's this?'

He shrugged. All he knew was to give it to Mo should she come by. He said to hurry or she'd miss the bus. They kept strictly to the timetable now they were Jiazhishi.

Mo climbed on. She was the only passenger. Everyone was home now, scattered across the countryside for the New Year celebrations. In a few days, when people returned to their jobs in the cities, there'd be queues at the ticket office hours before it opened, and standing room only on the bus.

But this journey was hers.

Mo took a seat away from the driver and his stream-of-consciousness chatter, away from the speakers and the crackle of 'I Love You, China', away from the bump of the back wheels and the burnt-out smell of the engine. On the other side of the window, darkness. Every so often, they passed a dim-lit village where the only thing that had changed in hundreds of years was the invention of the electric bulb. Mo took out the envelope, turned it in her hands, sniffed it for clues, and then opened it:

Dear Momo,

I have watched your lovely face in the days since Beijing and I could see you saw your chances fading. I thought you might slip away, leave us quietly exactly the way you came. Please, come back as soon as you can! And if you cannot, please do not forget us. Talk about us. Say our names aloud.

We remain forever <u>Pingdi</u>,

And yours,

Mayor Lin

At Yang'an Long Distance Bus Station, the Bright Nights hotel offered no-star hospitality to people with a few hours to kill. Mo pushed open the door to the smell of *baijiu* and a receptionist wearing shades against a violent neon strip. He took them off, brought his face close to Mo's, and looked at her with a gaze bewildered by light. 'I know you from someplace.'

Which she didn't want to hear. She was hoping that by now she was out of range of recognition, that here she could disappear.

'I know you from the newspaper.' He blinked water from the raw corners of his eyes.

Mo spoke in English. 'Do you have a single?'

He waved his shades at her, like a wand that might tell him where he'd seen that face before.

She said, 'For one night.'

'How many hours?' He glanced at the clock. It had a photo of a desert island with palm trees and surf, and was lit from behind where the sun would be.

Her bus to Guangzhou left at five in the morning. She'd like to sleep till then.

He said, 'I know your face.'

'Don't white people all look the same?' She scanned the counter for a price list, found a certificate of hygiene and payment of taxes.

He switched to Chinese: 'Can you speak Chinese?'

Mo knew the trap from *The Great Escape*. She looked blank. She said, 'Do you have a single? I need to sleep.'

Then a man tripped down the stairs looking beery and blurred and a woman followed in a tangle of dark chiffon, like a blackbird caught in strawberry netting. The receptionist's jaw thrust forward, flashing a till-full of burnished teeth. 'Just sleep? No karaoke?'

'No.'

'Want massage?'

'No.'

'Want sex?'

'I want to sleep.'

'You from the newspaper?'

Mo spent the night in a borrowed room. Bags of make-up and tubes of KY had been shoved under the bed. Clothes still hung in the wardrobe: tight skirts, loose blouses. On the sink, a packet of chewing gum, the kind that does for toothpaste.

And then the noise started, the clockwork thud against the wall, a hammering so hard Mo could feel it.

She shoved the bed to the other wall. Mo stared at the carpet, joined the dots of the cigarette burns. She counted the brown smears of slippered insects. Her eyes tracked the scuff-line on the wall. She imagined the cast of men that had been serviced here – skinny, fat, lonely, drunk, diseased, virgin, about to get married, just on their way home. She could see them holding on to whoever she was, scuffing the hair out of her eyes, crushing her shoulders, breathing her breath.

Mo got up. She went to the window. Outside, lights from the bus station lit a permanent dawn. Rats skipped across the forecourt, cleaners cleaned, and men pasted flyers for real estate and international friendship, for investment and reliable growth.

It was gone four in the morning when the last man left, and time to take the bus to Shamian. It was an island in the Pearl River Delta. You could breathe on the coast, but it also made Mo uneasy. It was where land stopped sea and sea ate land, where things changed each other, sometimes for ever.

The coast was where the O'Sheas had taken their summer holidays. They drove across to a nice part of Lancashire, and on the way up, stopped in Blackpool so Sue could pop in on her sister.

Selwyn used to drop his wife at Auntie Al's guesthouse. He waved from the car at the woman in the trouser suit with hair dyed the colour of coal, then took Mo to the seafront. They watched the plod of donkeys, and her father said, 'If I had

somewhere to keep them, I'd buy the whole lot their freedom.'
Then they queued at the Mr Whippy for a 99, and her father showed off with the numbers, such as: nine plus nine equals eighteen, and one plus eight equals nine, while Mo tried to decide whether to eat the flake first or last. And then they settled down to the Punch and Judy, and Mo watched her father grab his knees and his face crease up like a new-born baby's.

After that, they went to the beach. Selwyn sat in a deckchair, his top button done up. He read the *Telegraph* and checked the weather, which proved he'd chosen the right week to bring the family away. He turned heavy eyelids westwards, towards the sea, to Ireland, to where the O'Sheas came from. Mo had a bucket and spade. She sat on the beach and dug a trench in which to bury her father.

A couple of hours later, Sue came to find them. She always looked younger, more like a Moore, when she came back. Mo thought she might even have been laughing. Selwyn checked his watch because anything that needed to be said to Al could be said in five minutes flat. After that, it was just gossip and meddling. Also because in Auntie Al's guesthouse, there were women over from Ireland – women in trouble who needed somewhere to stay while they got things sorted out.

Al had helped Sue in that regard. Mo's mother had told her about that. Also, that she'd conceived on 21 December, in the Blackpool Picture Palace, to *Ill Met by Moonlight*. It was the matinee showing, when the tickets were cheaper, but dark by four on the shortest day of the year.

Sue was old enough. She knew what she was doing. And she was careful, which was why she couldn't explain how it had actually happened. But, with only his rough-cut fingers inside her knickers, semen had somehow got where it shouldn't. And by the time the British commandos had kidnapped General Kreipe, she was pregnant.

Sue didn't believe her missed periods. She didn't even believe her swollen belly. She put it down to rationing. It was months before she could no longer doubt that sometime after the Wall's ice-cream and before she caught the tram home, an egg had been fertilised.

Sue told Mo it was seven months before she believed it, which was far too late, even if it had been legal.

Also that it had been a boy.

She said the doctor had shown her the foetus, had stood at the foot of the bed, her legs still splayed, and held him up like a ghastly, bloody trophy. The child had been ready for life by then, had fingernails, lips, hair – her hair – and a wide brow dented with a question. Then the nurse had taken him away.

Those were the kind of things that happened at the coast.

Children were made. Children were lost.

What did you do with the baby, Judy? Whack. Whack. Whack.

It was late morning by the time Mo arrived in Shamian. New Year's messages caught the sea breeze and twinkled red and gold in the sunlight. Inflatable pigs swayed over the Bridge of England. Mo went to a café and ordered bacon, egg and chips. She went to the French patisserie and bought an *éclair au chocolat*. Then she found an internet café. The man at the desk took Mo's passport, wrote the number in a ledger, told her it would expire soon and she looked older than her photo. He got her to sign the Rules for Internet Users and checked her signature against her passport. 'You understand, yes? No? You break the rules, you break me, I break you.' There were twelve rules for internet users, and he dug with a biro under the Number One rule he said applied to her: *No looking up sensitive subjects.* 'You know what they are?' He meant Tibet, Taiwan, Tiananmen.

Mo said, 'Please tell me.'

'Sorry, too sensitive to say.'

She sat in the sound of digital gunfire, between a man losing at poker and a boy scrolling through catalogues of breasts, and looked up Selwyn O'Shea.

There were thousands of O'Sheas. Pages and pages of them. They were probably family, years back, centuries ago, when in-bred O'Sheas farmed sheep in dells in Ireland. Mo and all those people were related. She'd found all the family Gu could ever ask for in 0.26 seconds.

Though none of them was her father.

Did she mean *James Selwyn O'Shea, of Apple Tree Creek, Australia, our dear husband and father, eternal rest grant unto him O Lord*, the search engine wondered?

No. She meant Selwyn Roderick O'Shea, who was also dead and buried, but in Yorkshire.

She found a Roderick O'Shea, who'd left Dublin and gone into business, making aeroplanes in America.

Also, a John O'Shea, who'd worked in films and made *Runaway* and *Don't Let it Get You*, films she'd never heard of, but which seemed like a message.

She tried 'Roddy' because, to people who liked him, he'd always been 'Our Roddy'.

Then Mo hit caps lock and hammered at the keys, beating out his name the way it had been on the glass of his office door: SELWYN O'SHEA, BATA (PRES), HFIGATM.

But whichever way she tried it, whatever terms she used to look him up, there was no sign of that sensitive subject, the man who'd been her father.

Mo went out into the light and sat in the Ornamental Gardens. A bride was having her photo taken. She wore the kind of wedding dress that swept down Christian aisles, her train washing over the pebbles the old people used to massage their feet. A photography crew smoothed her silks, adjusted her jewels, and arranged her against her husband: head tipped his way, a gloved hand on his shoulder, a giving-in at the hip to let him take her weight.

Then a voice said in English: 'Excuse me please, Miss...'

Mo turned. A man stood crooked on a homemade crutch, his face so lined it could have been clinker-built.

'I'm not here.' She turned back to the wedding.

'You speak Chinese.'

'You cannot see me. I'm blending in.'

'Please, Miss.' He turned his empty pockets inside out and left them hanging against his thighs. 'I have no money. I haven't slept.'

'Neither have I.'

He held something out to her in short, rough fingers: a photo of a shaven-headed toddler. The child was in a striped jumpsuit, as if imprisoned by life already. 'Are you alone?' he said.

'Among a billion people?'

'But it's Chinese New Year.'

'But I'm not Chinese.'

'American.'

Not a question.

American couples filled the streets with height and ankle socks and matching T-shirts that said *Love* or *Luck* or *Happiness*. Mo had watched them take it in turns to clamp the girls they'd just adopted to their chests – to kiss her, whisper to her, then raise her to the sun and blink water from their eyes. Mo had seen grown men brought to tears by the fact of their new daughter.

The man said, 'Have you chosen *your* baby?'

Shamian rang with the sound of small-time quarrying, with young women tapping at slate, engraving portraits of just-made families. They copied from photos, chipping hope into stone and blowing away the dust.

'I'm not here for a baby. What would I do with a baby?'

He turned to the photo of his daughter. It was taken on her second birthday. In his pocket he had a picture from her first birthday and one taken on the day she was born. He was watching her grow up in photos sent by his wife.

'She's a chatterbox. I heard her first words.' Actually, they weren't her first words. They were the first words she'd ever spoken on the telephone. 'I'm going to see her soon. As soon as...' He cupped a hand. Mo looked at the cracked skin, the lines deep with dirt. She didn't need to be able to read palms to know what his palms said.

'Sometimes, my wife can't afford to feed her. Then she gives her away for a while. *Tongyangxi*. Do you know what that is? It's when a girl goes to live with her future in-laws. They feed her now and can have her later.' The yellow whites of his eyes turned wet. 'I come to Shamian because... because... Americans are good people. They are generous.' He took off a shoe, felt under the insole and pulled out a Disabled Person's Identity Card. It was brown, smooth, had been walked so far it was thin enough to see through. 'Some people are lucky. Some people aren't. It's just fate.' Close by, screened by a banyan, people were playing mah-jong. Under the warm January sun, they shuffled the pieces with a sound like chattering teeth. He said, 'Are *you* lucky?'

'I used not to believe in luck. Then I came to China.'

'Americans are lucky.'

'I'm not American.'

Mo looked away. Over the man's shoulder, cannons from the Opium Wars were aimed at the river: *Relics from the resistance to imperialist invasion...*

That meant Britain, France.

...weighing 6000 jin *and unearthed on Shamian 7 September 1963 and erected 30 December 1963.*

Too many details. Over-precise.

It was like the countdown to Hong Kong. Everywhere screens ticked off the days, hours, minutes and seconds till the UK handed it back.

And still the man was there.

Behind them, under the shadows of palm and eucalyptus, the shutters and pastel shades of the European past clung on. It was all so familiar and so strange: the trading offices and warehouses Mo knew from the Leeds and Liverpool Canal; the Our Lady of Lourdes Chapel; the Sacred Heart Church.

'I can see you're kind-hearted.'

Actually, she felt broken-hearted.

'And it's Chinese New Year.'

And Mo was broke. She reached into her pocket. 'I can buy you something to eat.'

'I can do without food. All I want is a bus ticket. The only thing that matters is to see my daughter.'

And Mo was broke. She reached into her pocket. 'I can buy you something to eat.'

'I can do without food. All I want is a bus ticket. The only thing that matters is to see my daughter.'

Then the sound of the Lord's Prayer drifted like an incantation from the open church door. He said, 'Do all Western people believe in God?'

'I'm only half-Western.'

'Does that mean you half-believe?'

'I've never believed in God.' But she did believe this man: that his daughter sometimes went hungry, and he was hungry for her. He was just like the mayor: they both missed their daughters and managed still to be kind. Men who could be sad without being angry, who could take a punch and not punch back.

Mo opened her palms, the lines different left and right; two fates, one chosen. Was that why Selwyn had left Mo all he had? Had Selwyn been hungry at the end?

Chapter fifteen

That night, Mo checked into a backpacker hostel, the cheapest she could find, on the far edge of Shamian with a view of the inner ring road. Mo stood at the window, and through the bars watched Guangzhou toss in its sleep. In the rooms of the restless, televisions flicked greys onto the ceiling. Someone was getting upset on the phone, someone rocking a baby, another drinking alone.

Mo took a shower in flip-flops that had been clipped so they weren't worth stealing. She got into sheets printed with the guesthouse name. She reached for the light switch and the gold-veneer came off on her fingers. Then she lay awake, listening to voices through the wall. She imagined what they were saying back home. Milton would say something like: 'Mo has a tendency to extreme solutions. I think we should report her missing.' The mayor would have found his Flying Pigeon by now and would be too upset to say anything. Mrs Su would say, 'She's *not* missing. She's just not here. She's just living her life.'

There was a phone in Mo's room, its thin tangle of wires held in place with masking tape. The wires disappeared through a hole in the wall, wound round washing lines and headed up into the branches of a palm tree. From there she lost sight of them. She didn't know where they went. They might have swung from telegraph poles in fragile curves across Guangzhou. They might have tacked their way underground. Or voices might have leapt up to a hard speck in the sky, then bounced back down to earth. It was her only link to the sound of anyone who knew her, and it seemed so effortlessly breakable.

* * *

Mo woke early to a bright morning and the gloom of a basement room. She went straight out and sat on a bench beside the Pearl River. The people of Shamian were just starting their day. Old men in slippers moved stiff arms through small degrees. Mo listened to the sound of a tennis ball slipping back and forth, taking its time getting over the net. In the distance, American voices and a flock of birds sounding like a typing pool.

Then, suddenly, the sun went in. A figure was standing over her. She didn't look. Another beggar. More money. 'Not today.'

'Please do not be alarmed.'

'I gave yesterday.'

On the bank of the river, fishermen examined grubs, turning them in their fingers as if they were diamonds, then hooked them onto lines and threw them into the river.

'Please come this way.'

Didn't she know that voice?

Mo felt a hand on her arm.

Sergeant Li said, 'Please stand up. Please keep close to me. Pretend you are disabled, or we are married,' and he took her in an invisible hold known only to possessive husbands and trained police.

If it'd been Inspector Gu, Mo would have tried to make a dash for it – a short lane with a sharp bend, dustbins she could knock over, traffic she could dodge and put between them, just like in the movies. But Sergeant Li had spoken so calmly, made a kind, breathless request.

He led Mo over the French Bridge. Men leaned on the railings and women leaned on the men and someone played 'Je Ne Regrette Rien' on a harmonica. He said, 'Please do not walk fast. I cannot keep up. My lungs are not good.' Now they were off the island and in the city. They picked their way through pavements gritted with bodies. Gangs of hard-faced children held out their stumps. Taxi touts smoked and played cards, careless of the outcome.

Mo said, 'Where are we going?'

'Please talk louder.' He squinted against the drivers caught in gridlock and beating out a protest on their horns. 'My ears are not so good.'

'Are you arresting me?'

'I am escorting you.' He cast his eyes across a mass of parked cars. 'Please be patient till I find it. My sight is not so good.'

'Escorting me where?'

'Pingdi.'

'But I've just left.'

'A return is a good thing. It is a lucky escape.'

And then, across a shimmer of roofs, Milton appeared. He was waving a white handkerchief as if flagging to surrender. When they reached him and before Mo could speak, he told her: 'Do not do anything silly. Do not run.'

'Why not?' Mo had always run. It was her answer to everything. And when she ran, it was for her life, her cricket-bat face flattened by the wind. That was how she'd run from her father, from England, from Strike Hard – recklessly, and till her heart burst.

Milton offered a wrist to Sergeant Li and let him cuff it. 'Because you are going to be locked to me.'

Mo raised a hand and took the other cuff. Then they shuffled together onto the back seat of the car, the foam hollowed with the weight of a thousand arrests. Sergeant Li got in the front. He adjusted the rear-view mirror, putting them in line of sight. He'd hedged his bets with lucky charms: a Buddha and dice and Mao Zedong that jostled as he pulled out of the lot.

They joined traffic at a standstill.

'No Inspector Gu?'

'He is at home in Harbin.'

Harbin was way up north, a city famous for its Ice Festival. Mo should have known he'd be a creature of cold blood.

'As Head of the Yang'an Office, he gets to take the New Year's holiday.'

On the other side of the window, Guangzhou was celebrating. Lanterns were lit. Bunting hung between the bauhinia trees. Purple petals lay in drifts against the kerb as if this were the wedding season. Mo stared at the handcuffs. She thought this was what marriage was like – chained to someone you saw every day but never really knew, being taken on a long and featureless road, all the way to divorce or death, whichever came sooner. 'What are you doing, Milton, in an unmarked police car, chained to an English woman?'

Milton held up the handcuff as if to admire it, as if *Yang'an PSB* was the latest name in costume jewellery. 'I am sticking by you.'

It wasn't the first time Mo had been put in a car and returned against her will. The same thing had happened the time Mo and her mother had gone up by train to see Auntie Al. It was that New Year's Eve, the last New Year of the O'Shea family, it turned out.

Mo couldn't recognise her mother whenever she stayed with her sister. It was odd the way her face collapsed as soon as they arrived, as if the elastic had been cut and it finally fitted. Al saw it too. She said, 'Ring Selwyn and tell him you've got the flu bug. Tell him you can't get back as planned. Tell him to go to Ted's for New Year.'

Sue never told her husband to do anything. But she did do explaining and apologising. And when she made the phone call, Selwyn did the listening. Possibly. Who knew, actually, what was going on at the other end of the line? Sue said, 'So, I'll see you soon, Pet, as soon as I'm on my feet again.'

Sue never called her husband 'Pet'.

When she'd put the phone down, 'What did he say?' Al wanted to know.

'Nothing.'

Al fiddled with her earrings, working her lobes as if tuning in to what his silence meant. She wore dangly earrings from

Oxfam that were bright and asymmetrical, the kind Selwyn said were OK in an African hut, but attention-seeking in Blackpool.

A couple of hours later, the telephone rang. It woke Mo, who was in the living room, asleep on her half of the pull-out sofa. She took the call in her sleeping bag. 'Hello?'

'Get your mother on the line.'

Her mother was upstairs in the TV lounge watching Max Bygraves' *All-Time Favourites* and swigging white wine from the bottle.

'She's not here.'

'Of course she's there. She's right there, doing something stupid, which is why her eleven-year-old daughter is picking up the phone at midnight.'

'She's asleep.'

'That's not hard to change.'

Mo heard footsteps – heavy and erratic enough to be her mother unsteadied by Blue Nun. She willed her not to come tripping down the stairs and burst in singing.

'I've got a message for your mother. Tell her to put her fucking arse in a fucking car and point it in my direction.'

It was the first time Mo had heard her father use that word. He said it sounding like the amateur boxer he used to be, the man in the photo who'd landed a one-and-done on Bradford Eric Boon.

'What if she won't come home?'

'She'll soon find out.'

He must have fingered the photo from time to time because he polished the frame with Brasso.

'What if she does?'

'She'll soon find out.'

Mo's eyes turned to the wall. Usually, when you had ducks, you arranged them so they were rising into the sky. But Al had hers sitting in a row, like the ones you shot in return for fairground candy.

'*Please*, Dad.'

'Since when am I your father?'

And the line went dead.

Auntie Al had a driver's licence but hadn't used the car in years. She took Sue and Mo back to the Quality Home at twenty miles per hour with warning lights flashing as if they were a funeral cortège. All the way back, they ate Polish Cake. It was the guesthouse trademark dessert because it didn't need baking. It was crushed Rich Tea in golden syrup and cocoa powder. Mo didn't know why Auntie Al called it Polish Cake. Maybe because they were too poor to have ovens in Poland. Or maybe a Polish guest who'd become a Polish lover had taught her how to make it. Several of her guests had stayed on longer than expected, and in the end for free. Polish Cake usually made Mo happy, but on that journey, it made her sick. Mo was never car sick because Selwyn had a BMW, and you only ever felt grand in one of those. Somewhere near Hebden Bridge, Mo opened the car door. They were going so slowly, Al didn't even need to stop. She trailed brown Polish vomit along the kerb. At least it was raining.

They got back at four in the morning. Al parked in the town centre, beside a telephone booth. If they needed anything, she said, just ring. They all got out to make guesses at the scratched-at call-box number. In the morning, when it was light, if she hadn't heard, she'd drive herself back home.

Al wrapped her knees in the tartan blanket matted from the dog that had gone paddling in the Irish Sea and been taken by a rip current. She got tissues and 10ps ready for the public loos. She kissed her sister as if she might never see her again. She said to Mo, 'For your mother's sake, be nice to your father. Show him how glad you are to be back.' She wished them Happy New Year and wound down the window and waved goodbye, her odd up-and-down wave, as if she were wearing a hand-puppet and trying to make them laugh. When Mo turned back, she saw Al had parked under hanging baskets full of pansies that were dead now and had been donated to the town by Selwyn.

* * *

Sergeant Li leaned forward and fingered the radio. The People's Army Number One Brass Band punched its way through 'Without the Communist Party There Would be No New China'. He drove at a crawl past cliffs of dark flats, the windows black with laundry. On balconies, houseplants stood sick in their pots, leaves still pitched at the sun. With her free hand, Mo explored the seat pocket. She found a blister pack of aspirin, a fine for overstaying a parking meter, and on the back, a poem someone had half-written about Time. 'What are we doing, Milton?'

'We are going back to where you left off. We are pretending you never left Pingdi.' Because the day before, Sergeant Li had rung the Palace and asked if she was missing. Milton had taken the call. Her passport had been used at an internet café on the other side of the country. He'd recited the searches Mo had made. It looked as though a Strike Hard target was trying to abscond. Milton said, 'You put a plane ticket to Kuala Lumpur into your computer basket.'

Well, yes, she had done that. But only to see what it would feel like. She wanted to be on her way to somewhere easier than China. Somewhere China-esque, but without Strike Hard.

'And there was an onward flight to Heathrow.'

Well, yes, there was. But only because she'd had time to kill and she'd wondered what England was like these days. Prince Charles's marriage was on the rocks, apparently. There'd been prison break-outs. Eric Cantona was in trouble for a kung-fu kick. And it was cold. Snowstorms had hit the country.

She'd also put a plane ticket to Hawaii in her basket, one way, no onward journey.

She'd looked up 'John Stonehouse' and 'consular assistance'.

'What were you thinking of, Mo?'

She was being unavailable for arrest.

'You were running. Hiding. It is classed as hooligan behaviour. You know what that means? Re-education Through Labour. It means learning the opposite of everything you know while working twelve-hour shifts. Writing confessions as if they are true. Singing Party songs. Do you know how many there are of those?'

Sergeant Li caught snippets of their conversation. 'Please do not talk political. Please just the weather et cetera.' Sergeant Li's eyes were addressing them in the rear-view mirror. 'Otherwise...' He patted a breast pocket for his walkie-talkie and found instead a packet of cigarettes. He pulled out a Red Mountain and lit it on the dashboard. Then they turned onto an empty cut-through that Milton knew from his delivery rounds and Sergeant Li said couldn't exist because it wasn't on the map. Li smoked with no hands. He bobbed his head in time to 'Without the Party', sending smoke signals to the top of the car. Mo was smoking too now – passively. She hadn't done that since her father had filled the BMW with Benson and Hedges. Her mother was a smoker back then, but only Embassy Extra Mild and only to keep him company. He used to say, 'One a day keeps the doctor away. Have a ciggie for me, love.' He'd wanted his wife to smoke so that whatever disease he got, she'd get too. He didn't want her to outlive him, to get to see things he didn't. He didn't like the thought of her on her own and possibly doing fine, thank you very much. It had to be both of them, or neither. So there she was, lighting up and working through her repertoire of poses, looking engaged with the cigarette without actually smoking it, while in the back Mo lay on the floor because that's what you did if your house caught fire, according to St John's.

Mo whispered to Milton, 'Didn't Sergeant Li *want* to arrest me? Locking up a hooligan would look good on his CV.'

'I appealed to his better nature. He has one, much better than Gu's. I asked him to return you to us, to act as if nothing had happened. I said it would be a gift at New Year to have just one more day with you. I said: What if *your* daughter just vanished? And he said he had a son. But the principle was the same, he believed that. Also it was the law, which he enforced as well as he could. He is a man with bad eyes and bad lungs but a heart that tries to be good.' Milton said, 'You should thank him.'

Mo wasn't keen on people telling her she 'should' do things. But if she said it to herself, it sounded less like criticism and more like a reminder. Mo leaned forward. 'Thank you, Sergeant Li.'

He nodded. 'Want different songs?' and he turned a dial and Jacky Cheung filled the car with Cantopop. He wound down his window and flicked his cigarette into a paddy-field that sparkled like a crystal ashtray.

Mo looked at the handcuffs. She and Milton were almost holding hands. The last time she'd held a hand was... a long time ago. Was it her last Dave? Actually, it must have been Mr Nash. Everyone held hands in a different way, she'd noticed, because it wasn't just the action, it was what you meant by it. Take her parents. They'd held hands at public functions – when her father appeared for his charity work with Vets and Pets for instance. Selwyn stood at the mic and made a speech about 'our brave boys' and rescue dogs, his wife's hand curled into a ball and his palm wrapped over it like a padded glove. It was hand-holding as wicket-keeping. Or else it was Scissors, Paper, Stone, and paper trumped stone, everyone knew that.

Selwyn never held his daughter's hand because that was his wife's job. So, if they all went out together, Mo and her mother trailed behind in the scent of Old Spice – which went quite well, Mo thought, with the rotten leaves and fresh decay of an autumn Sunday. Her father smelt of after-shave and her mother smelt of pre-wash. There was never a day when she didn't do a load. Selwyn had bought her a Bosch straight after they'd got married because the Germans were good at hardware, and if it hadn't been for the Russian Winter, Hitler would have won the war. It was a huge machine, too big even for the kitchen. It filled one end of the conservatory. Sue took the size of the machine as a sign that Selwyn wanted a big family. So she did a full load every time: bedding, towels, clothes that were already clean. In her head: *We can't have another child, love, there's no room in the Bosch.*

Mo looked at Milton, his long body zig-zagged into the back of the police car. She thought of that game with the folded sheet of paper. Consequences, they called it. She and her mother used to play it at Christmas when they'd lost at Risk and it was just Selwyn versus his brother trying to rule the world.

Milton Jin met
Mo Moore
In China
He said to her: 'If you can get here alone, knowing no-one, across oceans and rivers and through The Mist, there is nothing you cannot do.'
She said to him: 'Will you marry me?'
And the consequence was...

Because that was the thing: if Milton married her, she'd be married. She'd meet local conditions. She'd be normal. Or normal-ish. Or normal enough for Gu, wouldn't she?

Mo glanced at Milton. He was so delicately drawn. It annoyed her sometimes, how mild he was, how provisional, that he would just agree to anything. 'Milton, will you m...' She stopped. She turned the start of the word she was already regretting into a thoughtful *mmmm*.

Because what would be the consequence of the consequence?

Because that was the trouble with people getting together. It led to them parting. All hellos ended in goodbyes. It was best not to have them in the first place.

'Milton?'

He turned a face so blank to her that she wanted to take a pen and sketch in an expression to talk to. 'Will you marry me?' She'd never said those words before. Then she thought maybe she had – once – years and years ago, to someone who was drunk and whose answer was so slurred she couldn't tell if she was engaged or not.

Milton didn't blink. He stared straight ahead to the back of Sergeant Li's head. He'd shaved his own hair and missed a patch.

'No,' Milton said.

'Oh.'

'I am sorry.'

Mo turned to the window. Outside, fields were tiled with brown water and people crawled about in them knee-deep in mud. Slogans two-feet high urged people to be better. 'Is that a no in principle or a no to me?'

'I am already married.'

'No you're not. You *can't* be. You've never mentioned a wife.'

'That is part of the understanding.'

'With who?'

'The world.'

It felt suddenly cramped in the back of the car. Milton had long legs and they were taking up all the room. Mo would have got out and walked if they hadn't been tied together.

'*I've* never seen her.'

'Despite appearances, or lack of them, she is my significant other. The most significant thing about her is her otherness.'

He craned forward, taking Mo with him by the handcuff. 'She lives not far from here, actually, over that way.' He pointed their hands in the direction of tower-blocks, tiered like celebration cakes, cochinealed pink.

And now Mo had somehow ended up in Re-education anyway, because all along Milton hadn't been married and now suddenly he *was*. It was the opposite of everything she knew about him. There'd been no ring, no looking married, never mention of a name.

'What's her name?'

And he told her, and then Mo wished she hadn't asked because now she could put a name to a face she couldn't see.

Was she jealous?

Mo didn't get jealous.

But maybe she *was* jealous of Mimi. She minded, anyway, because Mimi had already taken Mo's way out. Also because Milton had kept quiet about her, and she and Milton told each other everything, didn't they?

Should she congratulate him? 'Is *she* tall too?'

'She works as a painter and decorator and does not need a ladder.'

'I'm happy for you.'

'Thank you.' A sad little nod. He turned his face to the window. 'She does not need a ladder, but she does sometimes need a husband. When I have a delivery in Guangzhou, I call in on the in-laws. They appreciate the gesture. Her friend, she plays double bass in a jazz band.'

The word 'she' came out like the gust of a long-held breath. They both sank back, abandoning their weight to the seat. The hardened foam of a police car suddenly felt quite comfortable.

'So your wife has a double bass player, and you have…?'

He raised their hands and placed them on a knee. 'I have Bucks Fizz.' He let their hands stay there. 'It is a love I conceived several years ago from someone I met while studying Irrigation. He was from the Gobi desert. It is from him I learned "Land of Make Believe".' He tapped a foot as if hearing it in his head. 'I was a hooligan once. "Hooligan", you know, is the technical term.'

'And since then?'

'And since then…' He counted them off on his fingers. '*Are You Ready… Hand Cut… I Hear Talk…* but then Bucks Fizz had the bus crash.' A sigh, deep enough for Sergeant Li to feel on the back of his head. He ran a hand over it, smoothing the patch he'd missed. 'But no matter. Passion, you know, it is not the only fruit.'

Dear Milton. Well, if *he'd* been a hooligan, then so had *she*. One time at college, someone had asked Mo if she thought she had a problem, an addiction maybe?

No, she said, she was just curious and not a time-waster. And she was going to prove, in every conceivable way – as Diploma Dave later psychologised – that she was *not* her father's daughter. Over and over, in everything she did, she was *not*-Selwyn. So Mo had sex in all possible combinations and with anyone and anything that consented and was legal.

Then she got an infection.

Her GP was young. She had the palest skin, unblemished by life or sunlight, as if she'd just come from a nunnery. She showed Mo a diagram of female genitals and the proximity of the urethra and anus.

'I know. I've looked.'

The doctor blushed.

'Many times.'

She was wondering, Mo could tell: with a mirror? Or had she seen other people's? She gave Mo the anatomical diagram, a line drawing, the uneven features splayed and labelled like an ancient map of Mordor.

Then she took a sexual history, which Mo simplified to save time and spare them both the awkwardness.

'Have you ever been pregnant?'

Mo had been careful. Even with all that abandon, she'd been scrupulous about her eggs.

Nulligravida, the doctor wrote, which made it sound like a crime.

In Freshers' Week, Mo had joined the Women's Group. Actually, there were several women's groups and they didn't seem to like each other. But Mo had settled, in the end, on the

Non-Male Union, led by Nick, who refused to be called the leader. Nick said the group was inclusive, and that everyone in it was defined simply by non-maleness, however that state arose – by birth or electively. It allowed for their commonality and their difference.

Selwyn, Mo knew, would have been more than 'not happy at all' about the Non-Male Union: he'd have wanted to take a machine-gun to them. Mo sat in the meetings and warmed herself in streams of long, careful sentences. And then she let her attention drift, and went round the ring and in her head had sex with everyone there. She spent most time with Nick, though. Nick had great bones and a profile like Leon Trotsky.

And then her mother died.

A few years later when she did her Death Diploma, Mo was told that grief often led to risky sexual behaviour. She studied stats and case histories that showed it. But it wasn't like that with her. When Sue died, Mo's body went quiet. She got herself a goldfish and took up quilting. She stayed awake all hours listening to the radio, which was how she knew the shipping forecast off by heart, and how she could chat so easily about cricket to the friendly bloke who in the end became her Radio Dave.

Mo and Milton and Sergeant Li listened to Hong Kong pop and laments for lost love till they reached valleys too deep for the radio signal. Then Sergeant Li hummed tuneless tunes. He asked Mo what British people sang to pass the time in cars. So she sang 'She'll Be Coming Round the Mountain' till an early dusk fell and the first firecrackers went up. It'd be the Year of the Pig in the morning.

It was dark when they reached Dadu. Even the lights of the hospital had been turned off. Mo thought of Lulu, who'd be allowed to stay up on New Year's Eve. If she rang him to say goodbye and see you sometime in England, he'd try to keep her spirits up and encourage her with a quote.

Mo said, 'What would Chairman Mao say to me at a time like this?'

Milton said, '"We shall heal our wounds, collect our dead and continue fighting."' He sounded tired.

Sergeant Li said, '"In times of difficulties, we must not lose sight of our achievements!"'

That was upbeat, for a policeman. Mo gazed out of the window, at the late twentieth century that had arrived in the village while she'd been away. New pylons carried fist-thick cables. Searchlights reached for the peak of Soaring Magpie Mountain. The road had been straightened and tarmacked, and was subject to a speed limit, and signs warned of the sudden appearance of cattle and pre-school children. Under brand-new street lamps, The Mist fizzed Fanta-orange. The mud track along the river was now a concrete Leisure Promenade. All the signs pointed to Jiazhishi, apart from the one at the South Gate. The last sign standing said: *Welcome to Pingdi.*

Bulbs were on in every house, lighting the way through the village. Faces came to the window at the sound of the passing car. Mo knew every one of them – all their stories, most of their secrets. In her head: goodbye Auntie Lu, goodbye Little Zhou, goodbye Uncle Ding. At least 'goodbye' was an honest word. It made no claims about ever seeing someone again. Unlike *zaijian*, and *au revoir*, and *auf Wiedersehen*. Did all the languages in the world hold out hope, apart from English?

She turned to Milton. 'What's going to happen tomorrow?'

'There will be the application of all applicable laws.'

'Which are?'

'As always in China, it depends on who does the applying.'

'What am I supposed to tell people? The truth? That I did a runner?'

'When in China was the truth ever a good idea?'

'So what, then?'

'Just say hello.'

'When I'm about to say goodbye?'

'Do you know what will happen between your hello and goodbye? A new year will start. People will be born. People will die. The whole of life will happen. The whole of life is always happening somewhere in the world.'

But Mo couldn't see the world. When she looked out of the car window, she didn't see the Land of Make Believe in which Milton found his happiness. All she could make out were the distant lights of the Palace and its dark hulk washed up in the fields.

Sergeant Li stopped at the gate and turned off the engine.

Silence.

Finally.

Home again.

For an hour or two.

At an upstairs window, a back-lit figure that had to be the mayor made wide sweeps of an arm. He looked like a man on a sinking ship, signalling the rescue boat this way. Because that's what it was, the Palace. A ship going down. It would belong to the Chinese state in the morning.

Orgasm

性高潮

Chapter sixteen

The mayor stood at the open Palace door, blushing under bright red lanterns. Mo wrapped her arms around him and tied her fingers together. She drank in Moonshine and mothballs, which was the scent of his Celebration Silks. The mayor squeezed her waist, squeezed again, and didn't seem to find enough of her. 'Have you eaten?' Over his shoulder, on the living room table, a steamed chicken, its neck broken, claws gripping the edge of the bowl. He placed an ear to Mo's chest, listening to the beat of her return. 'How long have you been gone? I was counting the hours till they turned into eternity.' Then a hardening of his face against a softening of his face. 'I truly thought I had lost anoth—'

'Thoughts that seem truly true are often false.' It was the boom of Mrs Su. 'Of course she came back. I had the kettle on already,' and she appeared, still dressed for Korea. 'No party dress because I am on duty. I show off fireworks at midnight.' And she offered Mo a cup of tea, half drunk and not quite warm.

Then the telephone rang. Mo answered. There were no introductions, but she knew that high-pitched rattle, the sound of authority talking through a kazoo: 'Good, you are caught.'

'Yes, Inspector Gu, I am home.'

'Technically speaking. But only until midnight. On the dot of twelve, you fail the Second Gross Deficiency. You are then illegally on Chinese soil. Your temporary presence is only tolerated under police supervision and from State goodwill.'

Down the line, Mo caught an eruption of laughter, the hubbub of a party.

'Any personal property left behind will be regarded as a gift to the Chinese people. The Palace is to be vacated. Whoever is there must leave.'

Mo didn't want this call. 'I'm keeping you from *your* family, Inspector.'

'In the morning Sergeant Li will escort you to Yang'an where he will complete the paperwork for your deportation. You will pay the fine for petrol from Jiazhishi to the border crossing. Doctor Long will secure the factory and the Palace.'

'He doesn't have keys.'

'The workers will continue to benefit from their ten-day statutory holiday—'

'I didn't give him keys.'

'—during which time, the Jiazhishi Voluntary Brigade will secure the site with electric fencing and defensive dogs—'

'How did Doctor Long get keys?'

'—while the State Takeover Committee for Failed and Failing Enterprises finalises the handover.' Inspector Gu was speeding up, getting bored of talking to a Strike Hard target whose case was already closed.

'Handing it to who?'

'I would like a word with Sergeant Li.'

'*Not* to Doctor Long?'

'Sergeant Li, I said.'

He was in the garden somewhere, helping Mrs Su set up her fireworks. 'I'll have to go and find him.'

'*Find*? Is he not attached to you? I told him handcuffs until you were expelled from the country.'

Mo called into the darkness that his boss was on the line. Sergeant Li took his time coming in. He wiped gunpowder down the sides of his trousers and held the phone in a fist. Gu talked and Li listened. He said yes, yes, he was taking notes. He reached behind his ear for a cigarette. Li blew smoke rings towards Harbin. His eyes roved the room. They stopped on Mo's certificate and her gold-lettered approval from the Chinese

Sexology Committee. Then a string of grunts and a morose 'Happy New Year to you too,' and he put the receiver down.

'What's going on with Doctor Long?' Mo said.

'I am sorry, but he is a surgeon. He has long fingers and they get everywhere. Also, he works in family planning. He is expert at neutralising women.'

Mo went upstairs to wash away the call with Inspector Gu and get the smell of police car out of her hair – the diesel, the leatherette, the Red Mountain. She changed her clothes. From her bedroom window, she looked down on a party that was just getting going. The whole village was on its way to the Palace. Mrs Su made traffic-warden motions to the patio where a fire burned for good fortune. Sergeant Li was circulating, serving Moonshine. The Pingdi Pipers played 'Hello, Goodbye'.

All Mo wanted to do was sleep.

She crept out the back way and went to the bottom of the garden, to where Lulu had built his hide-out.

Mo used to do that too, when she'd had enough of life in the Quality Home. She'd go to the woods on the edge of the Quality Estate and hide in the long grass and eat crab paste from the jar and wonder why her mother had married him. Mo had asked her once, and the answer came out bland and light: 'Because I love him' – because she'd asked herself the same question and that was the reason she'd settled on.

It was soft on Lulu's bed of hay. He had a collection of feathers, and he'd woven flowers into the wickerwork. Under a pillow of lavender, she found a pocketbook: *SAS Survival Guide*. She opened it where he'd used blades of grass as bookmarks: 'Facing Disaster,' 'Edible Tropical Plants,' 'Direction by the Heavens'. Was he planning on doing a runner?

Then Mo must have slept despite the noise of the party, because the next thing she knew, Milton's hand was on her shoulder and he was telling her the mayor was about to make his speech and could she come and hear it?

The crowd gathered and the mayor waited for a hush, and then, 'Tonight,' he said, 'is an occasion of many occasions – some happy, some sad.' First, he raised a toast to the Year of the Pig. Then to ample rain and abundant harvests; to new love – and a nod towards an elderly couple too engrossed in each other to notice; also to longevity because Old Mang would be a hundred this year; and to good marks in the high school exams. It would be years before any of the village children would take them, but already parents were asking for divine intervention.

And when all hopes for the future had been drunk to, the mayor reached for Mo's hand. Everyone knew what was coming and a melancholy fell over the grounds. 'In the morning, Mo is to be sent away – against the will of all of us...'

A thousand heads shook. The mayor had to raise his voice over the hum of discontent. 'She is to be deported to England. We do not know if we shall ever see her again. It is 9,000 kilometres away, and eight time zones, and a plane ticket way beyond our means.'

The crowd sighed, sounding punctured.

'Let us say it as it is: Mo is being condemned to exile. For what is England except a remote place, fenced in by water, renowned for poor food and unpleasant weather?' He turned to her, looking desperately sorry for England.

It was the kind of face Mo remembered at bus stops, on people weighed down by a bag of chips with too much salt and not enough vinegar, and the rain beating on the bus shelter roof, and the bus never coming, and cars spraying water up their shins.

The mayor said, 'We wish you a long life doing whatever English people do to make themselves happy.'

Was *Neighbours* still on? Did Tesco still do Breaded Chicken Kiev?

England. She'd have to get used to pound coins and portraits of the Queen, to pale skin and gloomy anoraks, and Mo knew that very soon it would all seem perfectly normal. She'd catch up with Spud, who'd have armfuls of children and say: 'Sorry I never made it over.' She'd have a weekend in Birmingham with Carol, who'd be done in from working nights and who'd chat the whole time as if Mo had never been away.

She thought that in the summer, when it was warm and the flowers were out – perhaps in June on the anniversary of his death – she'd go and say hello to her father. She'd pick at the weeds the maintenance man had missed. Put them in her pocket. She'd leave something – maybe a stone, something light but also heavy – something to show she'd been. Take a photo of the gravestone. Take several, actually, and get prints enlarged at Boots.

Finally, the mayor let go of Mo's hand. He forced good cheer into his voice and raised a toast. 'And so: to Mo's safe departure! To her adventures in England! To the wonderful fact of Mo!'

Milton bent down. Mo hooked her legs around his neck and he swaggered with her six feet into the air. It was odd, she thought, slinging her crotch around the neck of a man she wasn't going to marry. It was funny, sometimes, how close you got.

Hanging in the night sky, the red lights of *HAPPINESS*. She thought how sad she was. Sad that she was leaving. Sad that Pingdi was now Jiazhishi. She gazed over people's heads at the underside of clouds that, thanks to the Leisure Promenade and the glow of the fake gas-lamps, would forever be all-day orange.

Mo wasn't good at making speeches. Once, for school assembly, she'd had to stand at the front of the hall and give a report on a netball tournament. But all those faces, all that expectation. She'd stared at the ropes for hanging yourself from, at the climbing frames for falling from, at the giant hymn books strung from the ceiling like slaughtered birds, and said the first thing that came into her head. 'We won.' She got huge applause for that.

Now Mo turned her face to the sky. It'd be a new moon in the morning. And again she said the first thing that came to her: 'The moon is the earth's only natural satellite. It's moving away from us. It causes two high tides and two low tides a day. Its gravity is one-sixth of that on earth.' Mo felt weightless, as if lifting off from Milton's shoulders. She said, 'China's moon is England's moon. It's our shared landscape, in both our worlds. When I'm back, and on clear nights when the moon's bright, I'll go to my bedroom window and look east towards China, and...'

Mo didn't have the chance to finish. A handful of voices started the poem, and by the end of the first line, the whole village was with her. It was the Chinese anthem of absence, of homesickness, handed down across the generations for more than a thousand years:

> *Chuang qian ming yue guang*
>
> *Yi shi dishang shuang*
>
> *Jütou wang ming yue*
>
> *Ditou si guxiang*

> Bright moonlight before my bed;
>
> It could be taken for frost on the ground.
>
> I raise my head to view the bright moon.
>
> I lower my head and think of my old home.

And then, silence. Just the lisp of the river and a sigh so deep it could have been the wind. Mo scanned a sea of heads, all of them lowered – all, she noticed, apart from one. Sergeant Li was staring at Mo and flicking a finger across his cheek.

What do you do with a crying man? At Eden House, Mo had taken their hand and waited till the weeping turned to words. She'd dab at the wet as if staunching a wound, and sometimes they'd say it took them back to the war. Then they'd tell her about the war, and the friends they'd lost, and all the people they'd lost since. It was always about loss. And while they talked, Mo found the Roses tin and picked out their favourite soft-centres, and produced them like magic from up her sleeve until they felt so spoiled, they said. Mo was good at that: off-setting sorrow with sweetness.

Sergeant Li looked so innocent, so unlike a policeman. Mo slid from Milton's shoulders. 'As Guest of Honour, Uncle Li, would you come inside to cut the New Year's cake?'

He sank into a chair as if punched and dragged an arm across his face. He was sorry, he said, but it was always the same with that poem. As soon as he heard: 'I lower my head and think of...' But he didn't finish. The last word seemed to suffocate him. And then he told Mo that when he thought of *that place*, he thought of all the people that were not there. He dipped his chin to talk to his chest about The Ranch – bought for him by his son on the Grand Canyon Estate on the plains to the west of Yang'an. It had a white picket fence, a veranda and a cherry tree in the garden. He had a horse in poured concrete, a man in period costume to mow the lawn, and *no-one*.

He glanced towards the patio where the entertainments were starting. Tan-the-Acrobat, who'd performed for Chairman Mao, was now doing somersaults, roared on by the crowd.

Sergeant Li reached for a bottle and sucked brown pop through a straw. Between mouthfuls, he named the people that were not at The Ranch: his son, who was in D.C., a lawyer and a father, and too busy and successful ever to come back. His mother, who lived in a secure ward and was happy, in her own way, with houseplants, but alarmed by full-sized men. She was locked in her room with the jungle her son had given her. His wife was married to a merchant seaman, his father was dead, and his sister was in Canada with his niece, breathing fresh air and canoeing. Sergeant Li turned to Mo. 'It is strange, but when I look at you, and if take away the whiteness, I see my niece.'

She knew that thing with faces. In sideways glances and unanchored moments, everyone she'd ever known was here in China. She'd spotted her mother, and Auntie Al, and Carol and Spud. She'd seen teachers and Radio Dave. If she squinted through her lashes, Sergeant Li could be taken for a Moore.

'This Gross Deficiency...' He flicked a wrist. 'Mo, *I* have no family. *I* do not conform to local conditions.' He slid the empty bottle back on the table. Mo saw the sweat stains under his arms, caught the smell of single man, of hand-washed laundry put away before it was dry. 'And because of no family, every New Year, *I* am on duty. *I* have to sit by the station telephone and wait.'

'What for?'

'Drunken rowing and domestic fighting. Is not the festive season the most dangerous time for family relations?'

Mo offered him a knife for the New Year's cake and said to make a wish. He was exact with the angles and took his time with his whispered hopes. Mo watched while he ate. He seemed more and more absorbed, his jaws slowing, while on the patio Tan-the-Acrobat was building a human pyramid with the village children. When Li had finally finished and tongued the last shreds from his teeth, 'I have been assigned to your case for an entire month. I have had time to consider the evidence. And what I deduce is: what are families except exactly *this*? Is not everyone at this party family? Is not this whole village family? Mo, there is something I must do.' He rocked in his chair, gathering momentum and launched himself upright. He opened the patio door and stepped out. Over his head, the hook for the washing-line hung like an upturned question mark.

The crowd saw him and stilled.

Sergeant Li cleared his throat. 'I do not lie and I do not make speeches – except to criminal court, and then I read from my notes. So I will just say...' He looked unsteady, seemed to sway under the press of so many faces. 'This is the best New Year of my whole life. You have welcomed me like one of you.'

That was met with looks of bewilderment.

'I feel like a Su, like a Lin. I feel like a human being, not a police officer.'

Applause rippled to the end of the garden.

'I feel happy. I *am* happy.'

The applause went on so long that the mayor had to call for calm.

Sergeant Li studied his open hands as if they were his notebook. Then he turned to Mo. 'I therefore declare that this household conforms to local conditions.'

'Pardon?'

'You have passed.'

'No I haven't.'

The people in earshot gasped.

'I can't have. Inspector Gu said I was leaving in the morning.'

'And who is in charge?'

'But what will he say?'

Li pressed a palm to his breast. 'If I have to choose between Harbin and here?' Then he made a megaphone of his hands and broadcast his voice across the crowd: 'I. Hereby. Declare. That. Mo. Is. No. Longer. Struck. Hard!' And his face unfolded like a concertina at the end of a tune.

Mo knew she was supposed to be overjoyed. She was meant to be smiling and laughing and knocking back Moonshine like everyone else. But she didn't feel anything – except scattered by a wind that blew right through her. In her head, she'd already taken herself to England and China-Mo had died. And now, she'd been called back again, and the brief life of English-Mo was over.

She was nowhere and no-one.

She stared at the mist on the Menglang, which was denser than ever and swirling amber from the fire.

Then she felt a hand on her arm. 'Look up!' Mrs Su pointed towards the night. 'I saved this display for you. I knew we would need it.' And fireworks ripped from the ground, filling the sky with the shape of hearts – hundreds of them in pink and red, that thundered and then broke.

Mrs Su held her and rocked from foot to foot. Mo felt sick as she swung from one life to another. She fixed her eyes on the Palace door. It was solid and thick and made of wood that had taken three hundred years to grow. Said to herself but in Mrs Su's ear, 'I don't understand it. I'm so happy and so sad. And what makes me saddest is I won't find out what it says on my father's gravestone.'

'Whatever it says, it will be the wrong thing.' She took Mo by the shoulders, looked her in the eye. 'It will not be the one word you want to hear.'

'He never said that.'

Mrs Su brought her lips so close, Mo thought she was going to kiss her. 'Because they never do.'

The mayor pitched his way over, punch drunk with joy and telling everyone how speechless he was. He talked at length about speechlessness. Then he gazed up at the night sky. 'I thank my lucky stars! They are a constant, dependable. They have shone like this over humankind, ever since the sky was born.'

'Apart from the Intelsat satellite,' Mrs Su said, 'and the late-night flight to Rangoon.' Then she banged a pot to round up the troops and gather them at the gate. The mayor said, 'If you had gone, Momo, I would have spent the rest of my life looking at those stars, lost in a world of wishful thinking, my fading senses seeing you every day just across the river or coming down Soaring Magpie Mountain.' He took Mo's hands with a tender scoop, as if he would marry her. 'But the one word that presses itself upon me is a word I have uttered to no-one but my dear wife, my dear daughter, and to Chairman Mao in the old days of deep devotion. Mo, I—'

'Advance!' Mrs Su flung the Palace gates open. 'Let us claim what is ours! Let us retake *Happiness*!' and she threw an arm towards the factory and strode out of a poster from the Cultural Revolution. The whole village tumbled after her, swarmed across the fields, mindless of the stubble and the bleat of troubled sheep.

Everyone followed apart from Mo, who gathered up hats and toddlers abandoned in the rush. And the mayor, who was helping. And Old Mang, who was in the hammock, sniffing at the tail-end of sulphur, his cloudy eyes alarmed. 'No! Calamity!' he cried. 'I smell—'

'Nothing of the sort,' the mayor cried back.

Just before midnight, all the factory lights went on. It blazed like a launch pad, as if Mrs Su's Base 27 had moved here, to the foothills of the Shunhua mountains. The word *HAPPINESS* flashed on and off. Then, broadcast through speakers, the countdown from South-West Radio Farmer: *Ten, nine, eight, seven...*

Old Mang cursed. He wagged a finger and warned of The End.

...six, five, four, three...

Mo and the mayor clung to each other. They knew what was coming: an almighty thunder booming through the valley, the voice of fire launched into the sky, and shock waves shivering the core of the mountains.

Instead, what Mo heard was her name, high-pitched and frantic.

Lulu was on his bike. He was racing towards the Palace, and he was crying.

Chapter seventeen

Lulu's eyes ran. His nose ran. It was the kind of mess you saw on faces that were beyond consolation, beyond self-control – when the world has just come to an end. She'd never seen him look so young. The child that he was had finally arrived.

He threw down his bike, pulling so hard on his lungs Mo could hear them. He was too out of breath to tell her what had happened, but Mo knew anyway. She scanned the road for car lights, then picked up his bike and wheeled it inside.

Lulu was barefoot and dressed for bed. He looked overwhelmed by his grown-up silk pyjamas with their monogrammed pocket: *LJM*: *Long Jingming*. Bright Tomorrow.

Then the Palace door slammed shut.

Lulu sank to the floor. He crawled under the table and held his head in his hands like you do in a war when the bomb has dropped and it was just the wait to be hit.

The mayor said, 'Lulu, Strike Hard is over!'

He shrank further back, made himself small. Mo had seen animals at the market do that: press themselves to the back of the cage as a hand thrusts in.

The mayor took it for a game. He searched the room, round and round, circling in on the table.

Mo said, 'Is the gate locked?'

The mayor bent down. He reached out an arm.

Lulu whimpered.

The mayor said not to be upset, everything was going to be all right now, Momo was staying.

She said, 'Did you lock the front door?'

'We never lock the front door.'

Lulu choked.

'What are we afraid of, Lulu?'

Mo said, 'Please lock the front door.'

And when the sound of the mayor's footsteps had gone, from under the table Lulu told Mo what had happened.

When Mo had got on the bus at Dadu, Doctor Long had spotted her. He'd gone to The Cube after their last phone call to see what she would do. He'd watched the bus pull out of the station, and then he'd reported her to the police. A Strike Hard Target was on the run.

'How do you know?'

'Because he told us. Over breakfast. He looked so happy, so pleased with himself. "A fine day's work before I even get to the office," he said.' His mother had paused, her spoon suspended between bowl and mouth. Then she'd put it down, risen from her seat and removed herself from the table. Lulu had watched her leave the room – a silent glide towards the door. It was how she always moved. But Lulu knew that this time was different because she hadn't finished her breakfast. And it was a family rule to finish that. Because not finishing meant waste and weakness and was a bad omen for the rest of the day.

So Lulu had eaten on.

He'd spooned rice porridge, counting the mouthfuls, trying not to notice the sounds from their bedroom, the flit and scuffle, which meant his mother was not sitting quietly, being calm. His father had transferred his attention from his family to the newspaper. He ran his eyes over the business pages, up and down columns of figures. When he'd finished, he said, 'Your mother is not well. She is not herself. Please clear the table.'

The next thing Lulu heard was something flung against a wall – the dull, easy thud of an object light and empty. He went to his parents' room and found his mother slumped on the floor. Her handbag was upturned on the bed, its contents thrown about:

her make-up bag, her keys, her lucky red purse. Then Doctor Long ordered Lulu to his room. He told him to stay there and do his homework. And when he'd done his homework, he should do it again, only better. Between his father's legs, Lulu caught a glimpse of his mother. She was sinking. She seemed to be dissolving.

And then, this evening, his father had seen the fireworks. He'd stood on the roof of Golden Dawn Gardens and watched pink hearts popping over Pingdi. He knew exactly what it meant. That's when Lulu had made his escape.

'And your mother?'

'In the wardrobe.'

'Hiding?'

'Locked in. As punishment.'

'Since when?'

'Since their fight. Since you left.'

Which was ages ago. A lifetime ago.

But Lulu knew that she was alive because from his room he could hear tapping on the heating pipes. He stared at Mo, his big eyes bigger than ever. This exceptional child at The Exceptional School, who had already met so many of the world's wonders, looked at her with wonder that such things could happen.

But they did.

Of course they did.

And everyone knew it, really: that men threw their wives against walls; that they attacked them to stop them leaving.

Because that New Year, when Mo and her mother had left Auntie Al by the phone box and walked back to the Quality Home, Selwyn had been waiting for them.

Her mother had put her key in the lock and said, 'Whatever he says, just be nice,' and she'd pushed open the door. She left the key on the inside, because that's what they always did, it was what Selwyn wanted, 'a reasonable precaution when people out there are jealous of what we've got.'

The house was dark. 'Selwyn, love!' called brightly up the stairs.

Silence.

'Selwyn, love?'

Mo's mother bit her lip. She wasn't wearing lippy. She hadn't worn any for the whole of Blackpool.

Mo said, 'Isn't it better if we just let him sleep?'

Her mother turned on the hall light. It was sharp after the darkness, and glanced off the hardware of the English Civil War. She went into the kitchen and filled the kettle and fetched down three mugs. Mo sat at the table and ate from the tin of cinnamon shortbread her mother had made for Christmas. It was starting to taste of soap already. It'd be 1976 in the morning.

Then the kettle boiled and her mother warmed the pot and put on the cosy. She took the bottle of milk and gave Selwyn the cream. She was brisk and chirpy, as if it was seven o'clock on any weekday morning, and she was getting breakfast ready for when her husband came down.

And then, there he was, filling the doorway, dark and vast and in the gear he wore to footie: the black bomber jacket and steel-capped boots because the lads had big feet, and didn't always know where they were putting them. Mo caught the smell of polish. He always buffed his jacket for serious matches.

Her mother leaned against the heater, even though it wasn't on. 'I'm making us tea, love. Would you like some tea?'

'Thank you for keeping the appointment. I'm from O'Shea Estates.' He dangled Sue's keys from the tip of a finger. 'May I show you round the property?'

'Don't, Selwyn, please.'

'Here we have a highly desirable detached, four-bedroom house – the most expensive on the entire Quality Home Development – with all mod cons, double garage and a large, secluded garden. In a sought-after part of town with access to good schools, hospitals and transport links. It would make an ideal family home—'

'Selwyn, *please...*'

'—if the family deigned to be here. It comes rent free, with two cars, for life, for keeps, with a live-in husband who pays all the bills. It's your ideal Live-the-Life-of-Riley home. All you have to do is fucking *be* here.'

'*Please*, Selwyn.' She held out her hand. 'Can I have my keys back?'

'*Your* keys? *My* house. *My* keys. You!'

He meant Mo.

'Get upstairs.'

Her father's eyes were on her face, but not looking and not seeing. Her mother's eyes were on her back, she could tell, and willing her to get out of the kitchen. Mo kept her head down as she left, her eyes fixed on the Bri-Nylon carpet with the black treacle stain that would never come out, which you had to avoid when you came down in the morning if you didn't want a terrible day.

Mo got into bed in her clothes. Over her head, the Quality attic. Up there was all the stuff of their Quality life: Selwyn's boxing gear, demijohns from when he had a go at making beer, antiques he'd got bored of but couldn't throw away. Mo wondered what stopped the ceiling from crashing down.

Maybe nothing.

Maybe it would.

And then she heard a lunge of voices, and a door downstairs slammed. The sound of her mother's feet running up the stairs – the horizontal scuff of carpet, the kind of footfall honed over the years to keep the noise down. Mo heard the ping of the airing-cupboard, and a pile of linen dropped onto the floor.

And then silence.

Mo listened to the tick of her alarm clock, watched Minnie Mouse wave a bunch of flowers, back and forth once every second and smiling for all eternity. Then the thud of a neighbour's firework at the far end of the street. A brief gasp of light.

It was midnight.

Happy New Year.

Then boots took the stairs two at a time, and on the landing her father was saying, 'What the fuck do you think you're playing at?'

Mo heard the sound of metal slamming metal, bolts breaking apart and her father yelling. All his sentences began with 'I,' and in that furious assault of the self, Mo heard the spare bed being smashed to pieces.

He was calm at the end of it, and stilled. She heard him say: 'You *know* where the bed is.'

He was quick after that.

Mo listened to the sound of the bedhead against the wall. She never heard her parents. But this knock, knock, knock, knock had the same rhythm he'd used with the hammer. She imagined her mother, arms round his bulk, trying not to touch him.

Mo pressed her spine into the wall. Her eyes tracked the pattern in the wallpaper. If you were careful enough and concentrated hard, you could trace an unbroken line from the floor to the ceiling. It was a flower motif. She thought of the game with daisy petals: *he loves me, he loves me not, he loves me, he loves me not*, you never could tell.

One minute they did, and the next minute they were smashing things.

And where did that leave you?

Mo got up. She went to the window. There was the drainpipe she'd climb down if she had to get out in a hurry. There was the quince tree, and the apple tree, and the strawberries with the nets where the birds got tangled up and died. At the end of the garden, Mo's primary school, starlight landing on the netball courts. Her gym teacher said 'hard lines' when you'd done everything you could and still the other side won. Her voice came back to Mo: 'Hard lines, Simone, hard lines.'

The night was cold, and there was her breath draped in front of her. Breaths felt loaned then, and she wanted to count them.

She looked down at the patio. A girl in her school had fallen out of her bedroom window and landed on a patio like that. On her head, and she'd died. They'd said a prayer for her in assembly, and then she was gone. Mo thought: I can't even remember her name. She thought: children are dying all the time. She thought: I don't want to die in my sleep. If I stay awake, I have a chance of escaping. I must be ready to run till the daylight comes. So, she sat against the bedroom wall, listening for sounds from the next room. Sounds of anger, of panic. For hours, Mo listened for the sound of the end.

Then she heard her mother go to the bathroom – the brush of the door on the pile of the carpet, the click of the light-pull, the flush of the loo, the tap. Then Mo's bedroom door crept open. Her mother stood there, sideways lit by the bathroom light. She was in her slippers with the fluff-ball and her pink satin dressing gown, the belt tied, but the gown hanging open, her nightie looking soiled. She stood with her feet apart as if she needed air.

'He's asleep.' She said it flatly, in the quiet voice Mo remembered from bedtime stories, when they'd reached the last page and then it was The End. Her mother looked like a figurine taken from a wedding cake and left on the side of the plate with the strips of royal icing and marzipan that nobody wanted to eat.

'He put a knife to my throat and said he'd kill me.'

'Is it safe to be in there with him?'

'It is now.' Her mother blew her a kiss. She didn't want to come over, to do what she usually did, which was stroke her hair and tuck it behind her ears. She didn't want Mo to smell the smells, to get too close to what had happened between them.

The sound of Mrs Su's fireworks must have masked the approach of his car, because the next thing Mo knew, Doctor Long was hammering a fist against the window and telling her to release his son. He was in a suit and tie. He'd dressed formally for midnight, for the moment he'd lay claim to the factory.

'I'm not holding him.' Under the table, Lulu clung to Mo. She could feel his breath on her leg.

'Of course you are. Where else would he be?' Doctor Long leaned back as if scanning the front of the house. In fact, it was to gain momentum.

A fist flew through the window. Glass shattered into a thousand pieces and arced in slow motion across the room, strange and shocking and almost beautiful.

Doctor Long called through the broken window. 'Come out, Lulu. It is not safe in there.'

It was a face Mo knew well, but she'd never seen it like this before – so bleak and reckless. Doctor Long walked his eyes around the room, taking it in, placing himself in it.

'There are easier ways to take a look. Don't you have keys?'

He pulled them from his pocket and dangled them from a finger. 'Palace. Factory.' He inserted them through the window, offering them to Mo.

She raised a hand to take them, and he snatched them away. A smile that wasn't: his lips pulled back to bare his gums, a look she'd seen in dog fights. And that was when Doctor Long saw his hand was bleeding. He put it to his mouth and bit to stem the flow. He looked as though he'd savaged himself, he was eating himself alive. He fumbled for a handkerchief. For a moment, he was distracted.

Mo whispered without moving her lips: 'Keep to the floor. Use the back door. Stay in the garden.'

She felt Lulu slide from under the table, heard the catch of glass as he skidded over it, saw a shadow disappear.

Maybe Doctor Long caught the shadow too. He shouted through the window. 'Lulu! Final warning. Get into the car.' And to Mo, 'You will not get away with it.'

'Will *you*, Doctor Long?'

For a moment, neither said anything. Mo took in the coldness of his eyes. She knew that look. It could turn in an instant to anger. He'd played a long game. First the bid that Mrs Su had turned down. Then a foreigner had arrived and taken possession of his factory. Mo said, 'You were lucky with Strike Hard, though. Inspector Gu was very timely.'

'Fortune favours the brave and misfortune favours the opportunist.'

Mo didn't take her eyes off Doctor Long. She gestured over her shoulder. 'There's the certificate. Approved for ever and ever. Thank you for sorting that out. You meant it for you, but it's staying with me.'

Over their heads, rockets squealed with delight. The sky was raining Mrs Su's light. Then the chant of the villagers cheering on the fireworks: *jiayou! Jiayou!* – add oil! Add oil! and the clamour of ammunition. It was Mrs Su's grand finale. 'I'm sorry it didn't work out, Doctor Long.'

Across the sound of warfare and in a yellow chemical daylight, they saw each other clearly: a man who was denied what he'd decided was his, and... what? What *did* Doctor Long see?

A woman.

Therefore one rung down.

Young.

And so another.

Unmarried.

Another.

Childless.

He said, 'The Queen is never the last piece on the board.' Doctor Long strolled towards his car, no hurry, hands in pockets, as if he had all the time in the world.

Mo knew that walk. It was the walk Selwyn used, and Ted and Bernard and all the rest, when they'd been to the pub to watch a match, and they'd had a laugh and a couple of pints, and Leeds United had won. And now they swaggered to their cars, doing that thing with their hips, rattling the keys that were very close to their cocks. 'All right,' by way of goodbye. 'All right.' Because everything was all right in their world.

Doctor Long opened the boot of his car and reached for something heavy. He came back swinging a canister. It had a spout like a watering can. He bent down and worked close to the Palace wall, as if tending to the flower beds.

Then the fumes Mo knew from the factory van: heady, light, dangerous.

Doctor Long held up a box of matches.

He pushed it open, took one out, swiped.

He held it aloft, like a beacon, like a victory torch. Then a flick of the wrist, a spit of flame, and Doctor Long vanished.

And in his place: fire.

Resolution

消退期

Chapter eighteen

The villagers caught sight of the flames and came running. Mrs Su commanded chain gangs to bring sand from the banks of the Menglang and water to hose the wings of the building to stop the spread of the fire. In all the commotion, it took a while to realise the mayor was missing. It was Sergeant Li who found him. He radioed for help, but whoever was on duty had partied away all urgency.

When Mo reached Sergeant Li, he was on his walkie-talkie and in fast local Chinese. 'The body's prone and motionless.'

The mayor lay at the bottom of a flight of stairs. It looked as if he'd dashed to the patio late for his cue, thrown open the double doors for his grand entrance, and instead, it had been his grand exit. He lay in his Celebration Silks, his head resting on the step as if it were a pillow, his lips parted to deliver his lines.

'I've examined for injury.'

Blood wasn't showing except to mat the mayor's hair.

'Also for items to aid identification.'

Mo said, 'We know who he is.'

'I've searched for signs of forced entry and offensive weapons.'

'I know what happened.'

'Signs of life?' Sergeant Li hesitated, troubled by the question. So he recited police procedure: 'With apparent death, never assume death. The only exceptions are if the body is headless or decomposed to a point fully inconsistent with life. But the true state of affairs must be certified by a doctor.'

'There is no doctor.'

Because Doctor Long had gone. He'd put the empty canister back in the boot of his car, cast a casual eye over the Palace, then driven off – roared towards the village, his tail-lights jumping. Mo had followed his illuminated number-plate till it disappeared through the North Gate.

Then Doctor Long had vanished.

And the mayor was dead.

Mo was sure of that. She'd seen enough dead bodies to know. At Eden House, men often died on the night shift. She used to fill in the Deceased Removal Form, pressing hard with the biro because death was noted in triplicate. She wrote down the time of death to the minute. If she didn't know, because she hadn't actually been there, she just made it up: a round number, or a memorable one: 12.34, for instance. It made the family happy that the death had been so numerological, so meant to be.

And then, Mo sat with them and waited for the Co-op to come. While she waited, she listened to the sound of her own breath, to the sirens on the High Street and the thud of clubbers clubbing. She watched half-dressed teenagers pour into Grooves till the van pulled up with the pack ice and trolley. Sometimes, while Mo waited she talked, because who knew? The dead might hear. The sound of her voice might carry to wherever they were now – they couldn't have gone that far away.

The dead hung around leaving signs, Mo was sure of that. Such as her mother, who'd arranged on the day she'd died for the hospital canteen to bake rhubarb crumble. Selwyn was the only one who liked rhubarb. Her mother had made it whenever he asked for it, without complaint, while she and Mo scraped crumbs from the top and crushed them into the custard. Along with Old Spice, rhubarb was the quintessential smell of Selwyn.

When Mo got to the hospital, her mother had already been moved, and someone else was in her bed. Her charts were still there, though, with dated columns and scribbled initials, as if someone had trouble getting the pen to work. They were the kind of tick-sheets you found in public toilets that said: *all clean, no germs, all sorted.*

The nurse on duty said, 'Would you like to see her?'

'How did she die?'

'Quietly.' It was five in the morning. Coffee cups from the drinks machine were ranged like skittles along the ward counter. 'We didn't actually notice for a while.'

When the man in the morgue had been to the fridge, and arranged the Viewing Room, and pulled the cord that retracted the curtains, and activated 'Jesu Joy', there was her mother. She looked young and plastic, her mouth slightly open. Maybe she'd wanted to say something – ask for water, a pillow, pills – and finding no-one there because it was a weekend and reduced staff cover, she had died.

'What did she die of?'

The morgue man didn't know. 'Sometimes people just *do*, love.'

Later, the Registrar had listed 'a number of possible contributory factors.'

Her death certificate said 'pneumonia'.

But Mo knew.

What had killed Sue was Selwyn. Not directly. He didn't murder her – though he'd threatened to, though husbands sometimes did kill their wives. But for years, Selwyn had fought her, and impoverished her, and diminished her. Some men just killed their wives slowly.

Within hours, news of the mayor's death had spread across the county. The *Yang'an Times* curtailed its New Year's break to bring out a special edition: 'What Price Life in Jiazhishi?' The paper couldn't prejudice a criminal inquiry by naming the suspect but warned: 'Women of the Dadu Mountain Region please be aware that the Pre-Marital Health Check is suspended until further notice.'

Milton went to the hospital and took down the photo of Doctor Long from the High Achievers board. He used the photocopier in The Cube till the paper supply ran out. Rendered in black and white, Doctor Long looked hunted and haunted, his smile made shifty by run-down toner. Flyers went up on all the new lampposts put up to brighten the town. They said WANTED rather than MISSING. But then, Milton wasn't a journalist.

He went to the mayor's office and made the entry in the village register: *Event:* Death; *Name:* Lin Hongmeng; *Cause:* Blows to the head and soul.

If the mayor had been a member of the Su clan, he'd have been sprinkled with scented talcum powder and placed on dry ice in an open coffin in the Su ancestral hall. Around the walls, sprays of white irises would shiver with the turn of a fan, and prayers would be read in an ancient script that only paid monks could read. The bereaved and the curious would shuffle past, staring blankly at his blank face, then pinning money to the Money Board, and noting their donation in the Ledger of Condolence. And when, after many days, the wake was finally over, there would be a procession with drummers and weepers, and all the mourners in white. At the temple, the burning of the body, and incense, and paper casks of Moonshine – of all the mayor would need in the life to come. Then his ashes would be spooned into an urn and rowed down the Menglang and cast on a stormy day into the South China Sea.

Because the Sus liked drama.

But the mayor was a Lin.

At dawn on the day of the mayor's funeral, Mo was woken by cockerels with broken voices and goats that wouldn't look her in the eye. Down on the patio and at Milton's request, The Twins hummed a Bucks Fizz medley: 'Twentieth Century Hero', 'I used to Love the Radio', 'Now You're Gone', 'Where the Ending Starts'.

Mo put on all the clothes she had. It would be a three-hour trek into the mountains.

It was a small cortège – just the mayor's closest, his homemade family. Milton had rigged up the camp-bed with bamboo poles, and Mo took the lead out of the Palace and along the Menglang and up towards the foothills. They were starting on the track that the Nasu clan used when they brought cakes of indigo down to the factory.

At first, Mo focused on getting going, and finding a rhythm, and putting one foot in front of the other. She picked her way forward, feeling for footholds in earth that was slick with rain, through clearings cropped by wild sheep, and stonescapes greened with lichen. And after a while, the realisation came to her that this strange, otherworldly strain on her shoulders was the weight of the dead mayor. Still she kept on climbing. But now her feet fell as if on the pedals of a harmonium, like the one Granddad Stanley used to play in his old village church when he still had use of his ankles. Except, instead of hymns, Mo's feet pumped out tears. And when she'd blinded herself and had to stop to clear her eyes, she said, 'Milton?'

No answer.

She felt a quiver down the bamboo poles. She thought it was the wind, except there was no wind. 'Are you OK?'

'I am... I am... I am...' But it wasn't confirmation. It was the start of a sentence that caught in his throat and died.

Behind Mo and Milton came Lulu. It was the first time Mo had seen him out of school colours. He looked realer, less self-effacing, less defaced. In his white padded jacket and white skiing trousers, he could have been an astronaut climbing to the moon. He leaned on his mother's arm – though, when Mo looked again, it was the other way round: she was leaning on his. Mrs Long was bundled up in layers from her wardrobe – part kindergarten teacher, part mother, part wife – like a refugee from all her former lives.

Milton had gone to the Long's flat and released her.

When he'd jimmied the lock on the wardrobe door, he found what could have been an abandoned fashionable party. Mrs Long was curled on the sofa under a duvet of sable, and fancy shoes were piled on the floor. Then he was struck by the stench of toilets, saw the soiled handkerchiefs, and Mrs Long was murmuring that she was too cold to move. Doctor Long had turned off the heating, the front door was open and the January air had a bite. Five shoes counted the days she'd been there. And around the lock, hammer marks from a heel. But the door was made of snakewood: hard, expensive, stylish. When Doctor Long had moved to Dadu, he'd made sure that he bought style.

As they climbed, Lulu wept. Because who here would mind? He was catching up on all the crying his father had forbidden and that was against school rules. He swallowed his tears. He drank them. Because why not? He hardly ever tasted salt. It was banned in meals at The Exceptional School in case it hardened their future arteries. Lulu had barely stopped crying since New Year's Eve. He'd paused, briefly, when he'd escaped from his father into the garden, found Old Mang in the hammock and curled into the arms of a man who was about to be one hundred years old. Old Mang had distracted him by asking him to recite History, to tell him all the things this blind old man had seen. And Lulu stopped weeping for as long as it took to recite the twentieth century.

Behind Lulu and his mother, the unobtrusive step of Sergeant Li, who was new to the family and honoured to be there at all. And Mrs Su, being gung-ho and reassuring at the same time. She carried the axe, because this would be a sky burial. The mayor wanted to be eaten by birds, he'd always said, and be taken on their travels. And now Mrs Su was limbering up with unmeant swipes at a patter of dogs that were friendly but also hungry. Mrs Su was unafraid of the task because she'd seen everything. At Base 27, so many friends had embarked on missions as heroes and come back as body parts. She recited her Latin anatomy: *femur, spina, tibia, fibula.* She knew Greek too:

mania, nausea, psyche, trauma. She loved the Greek especially, because they were such masters of drama. She talked, filling the silence left by the mayor, doing what he'd have done if he were at this funeral – which he was, as she noted many times over, though in a special capacity.

Mo climbed up and up, over ridge after ridge. She glanced back now to see how far they'd come. Down there was a huddle of buildings that to the people of the village would always be Pingdi. The Palace – an open house and home to her new family. The Happiness Factory making sex aids that served all the people and was certified for the rest of time. And from this bird's-eye view, as the mayor had told her on the day that she'd arrived, what she'd bought with her inheritance read as *HU*: mutual, household, keep safe.

They were above the treeline now. The earth here was white, iced with a palette knife. Doctor Long was down there somewhere, probably working out a story, fingering someone else for the fire. She caught sight of Lulu. He looked more like his father than ever. She thought: Mrs Long can divorce her husband, put him behind her and start again. But Doctor Long is part of Lulu. He'll carry him for the rest of his life.

Gradually the air cooled and the sky blued. The light had a crunch to it now. The shadows looked ready to snap. Sharp gusts gathered spectres of dust. High over their heads, vultures circled on wind of the news. And then, finally, the climb stopped. Mo stepped onto earth that was flat and sandy, under a scythe of a moon that hung in the daylight sky. At the heart of the plateau, a slab of jade. A blade had fallen a thousand times there, some cuts sharp, some blunt, the strokes reading like hieroglyphs.

This was the source of the Menglang. They knelt on its banks and dipped their hands in ice-cold water, burning off the climb. Behind them, prayer flags bright and ragged, on staffs bent by the wind.

Mo whispered to Lulu, 'Do you know the Lord's Prayer?'

He leaned over the river, his reflection still and see-through.

Mo said, 'They were the first words of English the mayor ever spoke.'

Then Lulu began: 'Our Father, who art in... *where*, though, Momo? Who art in *whom*?' He stared hard at the water, seemed to commit what he saw to memory. Then he picked up a pebble, held it high over the surface and released it. His image shattered. Circles eddied outwards and died.

Mo had no idea where her father had died. She had no idea what he'd looked like, but in her head, the father that died was *satisfied*. She pictured him on his back, eyelids heavy and almost closed, hands linked on his belly, just as he did after Sunday lunch when he stretched out on the sofa, feet on the armrest, listening to Radio Two. That's what satisfaction was for him: Yorkshire pudding and gravy, cooked by somebody else, and the murmur of *Family Favourites*.

Selwyn was a happy man. As happy as a sandboy.

That's what he said.

He only ever did things that made him happy.

He said that too.

And one of the things he'd done, which Mo had never expected – which was so unlike the man she knew – was write a will to his estranged daughter and leave her everything he had. Which meant that, perhaps, Mo thought, over all those years her father *had* been happy, but not as happy as he'd have liked to have been. Not *entirely* happy. It meant he might, now and then, have thought of his daughter. He might have missed her, even. Maybe he'd wanted to get in touch, but he didn't know where she was now, what with young people moving around all the time. He had, perhaps, hoped that his daughter would feel time pass and the years quicken, and see her face change in the mirror, till one day, she glanced and, from the corner of an eye, saw her father there. Or at least, *also* her father there. And she'd decide that now he was too old to let the past stand in their way, and she'd get on the train and he'd meet her at the station, and they'd talk about the town and how nothing had changed, and how's life treated you, love?

And Mo never did.

Now, Mo stood. Soaring Magpie Mountain, pink in the morning sun, looked like a mitten abandoned in the snow. She said, 'I've never told you, Lulu, and now I want to.' She took his hand and led him to the edge, to where the earth stopped and the sky began, to a feeling they both knew. 'And I'd like you to remember it and, over the years from time to time, to say it out loud.' They stood in the chew of the winter wind and looked across the peaks of the Shunhua range that stippled their way to the horizon.

'My father's name: it is Selwyn Roderick O'Shea.'

Tiny in the bottom of the valley, Pingdi and Dadu lay scattered like children's building blocks. The finest thread of The Mist wound silver in the sunlight. They were nearer the sun than they had ever been. The air was so thin it ceded all the light and they could see for miles.

Acknowledgements

A huge thankyou to everyone at Bluemoose Books, and especially to Kevin for his boundless enthusiasm, and for grabbing this story and running with it; to Lin, who made editing a joy; and to Hetha, who let nothing through the net. You kept an author alive. My thanks too to Andrew Wille who pointed the way forward and never lost faith in the project. Without all of you, *The Happiness Factory* wouldn't have happened.

This story began life as non-fiction well over a decade ago. My thanks to Geoff Crothall, old China hand and old friend, for reading that early manuscript. Also to Ann Warden, who kept me company and kept me sane while I tackled Shanghai. I will always be indebted to Delia Davin, my mentor in the East Asian Studies Department at the University of Leeds. She didn't live to see the publication of this book, but I'm glad she knew it was on its way.

I want to thank the many kind and courageous people in China who shared their time and difficult stories. A special mention of Liu Hongsheng, known at work only as a number, who asked twenty years ago not to be forgotten, and is remembered here.

And my biggest thanks go to my lovely Guy, the gentlest of men, who makes me laugh and makes everything possible.